Make Me Shiver

COAL HAVEN, BOOK 2

MARIE JOHNSTON

LE PUBLISHING

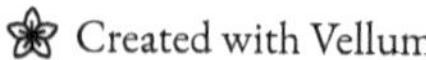 Created with Vellum

Have you ever gotten married without telling anyone? I did. Not telling anyone was the easy part. I had moved to a big city, had no friends, and wasn't speaking to my family.

I tried the whole "fake it 'til you make it" thing. I was the "fake" part and my husband, Archer, was concerned only with the "making it" part. When I got a call about a family emergency, I walked out on my hot-in-a-suit ambitious husband and my superficial life and ran back home to the family ranch. And I stayed, ignoring my husband's attempts to reach me—and I still didn't tell anyone I was married.

Then a year and a half later, I found Archer standing on my property, looking like a titanium rod in a pile of rusty nails. He came to end things but ended up staying to learn who he really married—the shy corporate woman with a perfect blowout or the sarcastic country girl with mud on her boots.

The longer he's around, the more I see I wasn't the only one who was disingenuous. The suit is gone, and my city slicker spouse is fixing fence, diving into muddy stock ponds to save calves, and calling in favors to get the cattle enough hay for the winter.

Yet none of that changes my family's need for me, and I'm not abandoning them again. It doesn't change the fact that the career he worked so hard to build is over a thousand miles away in Texas. Or that the life I want is exactly what he's run from. The only thing we're doing is making it harder to sign the divorce papers.

Author's Note

Dear Reader,

When I'm writing a book, I have so many thoughts and ideas I want to share with you. But by the time I finish the book, it's like an eraser has swiped across my brain and I'm filling it with thoughts and ideas about the next book. I jump from book to book; as soon as one is finished and off to the editor, I'm writing the next one.

I wanted to pause for a moment with *Make Me Shiver*. Please be aware that this book and this letter contain discussion about the aftermath of a suicide attempt by a side character. My goal is to write books heavy enough to give our emotions a bit of a workout and light enough to make the story feel like a nice escape. Each book is a combination of pure fiction scattered with lived experiences, observations, others' shared experiences, and research.

I didn't write Kane's part of the story arbitrarily, but as I was writing him, I was aware that readers may feel as if I took a serious, heartbreaking topic like suicide and made light of it by giving him an outcome that feels fantastical. My characters, like the story and the details within the story, are also pure fiction scattered with lived experiences, observations, others' shared experiences, and research.

I live where there's a high rate of suicides and suicide attempts. Kane is inspired by a real person, albeit someone I don't know well enough to confirm whether his gunshot wound to the head was self-inflicted or an accidental discharge. I do know him well enough to know he's in an at-risk demographic. We also know the family well enough to know they likely aren't going to talk about it—no matter how much we reached out to ask them how they're doing after the injury occurred. I suspect they'd be quite happy if we all pretended it didn't happen.

This guy survived. He's around for his kids, he still lives in the house where the injury occurred, he drives, and he waves every time he passes me. I see him all the time, but I still have a hard time believing it.

So Kane is part fiction, part life observation. I wanted to write his character because people like him are in the world around us. They might be called survivors or miracles, but at the core, they're still people who are going to let their dogs out and take their kids to school and grab groceries on the way home. I didn't want to reduce Kane to a harmful thing he did to himself, but I didn't want the other characters to pretend it didn't happen. I wanted to capture the reality of the topic but still keep the story light enough that you don't carry the heaviness with you when you put the book down. I hope I achieved that.

And because it can never be shared too much: The National Suicide Prevention Lifeline is 1-800-273-8255.

Thank you so much. I don't tell you enough how much I appreciate you.

Marie

One

LANEY

"No one asked you to come back." My mom's two-pack-a-day–roughed voice cut through the years to make me feel like I was seventeen again instead of twenty-seven.

Thanks for the reminder, Ma.

She was with me in the far pasture doing what ranchers usually do—fix fence. Another one of my shirts was ruined, thanks to catching it on the barbed wire on the section we were repairing. I was cranky after getting roused at the ass crack of dawn to go chase cattle off the road and back into the pasture.

Ma's dog, Portia, yapped around us. Portia wasn't the cattle dog we needed, but thanks to her prickly personality and sharp little teeth, we couldn't get another dog, and the only barn cats that stuck around were good at hiding and staying out of Portia's reach.

Now it was noon and already ninety degrees out in a dry-as-hell summer. The sun beat down on my ball cap. I had pulled my hair back in a ponytail and through the back of the cap. I rarely wore my hair down these days. The old habit of tossing it up with one of the eight hundred hair bands I left lying around had come back as soon as my plane from Dallas touched down.

No one from Dallas would recognize me. In Texas, I was more likely to be seen in sandals and a sundress. In Coal Haven, North Dakota, I had manure on my cowboy boots.

Thinking of Texas always made me think of *him*. I wasn't ready to think about him. I'd been avoiding thinking about him for over five hundred days. Someday I'd have to, but today was not that day. It'd been shitty enough.

No one asked you to come back. No, Ma. No one had asked me to stay in Texas either.

I shot Ma the saccharine smile I knew she hated. "You're welcome."

Ma took out her silver vaping pen and sucked in a breath as she glared at me. I'd had the audacity to complain about losing another shirt, and that unlike most people my age, I was running out of beater shirts while my nice ones hardly left the closet. I'd have to wear my three-hundred-dollar ADEAM top to brand cattle at this rate.

But Ma didn't like complaints and excuses. Rich, since she was full of both.

"We woulda been fine." She tossed the wire stretcher into the bed of the 1996 Silverado.

Woulda been fine. Sure.

I finished packing up supplies and started chucking them next to the stretcher. They clattered, and I didn't care where they landed. At one time, I would've been more particular, but I had a lot more stuff to expend my energy on, my mother being one of them. Sweat ran from my hairline, tracked down my collar, and soaked my sports bra. A tank top sounded nice right now, but I hadn't wanted a barb to the armpit. Once in my life was enough for that particular experience.

My jeans clung to my skin like they'd been sprayed on, thanks to the heat. Honestly though, I didn't mind fencing. It was better than sitting behind a desk. But I wouldn't turn down a little AC right now.

My stomach rumbled, but I sighed when I recalled what was in the fridge. Fifty-plus years of eating bologna sandwiches on white bread for lunch hadn't made Ma sick of bread or bologna. I couldn't stand either. But Papa worked out of town and used it as an excuse to eat out of town.

When I first came home, I'd bought what I liked to eat, only to have one or both of my parents tease me about my preferences or eat every last ounce of my hummus and pita chips. Papa had bitched about the fancy food as he chewed a mouthful of my chips, oblivious to the frustrating irony.

Since the ranch hadn't exactly replaced my previous income, I couldn't afford to feed the rest of my family the way I'd grown accustomed to eating. I choked down bologna and white bread every day.

I'd have thought I'd be used to the routine, but the longer I was home, the more I was reminded why I lit out of town as soon as I had my diploma in my hand.

At the time, I had thought it had been due to other motivations. Like breaking up with my longtime boyfriend and watching him go stupid over the new girl in town. But no. That ex had passed away years ago, and his widow, Kennedy, that new girl I had resented for years, was now my best friend.

Odd how things turned out.

Like how I'd come home to help keep the ranch from folding after my perfect brother, Kane, had tried to bury a bullet in his head and survived. Thanks to his low-caliber choice of destruction, the bullet had only grazed his skull.

He'd suffered a concussion, temporary hearing loss, and flesh wounds. But he wasn't taking over the Diamond UU Ranch like my parents had planned since the day they'd learned they were having a bouncing baby boy. Their expectations had driven him into a lonely existence.

It wasn't uncommon for young farmers to still live on their family land, but Kane hadn't been able to go to college when he'd graduated. He'd been stuck on the ranch, the fences as good as prison walls.

In the end, the suicide attempt had given him what he'd wanted—freedom, an out from an eternity of watching over cattle and a life under Ma and Papa's thumb. It'd finally gotten all of us to realize he'd been living in his own personal hell.

Guilt gnawed at my stomach as I climbed into the driver's side of the pickup. Would I have seen what was going on if I had stayed in Coal Haven? I'd never know, but Kane was alive and well now and that was the most important thing. Ma got in the other side and patted her lap for Portia to jump on. A cloud of vape smoke blew across the cab. Ma had the window open, but the breeze blew her strawberry-scented exhale right into me.

I opened my window until I could rest my elbow on the door and, if needed, hang my head out.

I hadn't minded the smell at first. Ma vaped as much as she had chain-smoked. I wasn't sure there was any benefit to the switch, but she loved telling everyone how she kicked her smoking habit. No one asked about her new strawberry perfume.

I bumped over the pasture, sticking to the tracks that were almost permanent after all these years.

Ma didn't talk on the way to the house. It was this way between us. Silence was better than bickering. Papa claimed we were too much alike, and that was why we argued.

Wasn't that normal between mothers and daughters? I wouldn't know. I didn't have close friends growing up to get a glimpse at anything else.

I pulled up to the gate. Ma didn't make a move to get out.

I suppressed a sigh and shoved the door open. "I'll get it. You rest." I'd learned the art of sarcasm before I learned to speak. It'd done nothing but bite me in the ass. The one time in my life I'd acted sweet and innocent, I'd been shut down. Hard.

Ma rolled her eyes and took another pull off the pen.

I opened the gate, pulled through, and hopped out to close it again.

I left the window open as I hit the highway. If I went straight, I'd pass Liam Barron's house. The illegitimate Barron. The Barrons ran this county. Siblings who were born into oil money. One of the sons ran the refinery outside of town. Another son, our neighbor, ranched on the other side of Liam. The only daughter of the group ran a ranch across the county and rivaled my mother for how many times she'd been called a bitch in her life. And the third brother was estranged to everyone in town. There was speculation about where he lived and how many kids he'd had and how old they'd be. I kept my mouth shut. The further I stayed away from the Barrons, the better.

I should've learned my lesson after high school. My boyfriend had been Liam's cousin. If we'd been from other families, we would've been two kids who grew up together and dated. But my boyfriend's family hadn't hidden how much they despised the Grangers or how they planned to take over our land, something the Barrons had been trying to do for decades.

I turned off the dirt road to our place and stifled a yawn. Kane had been out for his morning run—one of his new coping mechanisms—and called to let me know the cows were out.

Eighteen months ago, he would've saddled Papa's horse, Bolt, and waved them back in. But he'd distanced himself from all things ranching, lest Ma pull him back in, and I got to argue with Ma all day in his place.

I'd come home to help run the ranch. To keep both the business and the land in the family. To be there for Kane. I stayed because going back to my old home was no longer an option.

My stomach rumbled as I turned down the drive that wound past the house and into the middle of the yard, which was surrounded by the barns, a shed, and the house. I inspected the fence and corral gates as I drove by. There were a few weak stretches that would need to be repaired. Hopefully I'd have a chance to do the repairs before the cattle found them.

Ma grunted. "Who the hell is that?"

My gaze was drawn to a sleek dark sedan. "Someone who wants to wash their car."

She snickered, and I chuckled. Clean cars were a temporary luxury when living on gravel. Even the richest ranchers who had pickups worth as much as our house couldn't keep them pristine.

"Better not be that damn genetics salesman."

I wished it was, but Ma had run that guy out pretty hard. I thought it was a mistake, but what did I know? I'd only grown up working this ranch, done the finances all through high school, and researched how working with a bigger company to breed specialty bulls would improve business.

It was the direction Kane had been trying to go. Ma hated being told what to do, so she saw it as a hostile takeover, not the growth we needed to secure the ranch that'd been in our family for generations—the Diamond UU. We were to remain a cow/calf operation for eternity.

I coasted down the long driveway, tempted to block the fancy car in for no reason other than I was my mother's daughter, and pissing people off was a temptation I sometimes indulged.

I killed the engine but left the windows open. If it was going to become an oven, it might as well be a convection one.

I hopped out and walked toward the house.

"Laney," Papa called. Today was rare. Papa had actually stuck around to do some yard work. Most weekends, he was fishing, hunting, or doing extra repair projects. "There's someone here to see you."

Me? As I turned, the wind blew dust into my face. I brushed it away, willing myself to ignore the dirt under my uneven nails. Manicures used to be routine, but these days I only had so much money and energy to spare. I didn't miss them, but I missed not cringing when I saw my dirty nails.

Portia erupted in a frenzy of barks as a man walked out of the opening of the big red barn. His arrogant swagger was blazed into my brain. *No.* His dark gaze pinned me in place and his eyes narrowed. His full lips twisted like he couldn't figure out what he was looking at.

Because the last time he saw me, I'd been in five-inch heels. My freshly highlighted blonde hair had been in an elegant crown braid that paired well with the sapphire-blue Oscar de la Renta gown I'd been wearing. He'd told me that the color made my eyes look like the ocean on a sunny day and he hadn't been able to keep his gaze off my legs.

"Portia, quiet," Ma growled.

He tilted his head. As if that'd help. I'd told him I'd grown up working cattle, and sometimes I suspected he hadn't believed me. Like he'd been just shy of patting my hair and telling me not to worry my pretty little head.

There had been so many little signs I'd ignored until that day in my gown and my heels when I told him I had to leave his important work function, and he'd said *Not now*. I'd insisted it couldn't wait. Like a brainwashed idiot, I'd been trying to hold in my tears to keep from ruining his chance at a big promotion. And he'd shown me that what was most important to him was not me.

And here he was, in all his expensive-jeans-and-Tom Ford-polo-shirt glory.

Ma's bootsteps crunched the gravel behind me, and the dog raced between all of us. "You're looking for Laney?" Her incredulous question barely penetrated the booming of my pulse as my heart jackhammered my ribs.

Papa nodded and scrutinized me. "Actually, he said he was looking for *his wife,* Delaney Barron. Wanna explain what that's all about?"

* * *

Archer

The dusty vision in front of me was like a mirage, and I was a thirsty man who hadn't had water in a year and a half.

My wife wore jeans that hugged her hips, draping down thighs that had once gripped me around my waist as I... Nope. Not the place. I'd been delving into the past far too much on my drive up here. I took in the rest of her. Her shirt had a rip in the side, and it was all I could do to keep my feet rooted in place. A step or two to the right and I could catch a glimpse of golden skin. Her hair was in a ponytail, a grimy ball cap stuffed on her head, and she didn't have a hint of makeup on, unless I counted the dirt smeared across her forehead and down her cheeks.

Were those sweat stains on her shirt?

Even in the Texas heat, she hadn't walked around with a sweat ring down to her bra. But she wasn't exactly wearing expensive moisture-wicking fabric. The faded print on the old cotton shirt read *Coal Haven Fourth of July 5K*.

"Why—and I repeat—*the hell* would he call you Delaney Barron?" The woman who spoke had a voice that sounded like her vocal chords had been roughed up by forty-grit sandpaper. Was this Delaney's mother? She wasn't dressed much differently. Less sweaty, like Delaney had done all the work. The woman squinted at Delaney, a fan of lines spreading from the corners of her eyes. "Why would he say you're his wife?"

I didn't appreciate the hostility in her tone. Ironic, since I was here to give Delaney a hard time. "Because we're married."

The silence that descended in the farmyard was unexpected. Blood drained from Delaney's already pale cheeks. If she lost much more blood from her face, she was going to pass out.

Her mother's mouth dropped open, and the guy who'd chortled when I'd first asked to speak to Delaney Barron stared at me like I'd just gotten out of a spaceship instead of an Audi RS.

"You're what?" The woman took a silver thing out of her back pocket and puffed from it. Delaney hadn't mentioned her mother vaped. I hadn't realized how little I knew about her life in Coal Haven until now. The life she'd chosen over being with me.

Delaney's eyelids slid shut, and she swallowed. "Why did you come here, Archer?"

"Archer," the man said suddenly, like he'd deciphered

written code. This must be her father since he wasn't leaving the conversation. Didn't her family ranch have hired help? "Archer... Barron?"

The small furry dog sat on her haunches and eyed me. I wished I'd dug my old cowboy boots out of my closet and brought them with me. My ankles tingled, aware that the dog wasn't overly friendly and it was in a prime ankle-biting area.

I pushed down rising irritation. "Yes."

The man looked at Delaney, his eyes widening. "And you're... married?"

What the hell was the confusion about? Did I have to write it out in the gravel of the driveway? I studied the older couple. The way they exchanged glances. How their mouths flattened with the looks of shock and disappointment they shot Delaney.

"You didn't tell them?" I wished I could take back the incredulous tone enveloping my words. I was used to being cool under pressure, but this situation wasn't exactly normal.

Why was I so incensed? It wasn't as if I'd sent out notices I'd eloped to my family almost three years ago. The difference was that Delaney still talked to hers, yet they'd been clueless.

Guilt flashed across her features, but her shoulders went tight. "It's complicated."

"How complicated is it to tell your parents you're married?" *We can't let our private business affect our professional life. Let her go, Archer. If she wanted you, she would've given you the few minutes you asked for.* My boss's advice hadn't seemed pertinent until now. "Is there somewhere private we can talk?"

"Yeah, you'd better start talking," her mother said and folded her arms. Cheryl, the name came to me. Delaney had rarely talked about her family to me. She'd said they weren't as close as she'd like. Was it because they were so similar? I wasn't seeing a lot of the wife I knew in Texas in this woman, but side by side, they were a younger and an older version of the same hard woman.

"This is private," I reiterated.

Cheryl spun on me. The fire in her eyes nearly made me take a step back. Some of my clients were formidable, but this woman could make a bull cower. "And you're a Barron. On my land. Talking like you own my daughter as much as you wanted to own all this." She directed her blazing glare to Delaney. "Start talking, Laney."

"About what, Ma? That's the gist of it. He's a Barron and I married him. That pretty much tells you why I never said nothing."

This time I did take a step back. I'd never heard Delaney speak like that. The heat in her tone. That grammatically incorrect language. The way she freely confessed to not wanting to admit she married a guy like me.

I'd worked my ass off to get to where I was. To be proud of my job, my home, my appearance, and, especially, my last name. And Delaney spoke like it was the opposite.

Her father didn't lose his perplexed expression. "You went to Texas and found another Barron to date?"

"Another Barron?" I echoed. As if the rest of the conversation had been easy to follow. What the hell did that mean?

Delaney pressed her fingertips to her forehead and muttered, "I didn't get enough sleep for this." She blew out a breath and pointed to the space beyond her barn. Without looking at anyone, she announced, "That land over there is Bruce Barron's. Your uncle. I dated his son Derek all through high school until he dumped me to date Kennedy, who is now my best friend—yes, Ma, don't start. And Kennedy is married to Liam Barron." She rotated her arm to point past the house. "Your uncle Cameron's son, the kid not from his wife, in case you haven't heard the story. And I moved to Texas and happened to run across you. And no, I didn't tell you everything. You wouldn't have dated me otherwise." Her tone dropped to a sneer. "Too much of an embarrassment risk."

Yanked out of the weirdness of having my family— people I'd never met—described to me, I stared at the woman I'd married close to three years ago. The demure, put-together college grad I'd met at a job fair. Polished. Sophisticated. Accommodating. I'd had to have her, so I'd swept her off her platform-heeled feet.

This was not that girl.

"Wasn't getting dumped by one of 'em enough?" Cheryl asked.

Delaney cringed but folded her arms. "Okay, Archer. So you found me. What do you want?"

I'd been so busy soaking her in and managing the one-eighty she'd done on me that I'd forgotten what had made me drive from Texas to North Dakota in early July. Now that I was here, I didn't want to admit why. I didn't want to tell her about the papers in my car.

But I wasn't the one who'd left and stayed far away. She hadn't answered my calls. She didn't return my messages, other than the first one after she left when I asked if she was okay. Her reply had been "fine." That was my last communication with her since she'd walked out on me.

Despite my hurt feelings and resentment, my words tasted as sour as lemon juice. "You've been gone for over half our marriage. I came to get an annulment."

Two

LANEY

The heat of the sun blanketed me, but chills pricked over my skin. An annulment. Why did this feel worse than a divorce? My husband wanted to pretend we never were together. Like he had so many regrets, he wanted to pretend I never existed.

Shouldn't I be glad? My estranged husband wanted to be released from our vows and not look back. No messy divorce.

Were annulments messy?

I had no fucking clue.

Ma snorted next to me. "If I didn't believe you'd gone to Texas and found a Barron that'd marry you before, now I do. He's arrogant like the rest of 'em."

Ma had no idea. One of Archer's best friends, Briony, could grind Ma into the gravel with the heel of her Manolo Blahnik. Wilson, Briony's husband and Archer's coworker, would look at Ma's remains as if they were nothing but a snuffed-out cigarette butt. That was how they'd looked at me.

I'd had enough time to reflect on my marriage since I'd been home. I had wanted to be the girl I was in Texas so bad —until I learned no one cared about that girl either. More importantly, I'd realized how much I let the people in Archer's life push me around. Archer himself too.

Archer never pushed me physically. He didn't issue orders. He didn't stomp around and demand his way. He just expected it. He assumed I'd want to do nothing but please him, and he'd been so damn right.

No more. I wouldn't smile, nod, and spread my legs to make him happy. Although, that'd make me happy too. Archer was excellent in bed. Best I'd ever had, and while my experience had been limited to naive small-town guys, I somehow knew I could fuck every guy willing to jump into the back seat with me but Archer would still be the best.

The chill was gone, replaced by uncomfortable heat stoked by the blazing sun. Remembering how good it was with Archer wouldn't help this situation. The sex had been awesome, amazing, toe curling, but I didn't have to be the perfect compliant wife anymore.

"Look, I've had a busy day. I want to enjoy some AC and have lunch." I swung my hand out to encompass our property. I ignored the busted horse trailer sitting by the big shop with the half-open door, the gooseneck trailer with the back doors wide open and straw and manure hanging out, and the dilapidated vehicles that should be in a junkyard but which Papa managed to keep running. "Unlike some jobs, we actually get our hands dirty and work."

I spun on a boot heel and strode to the house. The burn of three pairs of eyes branded the area between my shoulders. As I went up the porch steps, wincing as they creaked under my heels, I spotted Kane staring out the kitchen window. Had he stopped by to talk to Papa? Kane didn't avoid Ma, but he was careful about getting her hopes up that he was ever going back to the way things had been and taking back the work I was doing.

His concerned gaze landed on me, and I gave him a small smile. I breezed into the house and the screen door slammed.

Kane asked, "Who is that?"

I toed out of my boots, wishing I could be storming into a new-build home that didn't have mismatched wood flooring that didn't look like any wood grown on earth, off-white walls and popcorn ceilings, or decor that was older than my rich-as-hell husband outside. At least a place with central air instead of a wall unit chugging away in the window of the living room.

Shivers traced over my body as I gulped down the cool air. I had walked away, but my troubles weren't over. "After graduation, I went to Texas and got married and didn't tell anyone because he's Allan Barron's son. Then I left when you were in the hospital, and he never even tried calling. And now he wants a divorce. An *annulment*." The second time I told the story was definitely easier.

Kane's dark-blue eyes widened. I hated the guilt flashing through them. He took a few moments to work through the same information our parents had just had dumped on them. Only unlike them, he processed it before he reacted—one of the many changes since his recovery.

"That sucks. I'm sorry." He offered me a supportive smile. I needed it.

It really did suck. Tremendously. After so long, I should be walking back out with a pen, asking where to sign. Only, every one of those days and nights that Archer didn't call, that he didn't show, and I wondered what was wrong with me, was validated. He didn't want me, and I was a fool to think he ever really had.

The backs of my eyes burned, but I managed a flippant attitude. "Yeah, well. Don't out-stubborn a Granger."

Kane stirred his coffee, which looked as light as weak chocolate milk. "You don't have to go with me today. Hang out here and ignore..." He lifted his chin toward the front door. I didn't know if Archer was still here or not. I'd left him at Ma's mercy.

Served him right.

"No, I'll go with," I said automatically. I'd forgotten his therapy appointment was today. Going along with him had started as supportive, but now I waited for him and then we went to the little bakery in town for a treat. At first, it'd been a way to take the sting out of therapy, a way to show him it was no different than any other doctor's appointment, no matter what Ma said.

When I told Ma I was setting Kane up with a therapist in town as soon as he was released from the hospital, she'd shunned me for three days. But Kane had continued his therapy long after he'd physically recovered. He was in a place to make his own decisions, and he wanted to keep seeing his psychologist. I had his back.

"Give me a few minutes to clean up and change." I disappeared into my small bedroom.

Bedroom was a strong word for it. As soon as my taillights had disappeared down the driveway after graduation, Ma changed my old bedroom into an office. All I had now was an inflatable mattress beside the messy desk with the computer. It worked well since I'd also taken over the book-keeping—an eye-opening experience.

No wonder Kane had felt hopeless.

I pressed my palms to my eyes. The door was shut, and the temperature was already rising, but I needed a flimsy piece of wood between me and the world right now. I'd sacrifice a little artificially cooled air to do it.

From outside, a car door slammed. Rare Archer. He didn't lose his temper. He never had to. The world flexed to do what he wanted, just like I had.

The screen door slammed. I pushed the stray strands of hair off my face as my muscles tensed, fiber by fiber.

Ma pushed open the door and stayed in the opening, one hand on the knob and the other on her hip. "Laney, what the ever-loving hell was that all about? Was that why you went to Texas?"

"No."

Maybe? All the talk about the mysterious Barron who had left town, gone to Texas, and never returned to Coal Haven was like my own personal fantasy. A new start where my last name and reputation couldn't drag behind me like reeds caught on a fishing hook. A place where I could be anything I wanted after a lifetime of being told what I wasn't getting. Yeah, that was probably why I'd gone to Texas.

"How?" For once, Ma wasn't berating me. She was genuinely confused.

My high school boyfriend had told me all about his estranged uncle, Allan Barron. Derek had said he'd never met his uncle or his two cousins, Archer and Ansen. "I went to a job fair and ran across him." I fluttered my fingers toward the window in the direction Archer would've driven. "I mean, look at him. You can figure out the rest."

Ma shrugged. Not even her cold heart could deny how good-looking Archer was. He looked like he'd walked off a movie set about a millionaire playboy who fucked young vulnerable women until they lost their damn minds.

That was pretty accurate, only he wasn't an actor.

She shook her head, her gaze still cloudy. "You mean

that man—and his family—didn't have a problem with who you are?"

Papa hadn't been raised in Coal Haven. Archer's dad might know who Ma was, but he likely didn't know Papa. My Granger maiden name wasn't familiar to him. "I never met his parents. His mom passed away when he was a teen, and he doesn't talk to his dad. When I told him I lived close to Coal Haven and he asked if I knew his relatives, I said I was familiar with them. After that, it was all about him."

Ma gave me a look, and yeah, I'd intentionally stretched the truth. We lived out of town, but we still lived inside Coal Haven city limits. Big difference, but I hadn't wanted to look like a stalker.

She stepped into the hallway. "You've got a helluva mess to clean up, kid. But I wouldn't mind being around when *your husband's* uncles and aunt find out you're part of their fucking family." Her cackle followed her down the hall.

That would be a show I'd rather skip. I'd had a front seat to their reaction when I dated Derek. But from what Archer had said, I wouldn't be part of their family for long anyway.

* * *

Archer

Rattler's Brewhaus wasn't the trendiest restaurant I'd ever seen, and it definitely wasn't the fanciest I'd ever been in, but it was more than I thought a small town like Coal Haven would have.

I scrubbed my face. I hadn't gotten out of my car yet. My nerves were shot, and my emotions were all over the place.

What the hell had I thought would happen?

I'd been encouraged to pursue an annulment. Less damaging to both my finances and my heart. I could've flown, but for some damn reason I'd driven right to an old address I found in the belongings Delaney had left behind. A long trek north through Texas, Oklahoma, Nebraska, and South Dakota landed me in the middle of North Dakota.

A part of me had wanted the time. Did I want to dissolve this marriage? How would Delaney act when I showed up? Had something happened to her? The closer I got, the greater the hope grew that maybe there'd been a valid reason for her to stay away from Texas. Had she been physically unable to leave Coal Haven and return to our condo overlooking downtown Dallas?

These were all questions that kept me from giving the lawyer a way to electronically send the documents to Delaney.

The girl I found looked like my wife, under the dirt and the ripped shirt and the worn jeans and boots. But she didn't talk like Delaney. She didn't smile at me like I hung the moon and stars like Delaney did. My wife would've told her family she was married. Right?

Our wedding had been the only impulsive thing I'd done in my life. Last-minute trip to Vegas. A few shows, a little gambling, a stop at a chapel. Neither of our families had been there. Wasn't that why we'd eloped? I hardly talked to my brother and hadn't seen my dad for years, and Delaney had gotten cagey about her family when we'd discussed tying the knot.

An impromptu Vegas wedding had been the perfect solution to keep from opening both our wounds.

And afterward? I'd launched into my work as a land broker, trying to earn a coveted partner spot. I had almost made it. I would've finally been the hick kid done good, partner in a land brokerage agency, with a downtown condo and an expensive car. And then my dream had nearly vanished.

I'd had to get back into my boss's good graces after the way Delaney left. One of our biggest clients had witnessed our exchange and told Mr. Truitt that NT Land Agency wasn't the family company she thought it was. Her deal would've pulled in eight figures.

I'd almost lost my damn job that night.

I tried to recall a conversation about her family. They were ranchers from North Dakota. They weren't tradition-ally close. She had a brother.

Kane gets everything. There's nothing for me at home.

Did Kane have everything? Or had Delaney gotten the ranch and that was why she'd left? My friends had asked me to consider whether Delaney was after my money. I'd argued. She'd had her own job at a marketing firm.

But I'd grown up hearing my dad rage about his oldest brother and how he'd been so greedy and pushed Dad out of the business. I'd grown up under the fallout of Dad losing everything—money, land, stability. Was that why Delaney had left and forgotten about me? For property she was too scared to lose in a divorce?

The idea didn't fit into the picture I'd seen when I pulled into the Diamond UU. The ranch didn't look like much. It looked like everything I'd worked hard to escape. Had she picked this place over me?

No matter what my friends thought about Delaney, I had held out hope that what she and I had wasn't a figment of my imagination. The more I thought back to the night she left, the more I recalled a frantic gleam in her eyes. I'd been under enormous amounts of pressure and stress at that time. Was I succumbing to wishful thinking?

Had I imagined the sweet agreeable girl I'd married?

I didn't have the whole story. I was starting to suspect

that I barely had one chapter of the story. So, yeah, I would stay. I needed the annulment, but I needed answers first. Too many questions to take back home.

I got out of the car. The heat was surprising. Delaney had occasionally mentioned how cold the winters could get in North Dakota. Once she'd wistfully mentioned how much she missed the summers and being surrounded by rolling green hills instead of concrete.

I'd been happy to be surrounded by glass and concrete if it meant I didn't have to break my will for an unforgiving, dusty and sparse landscape that was someone else's dream. A lot of my current surroundings reminded me of Texas, only a little lusher, a richer green that threatened to turn brown and dusty in the next week if there wasn't a good rain. The dry heat was similar to Dallas, but the buttes that jutted up in the middle of nowhere were a surprise, one that added character.

Inside the bar and grill, large windows allowed copious amounts of light to spill in. The lunchtime crowd filled most of the tables, but the bar had a few open spots.

This was nothing like the martini bars I went to with Briony and Wilson. I'd met them both in college, after I won a coveted scholarship Wilson's dad—my boss—sponsored. Norville Truitt had taken me under his wing as if he recognized a kid who was starved for a reliable father figure, one who didn't get lost in stale beer and rage about the unfairness of the world.

Wilson had proposed to Briony as soon as we graduated, and he and I had gone to work at his dad's company, NT Land Agency. Most thought it stood for North Texas Land Agency, but the company was Norville Truitt's very lucrative baby.

I waited for a hostess to show me where to go, but eventually figured the choice of seating must be as casual as the atmosphere. As I passed the empty hostess podium, a few men walked by. They were older than me, close to my dad's age.

One drew my eye. He was about my height, an inch or two past six feet, and the shiny black cowboy boots he wore with his crisp black suit boosted him higher. His eyes crinkled at the sides like he found something his companion said humorous, but otherwise the man gave the impression he didn't smile often.

The way his hair was cut and combed to the side reminded me of Dad. I slowed to a stop. Light-brown strands mingled with the gray. Dad had gray hair coming in on the sides of his russet hair the last time I saw him. Before Mama died, she'd forbidden him from dying it, claiming he got better with age.

Without her, he'd gotten worse.

A moment of longing tugged at my chest. When was the last time Dad looked as hale as the man looking at me with his head tipped to the side, like he found me as familiar as I found him?

This was Coal Haven, where Dad was born and raised. What were the chances? Nerves made me stand straighter, as if the first impression of my entire family rested on my shoulders.

If this was an uncle, then it sort of did.

He murmured something to the other two men in suits and veered toward me. He came to a stop and evaluated me as ruthlessly as I scrutinized him.

An unidentifiable emotion rippled through his gaze before he spoke. "Archer or Ansen?"

I had guessed correctly. Dad didn't have many photos from his childhood, but he and his two brothers had resembled each other in them, just like my younger brother,

Ansen, and I resembled each other. I didn't know what to think. "Archer. Cameron or Bruce?"

"Cameron." As I figured. He emanated power and displeasure, like a guy who could piss Dad off enough to leave the state and never come back. "Is Allan all right?"

My uncle barely knew who I was, much less why I was here. Of course he'd think the worst had happened to his brother. My wife had told no one about me. Cameron wouldn't know what else would bring me to Coal Haven.

"Dad's fine," I lied. Dad hadn't been fine since he'd lost the ranch and Mama died. But that was no one's business. Definitely not an uncle who could be as bad as Dad had made him sound. "I'm here for…" Well, damn. I hadn't expected to be in this pickle. I brushed my left thumb against the warm metal on my ring finger. I hadn't seen much of Delaney, but I'd noticed her bare ring finger. I clenched my fist. "Personal reasons."

Cameron's brow ticked up, but I didn't elaborate. "How long are you in town for?"

It was supposed to be a quick visit. Up and back. When I'd driven here, I was convinced Delaney was done with me. Why else would she leave on the most important night of my life? But after this morning and the way her mother told me I'd better sit tight *until Laney's good and goddamn ready to deal with you*, I had no idea. "About a week." I had planned a couple extra days after I returned to Dallas to file the paperwork and untangle Delaney's name from mine.

The thought soured my already disgruntled mood.

His scrutiny increased. Was he dying to know my reasons? Or annoyed I was being elusive? He surprised me instead. "Would you like to meet your family?"

"My family" had a weird ring to it. Mama's family hadn't wanted anything to do with Dad after she died, and I couldn't blame them. Dad hadn't been in a good place after she was gone. He hadn't been good company. They'd kept to themselves in El Paso while Ansen and I struggled to help Dad keep his job as ranch manager in northern Texas. And since they cut off two young kids because Dad had suffered the loss of his wife, I hadn't wanted to see them.

It'd been me, Ansen, and Dad for years. Until I left for college. But I had more family standing right in front of me. Family I had thought about in the abstract, almost as if they were a myth.

This situation differed in that Dad had been the one to sever ties, and at the time, no kids were involved. My father's side hadn't been a part of my life. Ever. They had been a distant thought as I'd made the long drive. Coal Haven was where my dad's family was from, but I'd lived in a town with more than a million people for over ten years. Long enough to forget what it was like to run into someone I knew at the gas station or while grabbing milk.

The chances of running into someone I didn't want to in Dallas were almost zero, and I preferred it that way. Coal Haven had what? Less than three thousand people? Better odds.

What would Dad think about me running into Cameron? And if I met everyone else? Dad had nieces and nephews here. Did he know about them? Uncle Cameron knew about me and Ansen. Did that make him more or less approachable? "I don't know, honestly. Do you want them to meet me?"

The muscles on each side of Cameron's jaw flexed. Was he upset? "I think the younger generation should decide for themselves."

He had a point. I took out my phone. "What's your number? I can let you know when I'm free."

If I decided to rattle my life any more than my wife already had.

He recited his phone number, tipped his head, and left.

I avoided eye contact with anyone else in the place and sat in a booth. An older server gave me a kind smile as she slid a plastic menu in front of me. "What can I get you to drink?"

For the curves life had thrown at me today, I'd need the good stuff. Anything but beer. "A Ballantine's on the rocks, please."

Her mouth puckered. "A what?"

"Ballantine's. Scotch?"

"Oh, scotch on the rocks?"

"Do you have Ballantine's?"

She scratched her cheek with the tip of her pen. "Uh, I can ask."

I was going to ask for whatever top-shelf scotch they had, but that was too close to being as undiscerning as Dad when it came to alcohol. "Just water is fine."

Her face crinkled with her smile. "Water on the rocks?"

I chuckled despite my sour mood. "Sounds perfect."

"Know what you want to eat?"

My room service from the morning had burned off hours ago. The eggs Benedict had been made to perfection, but the amount of food that had been delivered didn't fit the amount on the price tag. As much as I tried to shake the habit of determining whether what I spent my money on was worth it, I often fell back on habits that had served me well as a broke college student.

I'd have to watch that. I had enough money that I didn't have to worry about a roof over my head or check the prices of what I ate. "Do you have Wagyu beef?"

She attacked her cheek with her pen again. "Is that like Angus?"

Just two hundred dollars more a pound, give or take. I glanced at the menu and tried to find something that wouldn't remind me of my childhood. No soup, no canned vegetables, and no discount meat. "Prime rib sandwich?"

"We've got that." She scribbled on her notepad. "Anything else?"

She had no idea what a loaded question that was. "Actually, yes. Can you tell me if there's a hotel in town where I can get a room?"

Three

LANEY

I stepped out of the clinic and pushed my sunglasses down onto my nose. It was hot out, but there was a picnic table under some trees next to the building. If I could find a spot that wasn't full of bird shit, I'd rather sit outside than in the eerily quiet waiting room. Ma would lose her shit if she saw me sitting out where everyone could see a Granger was at a mental health clinic, but my nerves were too frayed to dwell on it.

My luck was picking up. Half the bench was clean. Dusty as hell, but better than getting bird poop stains on my shorts. I wiped the dust off with my bare hand, then brushed my hands together to get the grit off before I got it on myself. This was my favorite pair, and they were white.

After the morning I'd had, I dressed cute for Kane's appointment. A little boost for my raw emotions.

I sat down and tipped my head back. Heat gathered behind my eyes, but I refused to cry. Someday, when this mess was sorted, maybe I could think about how I'd fucked up in Texas. I could ugly cry and maybe even confess to Kennedy. I had a little. Told her I'd pretended to be like her to get the guy of my dreams since the other guy I thought I would grow up and marry and be happy with had dumped me.

Turned out guys just plain didn't want to be with me for the long haul, whether I was brutally real or fake as hell.

A bourbon-and-citrus scent curled into my nose before I sensed someone else in my little sanctuary. That smell was sophisticated, more expensive than what could be bought anywhere near Coal Haven. So damn familiar, my heart ached.

"Delaney." That voice. As rich as his aftershave.

My breath puffed out a "fuck." Today wasn't going to be my day, cute shorts or not. I opened my eyes and pushed my glasses up into my hair. I'd refreshed the ponytail but was far from the polished Delaney Archer was used to. "Archer. How the hell are you here right now?"

His brows lifted at my vitriol. But, seriously. Couldn't a girl have a pity party in private?

He gestured to the little ten-room motel behind him. The small twist of his waist made his polo cling to him and show off the defined muscles that still invaded my dreams. "This is the only place to stay in town."

Yeah, it was. Mostly used for family not wanting to impose when they were in town to visit and the many hunters and fishermen who came through year-round. I'd never been inside, but the place was as old as the town and probably more updated than my parents' house. "Find it to your liking?"

Surprise flickered in his gaze. At some point, he'd get over my sarcasm. It was as natural to me as my blonde roots.

"It's... adequate."

I snorted. The motel room would probably be the smallest room Archer had ever slept in, with the cheapest mattress and the least thought put into its decor. That wasn't a dig on the motel. It was just that Archer was accustomed to expensive quality.

His gaze raked over the clinic. I should have offered him a seat. Employ those snide manners his friend Briony used to chide me about. But he'd have to sit close to me to keep from getting dirty.

"Why are you here, Delaney?"

"You'd know if you'd given me two minutes of precious time on your most important night."

His jaw clenched, but his brow furrowed like he'd come to that same conclusion. "Care to tell me now?"

His drawl was barely there. It was subtle, more pronounced, depending on what Texans he had to impress. Archer was a land broker who didn't just buy and sell land —he bought and sold eight-, sometimes nine-figure tracts of land. Apparently, his boss thought a little twang would make him seem less intelligent and more incapable. Norville Truitt was the seediest man I'd ever met, and I couldn't believe Archer didn't see it.

My irritation amplified. The way Archer and his friends had flanked me that night, as if nothing going on in my life could ever be as important as their client dinner. That was Norville's influence.

He wanted the truth? I'd give him the truth. "My brother tried to kill himself."

His breath whooshed out. "What?"

"I'd qualify that as an emergency." I was a little too bittersweet, but I'd held on to these emotions for too long. "A reason to fly home on a moment's notice. Don'cha think?"

"Why the hell didn't you say something?" The audacity he had to look confused threw butane on my anger.

"Perhaps I realized my husband didn't take me seriously enough to listen to me over his friends. Perhaps I realized I wasn't as important to him as I'd hoped." Perhaps I'd realized it was all my stupid fault.

"You were important to me," he said defensively.

Past tense. "I was a doll you posed how you needed. Anyway, obviously Kane survived, but he's not taking over the ranch, so here I am."

"He's in therapy?"

I nodded.

"Good." Archer shoved his hands in his pockets and looked at the custom-made loafers on his feet. "Good."

A few moments of silence passed. The heat soaked into me, and I wanted to melt at his leather-clad feet. It'd always been like that with him. Once I was in his orbit, I didn't want to go anywhere else.

"I met my uncle."

This time, it was my brows that popped. "Which one?"

"Cameron. He asked if I wanted to meet the rest of the family."

"You gonna do it?" *Are you going to, Delaney. There's no reason to shorten words when you should be smart enough to enunciate.* Briony was a bitch. If I ever saw her again, I'd enunciate that.

Archer didn't seem to notice. "I don't know. I didn't realize how small Coal Haven really was. It strikes me that you know him better than I. That you know the rest of my dad's family when I don't."

I snorted. I'd told Archer I'd heard of them. I hadn't gone into detail, and he hadn't asked. Perhaps that should've been a big ol' red flag about our relationship. Archer had been cool with not knowing much about me or how I'd grown up, and I'd been the same. "Knowing them is different than liking them. None of them liked me. Even your cousin dumped me as soon as a new girl moved to town."

His lush lips formed a troubled line. "That you dated a cousin of mine is unnerving."

"High school sweethearts." Grief wove through me like it often did when I thought of my ex. I'd been so mad at him, so terribly hurt. But we'd grown up together. He'd been a friend in addition to my boyfriend. "He died a few years ago."

He frowned. "A few years ago? You didn't come back for the funeral?"

I looked away, staring at the slate-gray siding of the clinic. "No."

He waited, like he thought I was going to say more. Not coming home for Derek's funeral when I was supposed to be a happy newlywed had left me with complicated emotions. How did I tell my husband the situation? *By the way, not only have I heard of the Barrons, I was really close to one of your cousins for years. Grew up with him and thought I'd marry him. But meeting you was a total coincidence—mostly.*

I had considered how I'd arrive in Coal Haven for the funeral, and how while everyone was talking about what a tragedy Derek's death was and what an awesome guy he was, and oh, poor Kennedy, they'd still have the wherewithal to ask what I'd been up to. Where I had been.

I wouldn't have been able to answer the first question, much less the slew of them afterward. The land issues from my grandparents' day had spilled over to Ma and the Barrons as adults. The older Barrons weren't as well liked as they thought, but they were successful farmers and ranchers. They had oil money, and Cameron had a prominent position at the refinery. They were respected. Envied even. It'd been bad enough to have Bruce, Cameron, and Kira's disproval when Derek and I had dated, but I had also suffered the looks and the rude comments about not being good enough for Derek.

So, no. I hadn't come home. I'd added it to the giant pile of regrets.

"We need to talk, Delaney," Archer said quietly.

We'd had plenty of time to talk. "You want an annulment. I'll let you know when I'm ready to deal with it." *And with you.*

He made a disgusted sound. "Not the annulment, dammit. You're my wife. And I don't even know you."

I sent him an appraising gaze. "Do you think you would've married me if you had?"

His brows slammed together. "What the hell is that supposed to mean?"

I rolled my eyes. "Please. Pretty little arm candy for the southern boy climbing the corporate ladder. As soon as I stepped out of that role, you were done with me. The second I crossed you—done." He ground his jaws together, and I kept going. "You want to know me? People don't usually like what I have to say. Ballbuster, bitch, you name it, I've been called it. The Barrons fucking hate us and not just because we have land they want, but because we don't think their shit smells like roses and we're not afraid to say it. I get dirty when I work, and I stink, because that's what happens when you work in cow shit. If I never get another manicure again, it'll be too soon, but I don't mind dressing up. I just don't care whose name is on the label."

He continued to stare at me like he couldn't pair what I was saying with the woman he'd known.

I rose and brushed my ass off. "I'm going inside to wait for my brother."

"And the annulment?"

Of course he was still pursuing it—that was what he'd come here for. But a little part of me died. I'd been right.

A question rose in my mind. I hadn't thought of it earlier thanks to the shock of seeing him. "Why now?" The way he stilled made me push. "Why now, Archer? Why not last year? Last month? Why. Now?"

His expression clouded with guilt, and he glanced away.

A chill swept through me until it was like I stood in a freezer instead of outside in July. Just because I'd honored my vows didn't mean he had. "Let me guess. Briony found the perfect future little wife for you? Another one of her friends, so you can go on a cute little double date with her and Wilson? How nice for her you're going to be back on the market. I sure was a wrinkle in her plans."

"It's not like that, Delaney." The note of resignation didn't make me believe him.

Betrayal burned hot as a forge in my chest. "It isn't my business, is it?" I spun on a heel.

"Delaney, dammit." He cupped my elbow. "It's not—I'm not seeing anyone."

I shook my arm free. His touch was too familiar, too welcome. "What are you doing, then?"

His expression shuttered. "I'm not dating, but Briony and Wilson have a friend who works with Briony at the bank—"

"How nice of Briony and Wilson to preapprove your next wife."

"I haven't said I'd date her." His gaze hardened. "It just made me think... You left and never came back. I tried to contact you, but you wouldn't answer. You quit returning my messages. I get that I could've acted better, but you never gave me a chance."

I hadn't returned his messages. It hurt too bad. I was

afraid I'd hear exactly what he came here to tell me and the feelings of not being wanted once again would come roaring back. And they did.

Not one message said "I'm sorry" or asked "what happened?" I might've answered otherwise. "Aw, you poor guy. I hope you two are a good fit. Maybe when you marry her, you'll award *that* as the most important day of your life."

He recoiled, then clamped his jaw down. He hadn't realized how hurtful it'd been to hear him dismiss our wedding day like he had.

I strode away, calling over my shoulder, "Come by and try to catch me. Unlike you and your clients, we do more around here than jump on a horse in designer jeans and pretend like we know what the hell's going on."

If I'd thought I died a little inside earlier, now my heart was disintegrating into ash and blowing away.

* * *

Ma stood over my shoulder while I scowled at the computer screen. She'd brought the fresh scent of rain inside with her but had left Portia on the porch. I didn't hear the steady patter on the roof anymore. The hour it had lasted was the best music I could've listened to.

I'd looked up annulments in Texas yesterday, and my heart had sunk clear down to the bottom of a watering hole.

I hated having Ma in my private matters, but when I felt like it was me against Archer and his partners, I'd needed someone on my side.

Ma squinted at the screen. "What's the difference between an annulment and a divorce?"

"It's like our marriage never was." The memory of giggling and falling into his arms rose in my mind. We hadn't quit touching the entire weekend we'd gotten married. If I had to pretend I'd never been married, I wanted those memories to go away too.

"Meaning you get no money." No one ever accused Ma of being stupid. Stubbornness and pride interfered with her decisions, not a lack of smarts.

I'd be in the same boat if I wasn't careful. I tapped a finger on the screen. All the reasons why an annulment wouldn't be approved in Texas. "There're stipulations for an annulment."

Ma read over them. "Are they valid?"

Archer and I hadn't been intoxicated. Giddy on young love and champagne, but we'd knowingly married each other. I hadn't been underage. I'd met Archer after I finished college in Dallas, and we'd said *I do* before I turned twenty-five. Definitely old enough to know better.

But I hadn't been transparent. He could claim fraud. I'd lied about who I really was, and since Archer had access to better legal everything, I was screwed.

"Since I just now told Archer I dated his cousin for years and his uncle's my neighbor and I'd gone to school with a ton of his family, yeah, I'm sure they can claim I lacked transparency."

Ma propped her hands on her hips and cleared her throat. She did it so often, I doubted she realized she had that much phlegm. "Demand a divorce."

"I don't want his money."

She narrowed her eyes. I wasn't sure what look crossed my face. Panic? Obstinance? Pride? She rolled her eyes. "What do you want, then?"

Wasn't that the question? I wanted him to fight for me, but that ship had sailed. He was freeing himself so he could get it on with Briony's possibly gorgeous and legitimately sophisticated friend and not be the bad guy. Mostly what I wanted was to be able to pretend the marriage hadn't happened as easily as Archer would.

I took too long to answer, so Ma said, "Well, my two cents. Make 'em pay. One way or another. Lord knows Barrons can afford it. You ain't gonna get that kind of money here."

She left me alone to stare at the computer.

I let out a disgusted breath. Dammit. Why couldn't I just tell him to send me whatever had to be signed and walk away? I'd finally opened up and talked to Ma, but that hadn't helped. Or had it? She got me to realize I had feelings for a husband who wanted to want the person his arrogant friends thought was appropriate for him.

I'd known Briony had plans for Archer. He wasn't good enough for her to date or marry—she'd chosen Wilson, whose family was as affluent as hers. But he was clearly good enough for her friends.

When I'd met the Truitts, I hadn't been as awestruck as they thought I should be. I'd been raised around Barrons, who loved brandishing their land and oil money. And I'd seen the friendship with Archer for what it was. He was their pet project. Archer didn't talk about his childhood, but he hadn't grown up like them. He was their charity case. Rags to riches, all because of their goodwill.

I rolled my eyes.

Now, they had the perfect woman selected. Who wouldn't look at Archer and think he was God's gift wrapped in an Armani suit just for them? Why wouldn't Archer want her over me?

God, this hurt so damn much.

I wasn't a talker. I'd never had many friends. But I had a few now. Maybe it was time to talk to them.

I went outside. Heat wrapped around me, compressing the emotions I was already having a hard time dealing with.

My boots crunched through the gravel as I walked toward the barn. The sound dulled as I hit the mowed grass. Ma did a lot of the ranch stuff. Papa manicured the yard when he was actually home on the weekends. We had an older house. A worn red barn, and an even older white barn with peeling siding. But the lawn was on point. It was easier to keep a riding lawn mower going than to stick around home long enough to re-side a shop. Re-siding ate up too much fishing time.

But at least Papa hadn't asked Ma to pretend they'd never been married.

I crawled over the metal gate to the pasture and hopped down on the other side. Three horses nibbled the long grasses. The rain would help grow more food. Not enough to feed all the cattle, but I'd worry about that later.

The soft swish of the horses' tails reached my ears. They were grazing in the shade of the barn. Ma's old paint horse wandered away as soon as she saw me. It took oats and a prayer to catch that mare. Bolt the gelding watched me, his big, dark eyes interested. He was too high energy for an easy ride. My bay ignored me, tearing at the rapidly drying grass. I'd named her Target because of the white patch on her forehead. It was more round than oblong and made it look exactly like a bull's-eye.

The irony that I'd married a man named Archer was just mean.

"Wanna ride?" If I planned a longer ride, I'd skip it in this heat. But my trip would be short, and the grass she'd get at my destination would be worth it to Target.

I veered into the barn where we kept the tack. Target was as mellow as warm butter. Once she was saddled, I swung up and rode her across the yard, staying in the ditch along the driveway and all the way to my neighbor's house.

My friends Liam and Kennedy Barron. Friends who didn't know even half of my story.

I relaxed into the saddle, letting the sway of Target's easy gait chase away the tension that had been building since yesterday. I couldn't ignore Archer forever. He'd show up again eventually.

I rode next to the driveway, toward the shop. I never minded visiting Liam and Kennedy. Liam's grandparents had raised him on their ranch, but the operation had folded shortly after Liam moved out after graduation. He now lived in the house he'd grown up in and leased out the pastures to Bruce.

The shop doors were open. Liam's twins sprinted out, saw me, and ran for the house, calling for "Kenny," Liam's nickname for her since the first day they'd met.

I was almost to the main yard when Kennedy came through the door. She wore a loose T-shirt that was probably Liam's—they'd practically shared the same skin since they'd moved in together. Her denim shorts had been cut from an old pair of jeans. Another reason why I was so comfortable around her. She didn't put on airs.

When we were younger, she'd been a fragile little birdie. Cute and helpless. She'd been forced to come into her own after Derek died. Having a hot best friend turned husband who fully supported her while allowing her to do things for herself had helped.

I had the hot husband part. The support was missing.

Kennedy waved, her smile wide. I had never gotten that sort of enthusiastic reaction from anyone. Not from my shallow friends in high school, not even from Derek when he and I had been thick as thieves. Kennedy liked me for me, an outcome I had never imagined, one I decided I liked.

Eli sprinted for me, tripped over nothing, and cart-wheeled his arms, but stayed upright.

"Eli, what's the rule about horses?" Kennedy called in her calm teacher voice. There wasn't much the boys could do to get her worked up.

Eli stopped, and Owen pulled up short next to him with his face scrunched up and answered, "Don't charge them?"

"Right. So why don't we wait by the shop while she puts Target in the pasture?"

Liam had fenced off a small portion of the pasture by the shop just for Target. The thoughtful gesture made my chest tight. This was what having friends was like. To be wanted somewhere.

The pressure around my heart eased. "I put some carrots in the saddlebag for them to feed her."

Kennedy grinned. "You're their favorite aunt."

It wasn't much of a competition, but I preened anyway. Her sister rarely came to visit, and Liam didn't have siblings —not ones who talked to him, anyway. Cameron's other two kids had been trained to pretend he didn't exist.

She opened the gate, and I rode Target in. Eli and Owen dug out the carrots. Target was old and didn't get excited by the boys, but I made sure she attributed goodies to them anyway.

As Kennedy and I walked toward the house, Liam leaned out of the shop. He wore a thick apron and his hair was plastered to his head. He must have been welding one of the iron creations he made to sell at the furniture shop downtown. He said the owner marketed him so well that when she posted something of his, it was sold within twenty-four hours. I'd seen his work. It wasn't Hattie's marketing skills alone that sold them so fast.

"Hey, Laney. How's it going?"

I was about to say *fine* like I always did. Not today. "I've gotta talk to both of you, actually."

Liam frowned and stepped out. When I'd come home

after learning Kane was in the hospital, Liam had been the first to notice the tan line from my wedding ring. I had let him and Kennedy assume I was divorced.

"I, um, haven't been completely honest." I hadn't lied to them, and that had been good enough. Only one more thing I'd fooled myself about. I wiggled my ringless left hand. "So, funny story."

Four

ARCHER

I finished answering emails on my laptop. I had expected to drive to a larger town for decent internet service, but the motel had the best I'd encountered yet on my trip.

When I'd commented about the excellent Wi-Fi to the front desk clerk who owned the motel, she made a dry comment about being surrounded by energy industries. There was a coal mine not far away, the oil refinery, the coal gasification plant, and depending which direction I faced, wind farms. Stories-tall windmills circled in the distance. At night, their red lights dotted the horizon for miles. Those industries couldn't rely on crappy internet and cell service, and locals reaped the benefits.

I called Wilson. When he answered, I jumped right in. "I got the weather cycle reports for the Hernandez property and compiled the crop rotation and yield information. Tomorrow I'll dig into the water and mineral rights."

"It's done, then?"

"After I get the rights information and double-check the latest EPA regulations."

"No, Barron. The annulment."

I didn't want to talk about my annulment. I could picture him smoothing his pencil tie as he waited for my answer. What color did he wear today? As much as Briony tried to get me into the different colored suits her husband wore, they weren't me. Maybe I'd get there. Deep inside me was still that insecure country kid who got dumped for the star quarterback. Ansen and I hadn't been able to play sports. We'd had to help Dad every free minute we had.

"I've met with Delaney." I made our impromptu picnic table discussion sound like a corporate deal. "We have more to discuss."

"Discuss? It's yes or no." He made a knowing sound. "She's after the money, isn't she?"

I tamped down my irritation as thoroughly as I would a spark in dry grass. "It's complicated, Wil."

I thought back to our relationship. We'd dated for a few months before the trip to Vegas. Delaney hadn't asked to go on some expensive honeymoon. She'd been content with Vegas.

Since she'd been gone, she hadn't used our accounts. The last time she'd spent any money, it had been to buy a plane ticket to Bismarck the night she left me. When we were together, she'd seemed uncomfortable with my personal chef and the housekeeper. After we got married, I had insisted she get a better vehicle than the old rattletrap Corolla she'd driven when we met. That car hadn't moved since she'd last parked it.

Whatever Delaney had wanted out of me, it wasn't money. Not *my* money. Could it be something about my relatives?

"How complicated?" Wilson asked in the tone he used

that made him seem worldly and made me seem like the poor boy who had taken two-minute showers because the hot water hardly worked.

"She dated my cousin." I regretted telling him. He'd been ambivalent about Delaney when I married her, but afterward, he wasn't afraid to tell me I didn't need her anymore.

"Aren't your relatives rich? She's after his money, then."

"He died a few years ago." It was weird to say that about a relative I'd never met. Would we have been close? Friends? Would I have thought he was crazy when he dumped Delaney?

"Shit. I guess I can see it's not that straightforward. Let me know if you need any help on the Hernandez property."

Grateful he was willing to change the subject, I said, "Will do."

"But, Archer, don't let her get her hooks in you. Father has a good lawyer. If she's going to fight you—"

"Thanks, Wilson." I couldn't explain why I didn't want to hear Wilson talk about dragging Delaney through the courts. He'd been suspicious of her since I'd first told him I'd met *the one*. At the time, I thought he was looking out for me. I had assumed it was what friends did. I hadn't had many friends growing up. "I'll keep you informed."

"I'll be waiting to hear how it's going."

I hung up and stared at my computer screen. It'd gone blank. I wished my mind was as empty.

* * *

Laney

. . .

I reclined against the beam of the porch railing. Kennedy had asked me over again this morning, so after I finished topping off the water tanks, I rode Target over. She'd invited Aspen and Lyric. Lyric was besties with Derek's cousin, but she was younger than me and we hadn't talked much until now. Aspen had moved to Coal Haven a few years ago and worked with Kennedy.

"What would I have done if he'd showed up during the school year and you weren't here to listen to me whine?" I tossed my ball cap onto the wood next to me. The porch was shaded, and the temperature wasn't oppressive yet. It would be soon.

"Good thing summer school's done, or we'd have had to wait until the afternoon to hear how it's going." Kennedy rocked on one of the two chairs she had on the porch.

Aspen sat in the other rocking chair. Lyric was propped against another beam. She wasn't a teacher like Aspen and Kennedy, but she'd worked the weekend in the local clinic's lab and had the day off.

The four of us looked like we could be a group voted least likely to hang out. I was in my standard jeans and sleeveless top. Lyric wore a plaid skirt with a button-down white shirt tied around her waist like she was trying out her Sexy Schoolgirl Halloween costume early. Kennedy had on linen shorts and a tank top and was barefoot. And Aspen was in a jumpsuit like she'd walked out of New York Fashion Week.

Lyric had put her red-tinted hair into a ponytail. Three earrings lined each ear. The one on her left side was a golden snake that wrapped around the shell of her ear. "So, he, like, just showed up? Out of the blue?"

"Wants to date again," I said simply. "Just not me." The knife twist in the chest was just as sharp as when he'd told me the day before yesterday. Yesterday, he hadn't tried to contact me. I had slept shittily the last two nights and was perpetually hurt and confused.

Kennedy rocked her chair slowly and steadily. "If he wants to date so bad, why isn't he knocking your door down to sign the papers?"

"Maybe he thinks giving me space will make me more likely to be compliant." It was the only answer I could come up with.

"Do you have a picture?" Aspen curled one leg under her.

I dug out my phone. I wasn't a picture taker, so the ones I had of Archer weren't as far back as I wished they were. I scrolled to the photos of Vegas. Our wedding. Me in a white handkerchief dress and him in charcoal-gray trousers and a white shirt. I avoided looking too closely as I handed it to Lyric lest my heart fracture into a million pieces.

She accepted the phone and made a choking sound. "Holy *fuck*, Laney. This is him?"

Instead of grinning at her reaction, I succumbed to hopelessness. He really was the catch I thought he was. "Yup."

"I mean..." She handed the phone off to Kennedy.

Kennedy's brows lifted, but since she was the only one of us in a happy, healthy relationship, she wasn't as speechless. "I can see the resemblance, but I thought he'd look more like Derek."

Derek's hair had been more brown than black, and he hadn't been as tall as Archer. One of the things I cherished about our friendship was that Kennedy accepted that I was part of her first husband's life. She didn't try to erase my role as his ex or his friend. We could talk about him because he'd been important to both of us.

"It's Archer's mom. She died when Archer was a kid, so I never met her. But he said he gets his darker complexion and his dark hair from her." I hadn't met his dad either, but he probably looked like Bruce and Cameron.

Aspen stared at the photo. "You look happy."

We had been so damn happy. "Yup."

"This is your wedding photo, isn't it?" She handed the phone back.

I shut the screen off without looking at it. "Yes."

Kennedy frowned. "Why elope?"

That was one of the few questions about me and Archer I could actually answer. "He doesn't have much to do with his dad, and he hardly talks to his brother. I was still salty toward Ma and didn't want Coal Haven to know I'd stalked a Barron and married him. And his friends are assholes."

Lyric wrinkled her nose. "Fuck his friends."

"Right?" Of all of us, Lyric would understand how Archer's friends made me feel. She was best friends with Cameron's daughter, but as the science nerd with a punk streak, she hadn't been Cameron's or his wife Naomi's idea of a good friend for their little princess.

Props to Isla. She was ride or die with Lyric. But since Lyric was friends with Kennedy—and therefore Isla's estranged half brother, Liam—I didn't see them hang out. Isla was never part of our little get-togethers.

"So." Aspen switched which leg she had curled under her. "His friends are stupid rich, they want to hook him up with one of their other friends, and they encouraged him to get rid of you."

"Basically," I said.

"But he hasn't tried to end the marriage before that?" she asked.

I shook my head. He hadn't tried to save it either. "He tried to call the night I left. I didn't answer, so he left a message asking if I was okay. All I sent back was that I was fine. Then he sent me a happy birthday message like he was testing the waters. I never answered his calls."

Aspen glanced at Kennedy, then Lyric, before she said, "Then he might not want the marriage to end either."

I wrinkled my nose. "What do you mean *either*?"

"You would've answered and gotten the ball rolling." Kennedy's dark brows ticked up. "Do you want to stay married to him?"

"N-not like— Not when..." I leaned my head against the wood beam. "In another life, maybe. But he is who he is, and I am who I am."

Lyric was picking at a fingernail when she said, "But you two fell in love anyway?"

Was she reflecting on some deeper meaning she hoped mirrored the secret crush on Stetson that she thought none of us knew about? Did she think our circumstances would be similar if Stetson thought of her as more than his little sister's best friend? His family would also think he was way too good for someone like her. But Archer had fallen for me anyway.

I wasn't succumbing to a fantasy. "He doesn't know the real me."

"Just to be, like, devil's advocate"—Aspen rocked her chair like Kennedy—"you weren't rolling in a Mercedes, were you? Wearing Dolce and Gabbana every day after you bathed in Chanel No. 5?"

As if she sensed what Aspen was getting at, Kennedy asked, "You weren't telling him stories about how your coworkers pissed you off and you added salt to their coffee when they weren't looking?"

A smile twitched my lips. "Mr. Conlin had that coming when he insinuated I had someone else write my English paper. But I wouldn't have done that at my job. It was shitty, but I'm not childish. Anymore."

Kennedy's warm expression was supportive, but there was warning. "I just don't want you to assume someone like him couldn't fall for someone like you and write this whole marriage off because of it. The couple in that photo looks crazy in love."

"It was the alcohol." It wasn't the alcohol. Archer didn't drink very much. He had a scotch when he'd had a stressful day. He drank beer only if a client insisted, but as much as he seemed to like it, he didn't touch the stuff otherwise. And all I'd had that day was our celebratory champagne. "So what should I do?"

Kennedy rocked steadily. "Maybe figure out what you really want, and if he can't or won't give you that, then go ahead with the annulment, or a divorce, or whatever makes you happy."

I knew what I wanted. A guy who loved and supported me unconditionally. A guy I could be myself with and not see how he worried about what others thought. So, the hang-up was on whether he could or would give that to me, and I'd seen his answer so far.

Five

ARCHER

I was supposed to begin the drive back tomorrow. The earlier, the better. Yet I'd waited a full day to seek Delaney out.

The realization, followed by the resignation and betrayal, of what had brought me to North Dakota refused to leave my memory. The anger that had brightened her eyes and flushed her face wouldn't either.

Thinking back, I'd seen hints of her temper. Nothing of the magnitude to make me stop and think she had much of one. Depending on the situation, usually around Wilson and Briony, I had written off Delaney's flush as embarrassment. Maybe she was a little chagrined. But there'd been a spark in those brilliant blue eyes. A flash I'd anticipated but which had never amounted to anything.

She'd been hurt and pissed. And she'd tried to hide it.

Delaney had never gotten mad at me. She would always give me a big smile, and I had believed everything she said.

Was it the state of my sex-deprived brain that made it all crystal clear now? I'd been steeped in all things petite and blonde and was so trusting of my wife I hadn't questioned a thing, including her identity, her past, her family, or how she truly felt.

I hadn't asked because she might've asked reciprocal questions. And what would I have said?

If she had showed me her true self, would I have fallen so hard for her? Her looks were one thing, but had they been everything? She'd followed my business talk. I had thought I was boring her. Being a land broker wasn't exciting to someone out of the loop.

Wilson would say it was the dollar signs behind the shoptalk that held Delaney's interest. But she hadn't been lost. She knew about land. Its resources. Acres and how they related to farmers and ranchers. She'd followed every damn word.

Why had Delaney thought I would need a simpering, vapid woman at my side?

I turned off the highway and onto a gravel road.

I'd thought I was done with gravel. Hearing it kick up under the tires should have made me cringe. The car might get chips in the paint or the windshield or a flat tire from screws and nails hidden by all the rocks. Gravel roads were shitty on a vehicle, and my car wasn't just functional. It was a status symbol. I didn't kid myself about that. Clients who were trusting me to help them buy millions of dollars of property didn't want to see me in a beater.

What was this car's status in Coal Haven? Was it diminished to economical, a vehicle that got better gas mileage than the larger pickups that had to haul cattle supplies, trailers, and tools? The answer was all around me.

Cattle dotted the pastures. Simmental and Red Angus. I was pretty sure this was Delaney's family's land, and I wanted to see it all. Curiosity about my wife wasn't the only motivator. I dealt in land. Lived and breathed it. Whether my family had it or not had dictated everything in my life. I didn't own one square foot of land, but I bought and sold it for others.

As I crested a hill, I spotted a stock pond. Due to the drought, the waterline was down several feet, but thanks to the rain, the edges were a sloppy, suctiony mess. A little brown calf floundered, struggling to free itself while its equally muddy mother lowed from the edges. She must've been getting a drink and the little guy tried to follow her in.

The calf's attempts were weakening even as I slowed. It would die without help. I would've stopped anyway, but the way I grew up, I couldn't not stop.

I pulled the car to the edge of the road, parked, and tossed my phone and my wallet onto the seat. I would never leave my car and belongings like this in Texas, but the only people driving these roads were Delaney's family—or mine. On that odd thought, I ran down into the ditch. Broom grass brushed against my pants. I held down the top line of barbed wire and leaped over the fence.

I sprinted through the pasture, trying to remain upright on the uneven ground in my leather-soled dress shoes and keep from twisting an ankle in a gopher hole. The land sloped down from the fence, then up and down toward the stock pond. I stayed in shape. My condo had a gym, but I hadn't run on anything but a treadmill or a paved path in years. There was nothing in a gym that simulated barbed wire.

As I neared, the mama cow mooed, but she was more focused on her baby than on me.

The ground was soft before I hit the mud and life became instant slow motion. Mud sucked my feet deeper, and dammit, I lost one shoe and then the other. I probably didn't want either one back, but that would be hundreds of dollars lost to the earth.

I high-kneed through the muck until I reached the calf. It was tipped over, its face pushed into the mud, as it continued to attempt to free itself. Its struggles had only worked it deeper. Little bleats left it as I reached under its belly, ignoring the warm mud that was probably more than just dirt and water, and wrapped my arms around it. With one arm around its chest and the other around its behind, I lifted.

Two hundred–plus pounds came free. I gritted my teeth as Mama Cow's calls grew more frantic. At least with the mud, I didn't have to worry about being charged.

This would've been a hell of a lot easier on a horse, though. Like the time Ansen and I had roped two calves that had gotten caught in a mini mudslide.

God, it'd been years since I'd recalled that day. We'd been so damn proud of our scrawny selves. Dad too.

What would've made me prouder was if we had owned the ranch I'd grown up on instead of merely managing it. But the animals didn't care who owned it, and they were the most important part of the business.

I waded out and set the calf down as soon as I reached stable ground. On shaky legs, the animal wobbled toward the mama. I staggered away from them just in case Mama Cow thought I was a threat. Adrenaline pumped through my body. I couldn't outrun her with all the mud around my legs. I'd be sorer tomorrow than I had been from any workout in the last twelve years.

I glanced around. Cows stared at me, their tails swishing. I nodded at them and turned.

A woman on a horse gawked at me. "Archer?"

My wife wore jeans and a blue sleeveless shirt. Her worn cowboy boots were shoved into the stirrups, and she loosely held the reins. She looked comfortable in the saddle, more at ease than I'd ever seen her outside of bed.

My breathing was starting to slow. Grass poked through my wet and destroyed socks. I smelled like old fish and decaying organic matter. My clothing was ruined, and if I hadn't been driving by, that calf might've died. Not only was it a life that didn't have to perish, it'd be like burying money in the mud with my shoes.

"You need to give these cows a better water source."

Her surprised expression instantly morphed into ire. She smacked her lips. "Well, I'll just put up a sign by the pond. 'Please use the water tanks instead. Thank you, Management.'"

Of course they had better water for their cattle. They were seasoned ranchers, and I was acting like a dumbass.

I brushed my arm across my forehead, realizing too late that I was just transferring dirt to what probably had been one of the few clean spots left on me. "Sorry. It's just... if I hadn't come by, that calf might've died."

Her brows popped. There was nothing in her expression that told me she took what I said as an apology. "If only there was another rancher around." Her tone was as dry as the gravel on the road.

Right. I'd just insulted her. Again. On top of claiming my promotion was the most important day of my life. My wedding had been important. Even more, it'd been the best day of my life in a way that no client dinner would ever compete with. The client dinner would've changed my career and our lives for the better. I would've been partner. A level I never thought a hick kid from the country could attain.

I tried to make it better. "I mean, what are the odds that more than one person would've seen it?"

Her brows rose. "Probably the same as seeing Archer Barron's designer clothes covered in mud."

I clapped my hands together as if that would get the mud off. "You've said a few things that make me think you don't believe I've ever gotten my hands dirty before."

She kept a brow raised.

"I told you my dad managed a ranch." We'd owned none of it. It was what had gotten me interested in being a land broker, in why some people could afford all the land in the world, but families like ours could only be the hired help. "Ansen and I were his free labor."

She hmphed, and her horse shifted to the side. It was a nice-looking mare. Older, if I had to guess, but obviously a good quarter horse. I hadn't even known she had a horse. "What's her name?"

"Target." Delaney leaned forward and patted the horse's neck like she couldn't help herself. "She's almost twenty."

I could see a seven-year-old Delaney naming a horse Target. I could also see this Delaney charging off her horse and wading into the muck. I couldn't say that about the woman who was my wife in Texas.

I held my hands out and looked down at myself. "Can I clean up at your place?"

The moment of panic was fleeting in her gaze, but I felt like shit nonetheless. How had we gotten to this point? She was scared to bring me to her home.

"We've gotta talk anyway. All I need to borrow is a pair of shorts and a T-shirt." I glanced down again. "Any chance your brother or your dad have shoes that would fit me?" Anything to get me to my motel room, where my suitcase waited for me on the dresser. There'd been no luggage stand. There wasn't much of anything in the motel room.

Her lips were pressed together as her gaze dipped to my soggy socks. Would she send me on my way a muddy mess?

Was there a place here that would detail the muddy insides of an Audi?

"Fine." She slid down from Target. "But you're cleaning the saddle when you're done."

She wanted me to ride Target? Would she walk next to me? She had boots, I had nothing, but that wasn't acceptable. "No, I can walk."

"I don't want you dragging burs through the house. Target will be easier to clean than your car. I'll drive that back."

The car, yes. Adrenaline and my sexy wife were clouding my thinking.

She led Target to me, and I took a moment to let the horse get used to my presence. The mare didn't seem like she got bothered by much. Due in part to her personality, her age, and being ridden by a young Delaney, who was probably wilder than I had ever imagined.

"Thank you." Handing my keys to her felt like progress. The clock was ticking, but we could peacefully dissolve the marriage before I left.

"Yep." She stomped through the ditch and up to my waiting vehicle. I swung onto Target and breathed a sigh of relief. I hadn't gotten to ride nearly as much as an adult as I had as a kid. Muscles I'd forgotten about flexed and stretched, another thing the gym couldn't replicate. I missed riding.

I adjusted the reins in my hands. Target probably wouldn't need much encouragement to return home. I gave her a little tap with my heel. She started at an easy gait. The engine of the car fired up. Target tossed her head, but only as if to tell me she wasn't changing speed or direction. An easygoing horse with a streak of stubborn.

How much like her owner was she?

* * *

Laney

Ma's truck was gone. I figured she must have been in town running errands. Kane was nowhere to be seen. He was likely at his little place on the edge of our property. I had been surprised when he'd gone back. He hadn't hurt himself there, but I had wondered if it symbolized the prison he'd felt like he'd been in all his adult life.

I parked the car in front of the house so Archer could walk right in and leave after he cleaned up.

Archer waited with Target by the entrance of the barn. As I approached, he swung down. He'd made riding full of mud with no shoes look as hot as when he donned a felt Stetson, crisp black jeans, and his Frye Austin boots. Only with the mud on him, I almost believed he'd done more than play on the ranch he claimed his family had once run.

I hadn't seen that side of him. The corporate gig, the expensive condo, and the premium vehicle, yes. Dirty, hard-working cowboy, no.

I made him stand in his wet socks as I led Target into the barn. I took my time taking her saddle off and brushing her down. I needed a moment. I'd poured my heart out to Kennedy, Aspen, and Lyric. Weathered their stunned expressions, soaked in their worry over how I was taking this, and then had planned to ride home and be on my own to figure out what I was going to do. None of that had included my husband acting the hero for a helpless calf that wasn't his.

After I released Target into the pasture, I strode out of the barn and past Archer without a word. Maybe I should've spent more time with Target.

He rounded the gravel driveway, staying in the grass as

much as possible. I waited by the front door, dying inside with each step he grew closer. He was coming into the house.

I'd grown up here. I knew it wasn't some rustic lodge. It wasn't from this century and had seen quite a bit of the last. Not much different from many of the other homes in the county. Starkly different from a two-million-dollar condo.

"This isn't some fancy house in a gated neighborhood." As if it wasn't obvious, the only gates were between the pastures.

Archer glanced at the house and frowned. I bristled. Was he noticing the peeling Masonite siding he'd missed the first time he'd been here? Or the way the porch creaked when I took the first step? The overgrown flower beds Ma gave up on weeding by early June, if she tried in the first place? Papa would do it sometimes to get out of some other work, but he hadn't this year, and each tall blade of quack grass was like a tie-dyed flag calling for the eye's attention.

"I don't need it to be," he said.

I clenched my jaw. His place overlooked downtown. The walk-in closet was bigger than the room I was currently sleeping in, and his shower had six heads. In a few minutes, he'd enter a bathroom with one showerhead that had several clogged nozzles. "Are you sure about that?"

"Delaney, I grew up in a small house too. Doing chores and working cattle."

"Not like this."

"More like this than you know," he muttered as he went up the stairs.

"Doubt it." Had I claimed I wasn't childish only this morning?

He sighed, his arms hanging at his sides. "I wasn't the most open about my life either. The house I grew up in was better than a shack, but it wasn't..." He took in the weathered wood of the porch, the screen door with the half-ripped screen, and the crack in the living room picture window. "It wasn't much different than this. Worse, really."

The last part had come out reluctantly, like he hadn't wanted to admit it. I tried to picture Archer in a run-down house in the middle of Texas. The Archer I had married with his expensive suits and his thousand-dollar shoes would've helped buyers plan the demolition of old houses like this when they purchased the land they sat on. Muddy Archer, who had rescued a calf that wasn't his, looked like he might be more familiar with my lifestyle. Still, it was hard to believe.

"Sure." I turned to the door.

He reached for me but saw the mud on his hand. Clenching a fist, he pulled his arm away. "My dad's boss refused to put money into the house, and he'd only fork over for repairs on the barns and the shops if Dad couldn't fix them first. The year Mama died, he was going to dock our family's pay permanently until Ansen and I started doing her house-keeping duties at the main lodge." He pushed a hand over his hair and winced when it caught on dried mud. "When I was born, we owned everything. Then there were some bad years—Mama got sick and Dad lost the ranch. The new owner kept him on as ranch manager while Mama cleaned for the main lodge that used to be our home. We had to move to the piece-of-shit hunting cabin where no one could see us."

This was the most relatable I'd ever seen him. Pain was carved into his face, as if recounting how he was raised physically flayed him. "I didn't know. But it's nothing to be ashamed of."

He opened his mouth like he was going to say more but then shut it. Instead, he shook his head and said, "I was ashamed, for different reasons, and I sure as hell wasn't goin' to stay there. I know you hated that I kept a housekeeper, but I was over cleanin' toilets by that point."

The heat in his tone wasn't because he thought he was above it and therefore better than those who did it for a living. It wasn't the cleaning. It was how someone had made him feel about it. "People can be assholes, Archer. But it reflects on them, not us."

"Yeah, well, I wasn't proud of where I came from, and I wasn't going to stay there."

Didn't he see that was the big issue between us? "My surroundings don't dictate my worth." Neither did who I was with.

"I never said they did."

But in his mind, they determined his worth. I had been turning myself inside out because Archer didn't know the real me. Did I know the real him? "No, you let the Truitts decide."

His hard gaze pinned me in place as easily as his body. He kept enough distance between us that no mud got on me, but his body heat was more effective at increasing my discomfort. "Norville Truitt pulled a kid out of the gutter and made him think he could do something with his life."

Norville Truitt. The guy was as seedy as the cornfield down the road. "Did Norville tell you that before or after you kept his son from failing out of college? Because from what I saw, his help had conditions, and his help benefited him more than you."

Archer's brow furrowed. "Norville gave me my career. Everything I have is because of him."

"And he never fails to remind you."

The muscles at the corner of his jaw flexed. "It's not like that."

"Really? Did you make partner? Or did my 'scene'"—I

threw up air quotes—"give him the perfect excuse to keep you as his peon?"

"Jesus, Delaney." But he looked away.

Dumbfounded, I stammered, "Y-you aren't a partner?"

"No."

"Oh." Acid burned in my stomach. Was it because of me and the scene I'd made? I'd interrupted Archer talking to a potential client after I'd gotten the call about Kane from Papa. Wilson had sicced Briony on me while I was tugging on Archer's suit coat like a five-year-old child, and she'd dragged me out of the room.

And the person I'd been so desperately trying to be had complied. I had just heard that my brother shot himself in the head, yet I'd glued myself together. I could cry while I was packing. I could cry on the plane. I could cry when I was tucked into Archer's arms after I saw that Kane would be okay.

Then Archer had approached, his face full of thunderclouds, and he'd chewed into me about how I was acting, his voice low, anger reverberating in every word. And my world had caved. The paper palace I had built for myself collapsed under the pressure of the real world. So I came home to the real world and left my fake existence behind.

I hadn't thought about any repercussions for him, and standing on the porch while he was crusted over with ick wasn't the time. I opened the door. "Better get that shower done."

The intensity of his gaze grew like he wasn't going to let the conversation drop. But he relaxed and held his arms out and looked at himself. "You'll have to excuse my manners as I take all this off, but I'd rather your family see me in my underwear than track mud all over their house, as thanks for your hospitality."

My mind froze on the reference to underwear. "You don't have to—"

He shucked his socks first, then yanked his shirt off. He dumped it on the porch over his socks. The guy had ridiculous abs. A wide chest. No farmer's tan like I sported, but an even bronze over his chest and arms.

He flipped open the clasp of his pants and shoved them down. My mouth went dry.

It'd been too damn long since I'd seen this man naked. The land wasn't the only thing experiencing a drought.

He kicked his pants aside. "I don't think they can be saved."

I dragged my gaze to his dark eyes. They danced with humor. He'd busted me staring at him like we hadn't just had the deepest conversation of our marriage.

My stomach did the most traitorous flip. I spun on my heel and didn't bother holding the door open for him. I went straight down the hallway to the little closet we used for linen and useless junk Ma would never get rid of. I grabbed a towel and a washcloth. They weren't the super-fluffy, extra-soft, ultra-absorbent stuff he owned.

I turned, and he was right there. My fingers brushed against his warm chest.

The dank smell of the stock pond clung to him, but without his clothing and the smell of horse sweat, Archer's scent was able to break through.

Instead of closing my eyes and inhaling deeply, I said, "Geez, Archer. Give me some room, will ya?"

He was no longer looking at me like I was from another planet—the way he had since he'd arrived. The corner of his mouth kicked up. "I didn't want to be forward and assume which bathroom you wanted me to use."

"It's right there. Behind you."

He didn't turn. His gaze dropped to my lips. "So it is."

I swallowed hard, and his gaze darkened. The air thickened between us. This was why I'd pretended to be someone else. Because being around him, seeing him want me like that, was addictive, a drug I didn't want to live without and had been willing to leave everything I knew for.

I couldn't go back there. Neither could I move away from him, and it had nothing to do with the shelving at my back.

He swayed closer, crushing the towels between us, until his mouth was on mine.

Memories crashed into me. The way he could make me gasp. How he held me as he plunged into me. My cries when he made me come over and over.

I stiffened, but his kiss only softened; it didn't let up until, eventually, I was moving my lips under his, kissing him back. He didn't touch me, and I melted even more at the thought that he was being considerate about his dirty hands and arms. He had ways of making me feel precious. Another addiction. I'd never been precious to anyone.

The front door opened, and a dog barked. I jumped away, slamming into the shelves behind me. "Dammit."

Ma's rough voice called, "Hope I ain't interrupting nothing."

Archer's hooded gaze was purely for the bedroom. Not the middle of my house.

"No, Ma. Archer rescued a calf from the stock pond by the road, so he's cleaning up." I shoved him away. He reluctantly moved enough that I could edge by him. I pushed the towels into his hands and turned away, calling to Ma, "Think Papa would mind if he borrowed a shirt and some shorts?"

I left Archer in the hallway. He could find the bathroom easy enough. What I wished I could leave behind was how kissing him again only reminded me how good it was between us.

* * *

Archer

While I'd been cleaning off, the bathroom door had opened and closed. As much as I'd wished Delaney would slip in, take her clothes off, and come into the shower with me, it hadn't happened.

She still wanted me. And I spent too long in the shower pondering that news. We'd argued. I'd told her a little about how I'd grown up, but it hadn't dampened her reaction to me.

The girls Briony and Wilson had set me up with before I'd met Delaney hadn't been as stout. Those girls were from a different world. Dating me was more about the image we presented than whether we knew each other. I had lived through a time when Dad had forgotten to buy essentials like shampoo and toilet paper because Mama had been so sick and I hadn't been old enough to drive. And it wasn't like I'd offered up that information.

Hey, did your parents ever have only beer in the fridge?

I turned off the spray before I wasted more of the Grangers' water and stared at the white-tiled walls. Parts of several tiles had chipped and cracked, and the grout around the base by the tub was blackened in parts. The place was clean but so old that some areas just refused to look any more than they were. The bathroom in the house I'd grown up in had looked different, but the age and the wear had been similar.

I didn't miss having to fix handles that would no longer

screw into stripped-out cabinets. Plumbing that ran hot, then cold, low pressure or no pressure. Flooring that was a few decades past replacement. In my current place, everything was new and modern, and, more importantly, not broken. My housekeeper came in once a week to clean the nonexistent layer of dust that had accumulated. Simple.

It used to be.

I was supposed to drive up here, arrange an annulment, and then go back to Texas a single man and start dating again.

My stomach twisted. Over the last few days, the only part of the plan I was okay with was the "driving up here" part. I opened the shower curtain with the mermaids dancing on it to grab a towel. I'd had to stoop to get my body under the spray of the showerhead, but I was clean and mud-free. I pressed the towel to my face and inhaled a faint strawberry scent under the smell of fabric softener.

I dried off with the coarse towel. I'd get some added exfoliation. The clothing waiting for me was a pair of large black basketball shorts and an old gray T-shirt that read "Coal Haven Drillers" with a logo of a guy in a hard hat flexing his muscles. My lips curled up. In Texas, if you weren't playing a sport the moment you could walk, you ended up benched more often than not, and it didn't matter how much money your daddy had.

Since my daddy had had no money, we were all too busy working to spare time for something that wasn't going to put food on the table.

I bet Coal Haven was small enough to play every kid who wanted to try out. The trade-off for fewer opportunities in a smaller population was that more people could participate.

Was this what my life would've been like if Dad had reconciled with Uncle Cameron and stayed? He wouldn't have met Mama and put down roots. He might've learned what it took to run a successful ranch and hang on to it so when he met some young girl and had kids, he wouldn't rim the fucking drain of life. Would my life have been different? Ansen's? Mama's?

Would I have snatched up Delaney before my cousin had a chance? Would I have been smart enough to keep her?

I shook my head. Moot points. Mama was gone. Dad was nearly there. Ansen was fucking around somewhere in the country. I'd worked hard to get to where I was. Got my degree. Got a good job and had a chance at making partner with a man I admired. But I'd sacrificed my marriage the night of the dinner with Jaycee Henry. The following eighteen months had been some of the longest and loneliest of my life.

I pushed a hand through my hair and glanced in the mirror. A shadow of a beard graced my jaw. I could use a hair trim before I returned to work. Since I'd met Mr. Truitt, I hadn't let my clean-cut appearance falter. He was old school. His meticulous attention to appearance had rubbed off on Wilson and then on me.

I couldn't delay leaving the bathroom any longer. The shower hadn't helped to clear up a damn thing. All I knew was after that kiss, I didn't give a shit about an annulment.

I was still barefoot, and while it was weird to walk around someone's place without socks, it wasn't like I had shoes either.

I found Delaney in a little office with an inflatable twin bed behind a desk. She glanced up from an old laptop that ran like it was a jet engine readying for takeoff.

I frowned at the device. "You need a new computer."

"I need a few hundred dollars," she said flatly. "But we need food and feed more, so as long as this is working, I'm using it."

I could go buy her one. I doubted there was a computer for sale in Coal Haven, but it would be nothing for me. I could buy a hundred laptops before I flinched.

Note to self: order laptop.

I soaked her in. Her sleeveless top showed the curves of her muscles and the hint of a tan line around her bra strap. I could picture her throwing square bales onto a flatbed trailer. "Do you know where I can get a haircut and some clothes?"

Her gaze was wary, like she had no idea why I would ask. "There's a barber in town."

"Can I schedule an appointment online?"

Her lips adopted a wry twist. "You can stop in. And bring cash. I doubt Bernie has Squarespace in the barbershop. Otherwise, Dickinson or Bismarck would have more choices."

"I need to grab some pants." I had packed clothing that was better for the office, and I didn't feel like standing out like a throbbing thumb. "Does that place on the edge of town have clothing? Isn't it called Dollar something?"

She barked out a laugh. "No. Tractor Supply carries some men's clothing. The gas station has a few T-shirts, otherwise, Dickinson or Bismarck."

"Aren't they an hour away?" I couldn't even buy underwear in Coal Haven? "What about shoes?"

"I'm sure you can find flip-flops somewhere in town." She grinned like she knew I'd never worn flip-flops in my life. "Otherwise, Tractor Supply might have some, but I can't guarantee what kind of selection and sizes they carry."

I could take my chances with the tractor supply place or go somewhere I should be able to get everything I needed. And I had a killer idea I couldn't ignore. "All right, funny girl. Get in the car. You're coming with."

Her eyes widened. "Why?"

"Because we need to talk, and I need to buy some clothes."

"Aren't you leaving soon?"

"No." I held her gaze as I leaned back against the door frame and crossed my arms. My decision was immediate, and I couldn't take it back. "I want to get to know my wife."

She opened her mouth and closed it again. "You want an annulment."

"That was before you kissed me back."

Her eyes flared, and her gaze darted to the hallway. "Archer."

"Delaney, you told me I wouldn't want you if I knew the real you. Prove it."

Her gaze went frosty. "See, I'm not interested in proving anything when another woman's got her lacquered claws in you."

"What other woman? Briony's friend? No, she's got nothing in me, and I've had nothing in her or anyone else."

"But you want to. That's why you're here."

"*No.* I thought I should move on." Frustration roiled under my skin. "Everyone was tellin' me I should move on. I listened cuz I didn't know what else to do. That's why I'm here."

I dropped my hand to my side. I had believed them because it had seemed like a way out of the fog I'd been living in. Each message, each attempt to call, had put me in a near panic attack. Would she answer and tell me she was done with me? It was why it took eighteen months to do something. I didn't want us to be over. "Look, I don't know what to do any more than you do, but I haven't touched another woman since I first laid eyes on you, and I haven't wanted to. So how 'bout we start with you helpin' me get some clothes and a haircut?"

She considered me. Yeah, I'd heard the twang come out

too. Which I promptly forgot about when she said, "You're assuming I haven't moved on."

Her words were like an ice pick to the gut. "I— Wha— Are you datin'?"

Her back was ramrod straight as she gave me an imperious look. "No, but you seemed to assume it was impossible."

"I know it's not impossible. Look at you."

She cocked her head as if she was stunned I would think she was dead sexy in her work clothes. "I guess I assumed you were in the same place I was. Not sure what to do and waitin' for the other to make the first move."

"Well, you made the first move count." Hurt echoed through her words.

I wanted to shred those annulment papers. I wanted to go back to that conversation with Wilson and Briony when they discussed how an annulment was the best route, and, by the way, they knew a good lawyer. I wanted to have a long, hard talk with myself about what I had expected when I showed up here.

"I can't deny what I tracked you down for. But I also can't regret that I did. Can we at least spend some time together and talk? We shouldn't end this marriage as spontaneously as we began it."

Delaney dropped her gaze to her hands. I wished I could read her mind. When she looked up, she said, "We might as well go to Dickinson first. You can get both a haircut and clothing."

I forced myself to remain serious, but I really wanted to pump my fist in the air. "Yes, ma'am."

* * *

Laney

. . .

Archer walked out of the hair place, running a hand over his scalp, his mouth turned down. I had run into the dollar store and grabbed him a pair of black flip-flops. In his outfit, he looked like he was heading to the beach.

I held in a snicker, and he shot me a glare. I fought my laughter. "It's not bad."

"It's... okay. For a twenty-dollar cut," he grumbled. "And by someone who's barely out of high school."

His haircut was fine—a little closer to the scalp than he preferred on the sides, and the top was mostly even. The stylist had gelled and styled it to within an inch of its life. The look wasn't Archer. The backward ocean wave off to the side was Wilson's style. Archer preferred a clean part with minimal hair product.

He feathered his fingers over his head, his mouth curling like he couldn't help but be disgusted. "I tip my usual guy more than twenty bucks."

He'd tipped the young girl more than what the haircut cost too. He hadn't mentioned it, and I only noticed when her eyes had grown round and she'd profusely thanked him.

I found his generosity incredibly hot. So I switched my attention to the next items on his to-do list. "What do you want for clothing?"

"Does it matter?" he asked wryly.

On the way to town, he'd grilled me about what clothing Dickinson offered. The choices for men weren't as plentiful, and there weren't any Ralph Lauren or Neiman Marcus stores.

"Take your pick—skater boy, cowboy, or schoolteacher. Which look do you want?"

"When in Rome." Archer opened the passenger door for me. "I'll go with cowboy."

I got in and waited until he was behind the wheel before I said, "Boot Barn, it is. But you're just wearing them for a day or two." He didn't say, but I assumed he didn't want to get his good clothes dirty. In case he played the hero for any more cattle. "Why don't we just go to the thrift store—"

"No." He stared out the windshield, everything about his demeanor hard. "I'm never stepping foot in a fucking thrift store, secondhand store, or flea market."

Embarrassment flooded my cheeks. Ma used to bring Kane and me to town for back-to-school thrift store shopping, and I had enjoyed the trips. "Some of us poor folk sometimes have no choice but to shop there."

He let out a long breath and closed his eyes. "You think I'm sitting here hating on everyone who goes there?"

"Sounded a little judgmental." Sounded like what a Truitt would tell him.

"It's not judgment." His jaw worked. "When I started making my own money, I swore I would never buy used clothing again. Never."

"Why was it so bad? People love their thrifty finds. I once scored an almost new Columbia coat for twenty bucks."

"Maybe it depends on the kids people go to school with. My classmates weren't as open minded." His gaze turned faraway, like he was lost in the past. "It was a small school, and while everyone seemed closer because of it, my brother and I were always on the outside. Between our bathroom situation, the clothing that never fit quite right or was out of style, and our shaggy appearance... we just couldn't win."

I pictured a dirty, haphazard young Archer, and my heart cracked. "Kids can be cruel."

"Yeah." He went to put the car in gear, but he didn't. "I actually had a girlfriend in high school."

I wasn't surprised. Going a few days without a shower

and long uneven hair wouldn't diminish his looks. But his tone didn't make it sound like the girlfriend situation ended well. "It didn't end well?"

"To her, it probably seemed like it ended with a mutual understanding. Sure, it was reasonable that she'd want to go to prom with a guy who could afford to at least rent a tux. Those photos last a lifetime, after all." Bitterness hung off his words. "She thought I should be fine staying at home while she went with someone else. She claimed it was just one night. I was gutted."

I made a disgusted noise. "Fuck her." He lifted a brow, and I shook my head. "She was awful, not you. And if you want to buy brand-new stuff you'll never wear again, that's fine. I get it."

I also got why the Truitts had such a hold on Archer. They were refined and polished, and they hadn't dumped him for a guy with a nicer tux. But that was because Archer made money for them. I was sure if he'd raked in the cash for his high school girlfriend, she might've kept him around. Norville Truitt was just a slicker version of that girl.

He put the car in gear. The conversation was over. "How do I get to the western store?"

Six

LANEY

This had turned out to be a weirdly normal afternoon.

He didn't mention saving the calf. He hadn't once checked around his car to look for dings or chips. But he had taken it through a car wash. We both knew it'd get dusty as soon as he took me home, but the car wash was like the new clothes. Some things he had to do to keep the insecure kid from taking over.

We were on our way back to Coal Haven. He wanted to see the countryside, so I directed him through the back roads, taking county highways instead of the straight shot off the interstate.

Trees concealed the golf course on the edge of town. Houses spread out from there, mostly on one side, as the highway curved through. I was staring out the window. It was better than seeing Archer in the snug green T-shirt and the dark-wash jeans he'd gotten at the Boot Barn. He'd even bought a pair of boots. Not flashy ones. These were made for work.

I hadn't asked what he planned to do with them. Maybe it was a treat for him to buy new western clothing, down to the boots, when he was leaving soon. Briony would faint if she saw him dressed like this. She'd probably ban him from the state until he changed clothes.

"It's really beautiful here." Archer's wrist was propped over the steering wheel. His gaze swung over the rolling hills, touched on the pasture dotted with cattle on his side, and the field full of leafy corn on my side.

Pride swelled in my traitorous chest. His enthusiasm was genuine; he liked the place I called home. "It's a dry year; otherwise, it'd be really green."

"How are the cattle handling the drought?"

Anxiety burned in my gut. "It's so dry. We're cutting hay next week, and I think we'll pull the cattle from the pastures early and feed them like it's winter." I leaned my elbow by the window. "I've heard that the dry weather has brought out the blister beetles. I'm going to go look, but we can't feed the horses that hay. It could kill them. We can cut it with silage for the cattle and save us some extra cost buying clean hay."

He whistled. "Blister beetles are nasty."

I wasn't surprised he'd heard of them and the damage they caused. Some parts of Texas had them bad, and Archer's business was to know the good and the bad of the acres he sold. "Yep. And when hay's short, the price per round bale can triple." It was nice to vocalize my worries with someone who understood. Ma liked to pretend everything was fine until she was cussing out a potential hay source on the phone. *Ninety goddamn dollars. Did you bale pure fucking gold?* Instead of seeing the problem and working to solve it, she complained until it got worse.

"So, your brother's done with ranching?"

I nodded. Another sensitive subject, but one long past due to discuss with my husband. All the things I'd wanted to talk to him about when we met welled up. It felt good to tell him about my life and my situation, even if we might not be married much longer. We'd end this marriage being transparent, and I wouldn't live with the guilt of holding out on him.

"Ever since Ma was pregnant with him, he's been assigned the task of taking over. There was no college money for either of us, but there was no talk of anything but taking over Diamond UU for Kane. 'The double *U* is yours,'" I mimicked in Ma's growl. Something I'd heard her say so many times. "All he had were expectations and obligations for a career he didn't want on a ranch she couldn't quit controlling."

"Your dad isn't part of the business?"

"He's a mechanic in Mandan. He'll fix what's broken on the ranch and do some yard work, but that's about it. The rest of the time, he's fishing or hunting. It's Ma's show." I sat up with a frown as he turned off the county highway. His motel was on the edge of town, but he needed to stay on the highway to take me home. "Where are you going?"

"I haven't seen Coal Haven yet."

"Archer." What if we were seen together? He'd said he hadn't told Cameron why he was here. His uncle would have all sorts of opinions about how quickly we should annul our marriage.

Archer wasn't swayed. He drove past the gas station and curved around to the residential area between the highway and downtown. "Where'd you ride to earlier today?"

"Kennedy and Liam's." Would anyone recognize me in an Audi? A grass fire in this drought wouldn't spread as fast as news of me with the new guy in town.

"Call them up. Ask them to meet us somewhere."

I stared at him. "Why?"

"So I can get to know your friends, Delaney."

"In public? What do we say when people start asking about you? 'Oh, yes. We're married, but he's here to end it. Can I have an order of frickles?' This is Coal Haven. The teller at the bank and the cashier at the grocery store are going to wanna know."

His expression hardened for a second before he said, "What the hell is a frickle?"

I put my hand over my heart, grateful for a change in subject. "Only the best appetizer ever created. Fried pickles."

"Fried? Pickles?"

I couldn't tell if he was teasing or not. "Mm. Hardly the fine dining you're used to."

"I've only used a personal chef for the last five years."

I tipped my head and gave him an *exactly* look. "And how is William?"

His lips twitched. "Still makes the best beef Wellington."

I hadn't gotten used to the personal chef. William had been in and out while I was at work, but it'd been nice eating sandwich-free for over a year.

"It might surprise you," Archer said, "but I've heard of them before. I've just never heard them called frickles."

I like that he teased me. It wasn't something we'd done before. "My personal favorite is the fried pickle spears in a wanton wrapper with Havarti cheese. Add a cup of knoephla soup and I'm in heaven."

"I have to ask."

"You don't know what knoephla is? You probably don't even know it's spelled with a *K*. And that 'eh' sound is an *O* and an *E* next to each other, but no one really knows what order they go in."

"You'll need to enlighten me on all things knoephla." My stomach picked the unfortunate moment to rumble. Victory lit Archer's eyes. He pulled away from the intersection. "Does Rattler's serve frickles and the soup?"

"They do, but…" Everyone went to Rattler's. Especially Stetson and Holden. The sons of Cameron and Kira didn't hate me, but we weren't buddies. If they thought I'd tracked down Archer for his last name, they'd hate me soon. They'd lump me in with women like Liam's mom. She'd been willing to destroy Cameron's marriage before she died.

"Dammit, Delaney. Do we have to try not to be seen together?"

"Yes, Archer. Because I live here. I've been the subject of significant gossip my entire life. I don't want my marriage to be part of it, especially if it's so everyone can nod their head in understanding when they learn it didn't last." In the time since I'd come back, Coal Haven had been more like the home I wished I had growing up. Hearing all the same things as when Derek dumped me would make me feel more unwelcome than before.

"Jesus. If it's really that bad, why do you want to be here?" His unspoken question resonated between us. *Why did you leave me?*

"Because these people have the decency to whisper behind my back and be nice to my face. In Dallas, I didn't have either." I mimicked Briony's twang—an exaggerated hick accent she saved for me—saying, "'Delaney, *huuun*. That suit be fittin' you like burlap on a rutabaga. Why don't you give my personal shopper a holler? She's been *ah-prized* of the situation.'"

Archer stopped at another stop sign and stared at me, shock in his eyes. "She doesn't talk like that."

"Not when you could hear," I said sweetly.

"She doesn't have a pronounced accent."

"She turned it on to make me feel like shit, and I think she liked insulting not just me, but whole groups of people. I'm surprised she didn't use that on you when she and Wilson made you their little glow-up project."

He didn't reply, and his silence told me everything.

"She did the same thing to you, didn't she?"

"No." He didn't meet my gaze. "Wilson liked to give me shit though."

"Until he bullied it right out of you. They were probably upset that they had to go from their private school to a private college and not an Ivy League school and took it out on you."

"Their parents wanted them to go to a Texas university."

"Mm. I'm sure that was why they didn't land in Harvard. Anyway, Ma might be bad, but at least I know where I stand with her." Since I was on a roll, I pressed on a subject almost as raw as his partners. "Why didn't I ever meet your dad? I'm learning how you grew up, but did you even tell him you got married?"

A cloud of fatigue formed around him. "After I left home, it was harder for him and Ansen, and then Ansen left and Dad got fired. He couldn't keep up with the work. How could he, with my brother and me gone?" Guilt flashed through his features.

We were still sitting at the stop sign, but Coal Haven being so small, no one had come by yet. "Ansen blames you."

"Maybe. I couldn't afford to drive four hours to see him when I was going to school, and then he moved, and we sort of lost touch." His hand tightened on the steering wheel, and he rolled through the intersection. He didn't take the turn that would lead out of town to my parents' place.

I glanced around, but there were no vehicles to prompt the move. "Where are you going?"

"Let's order dinner first. We'll pick it up and eat at the motel."

"Why?" Apparently, that was all I would be getting on his dad. Archer had opened up more than ever today, but his family remained a tender subject. I didn't take it personally. I thought Archer was doing that enough himself.

"Because I'm hungry."

The idea of sitting in what had to be a cozy motel room dominated by a bed twisted my insides into a honda knot. I couldn't let myself get roped in by him again. I'd been willing to sell myself out when I had nothing and no one depending on me. But now I had Diamond UU. I had a place where I was needed. A place where I fit by just being me.

"I should get home. I've been gone most of the day." That was reasonable and not a desperate attempt to get away from how his bourbon-and-citrus scent branded my skin.

He snagged my hand, threading his fingers through mine. His thumb ran over my bare ring finger. Hurt darkened his fathomless eyes.

"Ranching and jewelry don't go together." It was a good reason, but I hadn't taken my ring off to do chores. He wore his, but I wasn't sure what to think of it.

"Food and discussion, Delaney. We don't have to make our decision tonight."

When, then? I'd lived with this anxiety long enough. With him next to me, making me like him even more, the stress might topple me. But all I said was "All right."

* * *

Archer

. . .

The motel room used an old-fashioned key on a large blue oblong key ring. I let Delaney in. She carried the soup, and I held the appetizer and drinks. I'd respected her concerns and parked at the edge of the parking lot and run inside to grab the food. I didn't see my uncle, and if any of my cousins were in there and figured out who I was, they didn't make themselves known.

She went right to the little round table flanked by two chairs and set the food down. The inside of the room didn't give her pause like it'd given me.

It'd been years, probably when I'd been single digits old, since I'd stayed in a motel like this. One with doors on the outside and no room service. I doubted anywhere in town delivered food. Mini blinds graced the square window, a picture of a sandhill crane taking flight hung over the bed, and a small flat-screen TV sat on a dresser that matched the end table. The queen bed with a white duvet dominated the room. The bathroom was tiny; the toilet was positioned between the tub and the counter. The one sink unearthed memories of brushing my teeth while elbowing Ansen out of the way and Mama yelling at us that the bus was coming.

A blissfully normal memory. I didn't get those too often.

My wife positioned the food. I got a cup of soup with large hunks of something floating at the top, and the pickle spears were placed between us. She'd already dug a fried pickle out and slumped in her chair, legs spread and chewing.

When she saw me staring, her chewing paused. "What?"

"Nothing." I bit back my grin. "Make yourself comfortable."

"I did." She continued munching.

I sat and inspected the soup. "What's in this?"

"The secret ingredients are cream and butter. Lots of

both. The dumplings are made of flour and milk. Then there're potatoes, celery, carrots 'n' shit. Those don't really matter. The dumplings are the only reason anyone eats it."

I took a hearty spoonful. Savory flavors wrapped in buttery creaminess burst over my tongue. "Is this homemade?"

She nodded and snagged another fried pickle egg roll. "Remington Durant, one of the owners of Rattler's, uses his grandma's recipe. Word on the street is that Beverly, the owner of Main Street Diner, was pissed when Durant started serving this."

"Rivalry of the recipes?"

Delaney polished off her pickle and grabbed another. I'd never seen her eat with abandon. I enjoyed seeing the real her. Getting to know the real her.

Texas Delaney had been full of manners, was my biggest cheerleader, and was, of course, gorgeous. Coal Haven Delaney was real, down to earth, and had a lot of responsibilities stacked on her slim shoulders.

And she was hot as hell.

I hadn't spoken about much of my life to Delaney before tonight. The few times I had said something to Wilson or Briony, their aghast responses had clammed me up. Delaney hadn't batted an eye. She was angry on my behalf, but not embarrassed. She didn't act like knowing me then might've ruined her social standing.

I'd known my friends hadn't grown up like me and weren't interested in that life. But I'd forgotten somewhere along the line that while there were several things wrong with how Ansen and I had lived, it didn't mean anything in regard to my character or how I should've been treated.

Fuck her.

Delaney's simple response had said it all. Fuck my high school girlfriend and how she thought I should consider letting her go to prom with another guy and then come back to dating me.

"Not so much a rivalry," Delaney answered, yanking my mind back to the soup. "Beverly claimed that Grandma Durant got the recipe from her in the first place."

"Do the soups taste alike?"

"Not even close. Jocelyn, the waitress who's been at the café forever, said Beverly adds leftover chicken from the week's specials, and the soup is so thick you're worried you're going to break your spoon. It's good, but it's not Grandma Durant's."

Delaney wasn't guarded when she talked about these people I didn't know. What if... Shit. What if she hadn't been shy when we'd gone out with Briony and Wilson? What if she'd been guarded?

The way she'd mimicked Briony. I'd heard my friend talk that way when ridiculing others, but when I called her on it, she managed to make it sound like I was the sensitive one. I had been sensitive, so I'd fallen back.

I cupped my bowl and reclined in my seat. I had a few things to think about. After spending much of the day with Delaney and talking, really talking, I had come to a conclusion, one I wasn't sure she would like or that my boss would like. "So, about tomorrow."

Her head popped up, and she quit chewing. She brushed her fingers off on the napkins Rattler's packed for us. "Do I need to meet you somewhere before you leave?"

She thought I was still pressing for an annulment. If that was what she wanted, she would've signed the papers. When I'd told her we shouldn't rush through destroying our marriage, I meant it. Nothing had sounded as true, and I'd thought she agreed.

"I'm not leaving tomorrow."

She stared at me, confusion filling her expression. "What?"

"I'm not leaving. But I won't take you away from work. Give me a job. I've still got skills."

Never in my adult life did I think I'd be willing to jump back into the dirt and work someone else's land. I'd built a life where I could afford quality, and I had the stability to keep it mine.

This was only temporary. I was asking for Delaney's time. Our drive back had been nothing but miles of farms and ranches. Some were large operations that had hired help and stayed lucrative enough that drought years like this one were nothing but a blip on the radar. But several were like the Diamond UU. Small. Old buildings. Single-family operations that weren't stable despite being in business for generations.

She hadn't stayed away because she'd found some rich rancher to latch on to. She was struggling to save her family's livelihood. A task that had taken its toll on her brother, but one she was thriving under.

She was still staring at me, as if she waited for me to say, *Nah. I've seen what I needed to see, and I'm out.*

"Are you going to cut hay if there's blister beetles?" I pressed, willing her to accept my help instead of informing me she planned to agree to the annulment, just let her grab a pen.

"We'll salvage what we can," she answered carefully.

"Give me a hay mower and point me where you want me to go."

She munched the rest of her pickle, still not answering.

"Got fencing to do?" All the tasks of a ranch clicked through my mind. Putting up hay. Fixing fence. Working cattle. Giving my brother hell until he tackled me. Mama getting after us for dragging dirt through the house.

The fondness behind those memories swelled until I itched to jump in and experience it all from the front seat again.

Delaney finished her mouthful. "There's always fence to work on. Just once, I'd like to get to a weak section *before* the cows get out. We've really needed to replace the posts on an entire quarter for years. It's like a jigsaw puzzle." She paused and picked up her soup, holding it like me. "What's ol' Norville going to say when you tell him you're staying longer?"

I stirred my soup. The food tasted so good, I didn't want my appetite to disappear. "I don't know. But I'm not just an employee, I'm a family friend. I expect they'll take that into consideration if I tell them I need more time."

"What if he doesn't?"

"He will." The confidence I spoke with was higher than what I felt inside. I should have more faith in the Truitts. I did, but this was new territory. "I'll explain us, and I'll tell him about meeting my uncle for the first time."

She considered me for a moment. "Why did your dad leave?"

The change in subject wasn't jarring. I had brought up my uncle. But I wondered if she thought that somehow the two were related. Dad left for Texas, and Texas was now my home.

"Probably because of his pride." I didn't know specifics, but that would be my guess. After meeting Cameron and getting a sense of his unyielding authority, I was certain that had chafed Dad his entire life. Dad didn't like being told what to do, no matter how much he needed to be guided. "And he stayed gone because of pride." Regardless how much it would've helped our family to slink back to North Dakota where we might've had some support. It was hard to think things would've been worse if Dad had gone back to his hometown.

"Your grandparents tried buying out mine."

My brows popped, more from the realization that our families had been intertwined somehow for so long. "Obviously, they said no."

Her lips twisted in a wry smile. "I think there was a lot more said. Your family tends to be on the arrogant side. I can't imagine what your grandparents were like rolling in all that oil money. My grandparents wouldn't budge, insults were traded, and I think even the county got involved as claims were made about my grandpa rustling cattle or something. Ma has harbored a grudge ever since."

"That's why it's a big deal I'm a Barron." I used to care about my last name in that I didn't want it to be associated with a broke-ass family. The meaning of my last name in Coal Haven was different, and it was highly annoying that it was an issue in how people accepted the idea of me and Delaney together. We had enough of our own shit to work through.

She nodded and dug into her soup. It was a bigger deal than she let on. I'd run across some family drama in my time making land deals, but I hadn't expected to find it in my own history, to have it rear its head and affect my marriage. As if we didn't have enough to get over.

We finished our food. Delaney gathered up our trash. "Well, I guess it's about that time."

I didn't want the evening to be over. I didn't want to take her home while I came back to an empty bed. The optimism I had felt before had leveled out and dipped a little. Delaney had been raised to think being a Barron equaled being an arrogant jackass, and I hadn't done much to show that I was different other than to let her in on the reasons why I lived my life the way I did.

She rose to stuff all our garbage in the plastic to-go bag. I was seated, but she didn't tower over me. She adjusted her worn ball cap, and her blonde ponytail sticking out swung like a pendulum. She was dressed like she'd worked all day, and she had for part of the day. The rest had been spent on the most relaxed afternoon I'd had since the last time I was able to lounge in bed with her and ignore the world.

I lazily drank in her lithe body as the concerns I harbored faded against my desire. Her slight curves had always captivated me, but knowing they came from hard, honest work sent blood to my dick faster than ever.

I snatched her wrist and tugged her toward me.

"Archer!" She fell onto my lap, bracing herself by pushing against my chest. Her legs straddled mine. She was sitting too far away to feel my growing erection, but my dick noticed her.

I circled my arms around her waist. "Can I hold you?" I'd let her go if she said no. *Please say yes.*

She was tense. "I've been up since five and I smell like horse sweat."

"A little horse sweat never scared me off." I leaned forward and gave her a sniff that ended at the base of her throat. Subtle hints of strawberry, like what I'd smelled her mom smoking, the horse sweat she'd mentioned, and the faint floral fragrance of her favorite lotion. I relaxed into the chair but didn't let her go. "I wish we'd talked like this earlier."

Her tension leaked out, and her expression turned troubled. Defeated. "It doesn't matter though. Does it?"

"What do you mean?"

"I mean that my life is here, and yours is in Dallas."

She'd hit on the crux of the issue between us. She was a Granger before we married—an unexpected issue. She'd left without an explanation, and I hadn't chased her. Another major issue. But in the end, we'd each felt our place was across the country from the other. A startling concept I'd failed to ponder before now.

I didn't quit holding her. If she wanted off my lap, she'd get off. I'd learned that about her since I'd come to town.

I refused to give up. "I think it's still too early to trash what's between us."

"No, it means there's no point. You have all the proof you need to justify an annulment."

Irritation swept through me like a brush fire. "I don't want a fucking annulment. Jesus, Delaney. I want my wife."

"A wife who lives in another state—"

I pressed my thumb to her lips. "But we're here. Together. You're straddling my lap right now. Wearing dirty jeans I'd love to strip off. Trying to hide your hat head. Don't think I don't know that's why you're not taking your cap off."

Her brows drew together as I flipped her cap onto the table. Her pale hair was plastered to her head, and several strands stuck up. My lips curved up.

She scowled. "Quit laughing at my hair."

"I'm not laughing. It's adorable."

There was the eye roll again.

"Your mama gave you hell for that eye roll, didn't she?"

Her smile faded. "Ma gives me hell, period. She always has."

"Cuz you give it back." Yeah, there was a lot between us we had to address. Much of it made it difficult to create a successful marriage. I'd spent most of the drive from Dallas steeling myself against seeing Delaney with her bright-blue eyes, her soft smile, and her blonde curls. She was gorgeous and sweet, but I was supposed to get out of our marriage.

I hadn't been prepared for a wife who hid our vows, bit my head off, and ate over half of the fried pickles.

I was supposed to get out of our marriage. But it was the last thing I wanted to do. The first thing I wanted to do was capture those naked pink lips that hadn't seen a swipe of gloss all day.

* * *

Laney

The heat level in Archer's malt liquor–brown eyes increased, and his gaze stuck on my lips. I'd been trying to ignore how good he felt under me. Solid, warm, and strong.

Familiar.

Achingly familiar. I missed how it was when he was under me, over me, in me, with every fiber of my being. I missed waking up in the middle of the night and having his wall of heat behind me. All last winter, I'd tried not to think about how nice it would've been to snuggle against his hard body when the drafty window let in too much of the bitter north wind.

His embrace tightened until I was tipping forward and offering no resistance to do otherwise. He captured my mouth, and my arms were around him before I realized I had moved.

He splayed his big hands against my back. And wasn't that what I'd always loved about him? He was tall and broad. I was short and wiry. I was used to being towered over, people trying to dominate me. But with Archer, it'd been nice to sink into his shadow. To still be seen by him, to be protected.

His hot tongue licked along my lips, seeking permission, and like always, I automatically gave it to him. I cursed the choice of fried pickle spears and knoephla soup, but they tasted better with Archer's flavor.

I groaned and sank into him. My body ignited. I was pressed as close as I could possibly be straddling his lap.

He rubbed his hands up and down my body, starting a blaze wherever he touched. Stroking my torso, his thumbs brushed under my breasts, then around my back. He cupped my face with one hand and my ass with his other. I ground down on him, scooting close.

God, that erection. The guy was gifted in that department, and he knew how to use it. I was heavy with need. Every nerve knew this man and wanted what he could give.

I'd progressed from small-town boys with no experience to college guys with too much confidence to a master. He had the confidence, but he also had the maturity and patience to go with it. And while I'd been convinced that I was lucky to orgasm once with bonus points for me not having to assist, Archer had proven that he'd take care of it all. He'd taken care of me beyond the bedroom, and damn, that'd been nice.

Too nice. The relationship I'd had with Archer had been an illusion, a fantasy I'd helped to create. It hadn't been fair to him. Or to me. And I couldn't go down that rabbit hole again.

I pushed against his chest, breaking our kiss. He gazed at me with lust-filled eyes and leaned in. I swayed back and put my fingers against his lips.

"I can't do this." There was no point. He had to go home, and I had to stay.

He didn't let me go, but he put space between us. Was his expression disappointment or fear or both? "Do you want to stay married?"

Hot pressure pricked the back of my eyes. "It doesn't matter. I told you."

"It makes all the difference in the world."

I slumped on his lap. "I don't see how it could work out."

"Me neither."

My heart sank. Oh, God. This was it.

"But that doesn't mean there isn't an answer out there. We need time, and I'm going to be here for a while. I haven't used any vacation days since our trip to Vegas."

All the reasons this wasn't a good idea clambered into my mind. My personality, which hadn't scared him off—yet. The Truitts. My family and my work. Where we lived. But sitting on his lap after he'd kissed Laney Granger and not some image of a perfect woman wasn't the best time to turn him down.

"Fine. I've got a ditch waiting for you to hay." I wasn't sure what I was excited about more—having some help around Diamond UU or seeing Archer drive a tractor instead of a high-end car.

The smile I was rewarded with wormed its way into my belly and moved south. I had to push completely off his lap before I started grinding into him. I stood and grabbed the last pickle spear. He'd had only a couple, but the guy had to learn he couldn't leave food sitting around me.

He rose and adjusted his pants around his impressive erection. "Tomorrow, then. I'll be ready to work."

ARCHER

The tractor Delaney put me in was an old red-and-white monster that required me to wear headphones while I was in the cab to protect my hearing. It looked rough on the outside, but unlike the tractors I drove growing up, it ran well. The perks of having a dad who was a mechanic.

Bumping through the ditches my wife had outlined as Diamond UU, I spent the morning cutting hay. Currently, I was hoping the tractor had a low center of balance as I mowed at an angle between the road and the lowest point in the ditch, the most thrilling thing I'd done in a while.

The financial podcast I was listening to paused as my phone rang. I tapped an earbud and hollered without looking to see who it was, "Yeah?"

"Lord, Archer." Wilson's alarmed voice flooded my ears. "What is that racket?"

I brought the tractor to a stop and let it idle. The noise

of the engine didn't decrease by a lot, but it evened out. "I'm haying."

A beat of silence passed between us before he said, "You're what?"

"Cuttin' hay. Resurrectin' those skills you recruited me for." I'd been the country boy who could pass as sophisticated. Mr. Truitt and his son had connections, ambition, and more money than I did, but I had real working knowledge that had slowly morphed from personal experience to spreadsheets and reports. Our clients sensed I possessed more than book knowledge, and it had increased their trust in me.

"How did you end up utilizing those skills?" His curiosity was touched with a small amount of disdain. Wilson's people skills were stronger than his arrogance, but I knew him well enough.

"Listen, I was going to call you. Is your dad around too?"

"He's with a client. Something wrong?"

"I need to be gone longer than I thought."

"Seriously? You've been gone for almost a week."

"I know. I'd like to use some more of that vacation time I have stored up."

A subtle point, but one I needed to make. I hadn't taken sick days, much less vacation days. Wilson would call in after a long night out with friends, but I'd always been one of the first in the office. My wedding and this past week were the longest I'd been gone since I'd started working with them after college.

"Yeah," Wilson said in the tone I recognized as fake nonchalance. His way to play off being cool when he wasn't cool. "But I gotta tell you, my plate's pretty full with the Neuman subdivision and assembling a parcel for Kramer Energy's proposed carbon recapturing plant."

Wilson liked to drop facts. All he had to tell me was that he was busy, but he liked to point out the important people he worked with. The farms and ranches I brokered weren't small game for the company, but sometimes he and Mr. Truitt acted like it. Usually, I let it roll off me like water over duck feathers. Today, it stuck in my craw just a little longer than normal. "I have my laptop; I can still do some work here."

"You won't be here for the meetings."

"I can video in."

Wilson blew out a sigh. "How long are you planning to be gone?"

"Another few weeks."

"That'll be a month total, Archer." His tone was flat, as if I hadn't done the math.

"It's my marriage, Wilson."

"Y'all working it out or what?"

Since he sounded like my answer might make a difference in how he told his father, I answered, "It's more complicated than I thought. She has family here. If we work things out, I have to convince her to move back with me. It's going to take time."

"She left you."

It was on the tip of my tongue to tell him why, but it wasn't his business. "Just trust me. She had a good reason."

He grunted as if he doubted any reason could be good enough. "You're going to owe me for telling Bri. She's not going to like this. She really talked you up to Phoebe."

Briony wasn't in charge of my personal life, and it wasn't like I'd hid being married when she said whatever she said to her friend Phoebe. She hadn't asked me beforehand, or I would've told her I didn't want to be set up. "I appreciate it."

"Three more weeks?"

"Yes." It wasn't much time, but I'd make it work. "Remember I told you my dad was from this area? I also met my family."

"Oh, yeah?" Wilson summoned a hint of interest. "Are they like your dad?"

"No." I couldn't speak for all of them, but if they'd been like Dad, Delaney would've had more stories to tell. "There's generations of oil money up here. One uncle is the CEO of the refinery, and my dad's other two siblings run big successful farms and ranches."

"Yeah? The pauper's actually a prince?"

I bristled at his description. I was no longer poor, but Wilson often reminded me of it. I'd been the kid with long hair and old clothes in class he borrowed notes from when he'd partied too late the night before. "No. None of it belongs to me."

"Well, I'll pass on the information to Father. I'm sure he'll be interested."

Interested that I was trying to save my marriage? Or interested that my family had money? I hated that I thought Mr. Truitt would nurture one relationship over the other.

As soon as I hung up, my good mood from earlier pushed out the lasting irritation from the call. The podcast filtered through the earbuds, and I finished the mowing.

I rolled to a stop when I spotted Delaney's old Chevy kicking up dust. I killed the engine and hopped out. She lumbered to a stop. "Something wrong?"

"No, I just finished and was heading back. Where are you going?" The sleeveless shirt was gone, replaced by a frilly tank top, and her long platinum hair was brushed out.

Her lips pursed. "The insurance office."

"Want company?" I'd get to see more of Coal Haven, and maybe she would think that being seen together in broad daylight was a better way of introducing me to the town.

"Not for this. You don't want to witness this."

I propped one hand on the door and the other on my hip. "Now I'm intrigued."

"Don't be. Just an asshole from high school who thinks he can jerk me around as an adult."

"Moving to another agency?"

She pushed up her sunglasses and glowered out the windshield. "I wish. No, our agent is dragging his feet. It's a drought year. I know there're claims we can make and programs we qualify for, but he's always 'looking into it.' I'm going to tell him what I think of that."

I didn't want her to have to deal with assholes, but I also didn't want her premiums to climb high if their family business was already struggling. "You have an appointment?"

She nodded, anger flashing behind her dark lenses.

So this guy couldn't run her out of the office with a no-appointment excuse. Her quick description of her agent told me enough about the guy. I'd grown up seeing people like him treat my dad like crap. And the stories my clients would tell. Delaney could handle it, but I might be able to get her what she wanted without burning a bridge she hadn't made an alternate route for. "Care to let me give it a shot?"

"You want to tell off a guy you've never met because I said he's an asshole?"

"I negotiate for a livin', honey," I drawled. "And I have to do it in a way that they want to work with me again."

She tapped her unpolished fingernails against the steering wheel. "How am I going to introduce you?"

By telling people I was her fucking husband. "With the truth. I'm staying for another three weeks."

"Three *weeks*?"

I grinned at her shock. Maybe I should've talked to her first, but I couldn't help myself. I wasn't ready to leave, so I'd gambled that she wasn't ready for it either. "I said I wanted to work on this, and I'm here. It's going to get out, Delaney. I've been here for a few days. I think I saw Uncle Bruce, and he's going to be wondering why the hell the nephew he's never met—the one who his brother told him was in town—is working for the Grangers. People in town are going to keep seeing me. Let's use the surprise to our advantage."

She mulled it over, mouthing *three weeks*. "I feel like I should have some pride and tell you about how I don't need to be rescued by a man, but I'd really love to see Chad get talked into circles like he's been doing to me and Ma." She jutted her chin toward the tractor. "Leave it. We'll get it later."

I wasn't used to abandoning equipment, but I hadn't seen more than two vehicles in the hours I'd been working. One had probably been my uncle Bruce since he'd stared so hard I thought he'd climb out of the window. The other had been Cheryl, and she had ignored me.

I hopped in, and Delaney took off for town. I tried to keep from grinning the whole drive. She hadn't argued about me staying.

"Tell me about Chad."

Her grip tightened. "So... I said he was an asshole in high school." She cringed. "But we also had a fling."

The jealousy flaring hot in me was unexpected. High school was a long time ago, but I hadn't prepared to meet any of her past boyfriends. "He's dickin' you around because you hurt his little teenage feelin's?"

"I didn't—" She chewed the inside of her lip. "I mean, I didn't go out with him again, but it's not like I said, 'I don't care to experience thirty seconds of random thrusting while you grunt in my ear again.' I let him down easy."

I wasn't going to pretend that I didn't go through the thirty-seconds-of-random-thrusting phase. It didn't last long, and thankfully, my girlfriend at the time had been just as inexperienced as me. She'd held how I dressed against me, not how I fucked. Neither of us had known better, but had she walked away, I couldn't imagine being crusty about it ten years later. Probably meant he was still random with his thirty seconds and hadn't worked on his before-and-after technique either.

"You'd be surprised how many clients I work with are like Chad."

"So you think you can handle him? Because if not, maybe it's not worth it. I can tell him off and price other companies again. Maybe Ma will listen."

I'd be insulted, but Delaney was turning the situation over to me in addition to passively revealing to the town she was married to a Barron. "Do you trust me?"

She drove down Main Street and parked in front of a long, flat building. She stared at it for a moment, then scanned the rest of downtown. Indecision left her gaze, and she nodded. "Yes. I trust you."

* * *

Laney

He'd said to trust him, and I had.

And I sat through the meeting, stunned. My friends hadn't betrayed my confidence. Chad got the distinct honor of being the first person to publicly know I was married. To a Barron.

I didn't care for Chad. He had morphed into an ass after I quit seeing him, and I hated that he was the only insurance agent in town that Ma would let touch our account. She wanted an agent she could talk to face-to-face, even though she sent me to all the appointments. Other companies would be more expensive. But we'd also get better service. Ultimately, it was Ma's decision. Diamond UU was still in her name; she had been going to sign it over to Kane when she retired.

I didn't have to worry about better service today.

Chad's smug gaze had landed on Archer and darkened when we'd walked through the door. Before I got Archer's name out, my husband was pumping Chad's hand like the insurance agent was some sort of small-town rock star. Then came the quiet bomb of "Hey, we're married." Only, Archer spun it like it was Chad's biggest honor in life to be one of the first to know.

After that, Archer controlled the show. Chad might have thought he had some power, but it was all in Archer's strong, capable hands. Archer's knowledge of possible insurance claims during all types of weather shouldn't have been a surprise. It was his job, but it was the seamless way he presented options. He didn't need to "look into it," because all the information was there. Then Archer manipulated each sentence like it was Chad's intelligence that helped us out, and eventually, Chad was gathering information about federal programs I could talk to the bank about and filling out forms so we could have some financial relief during a drought year.

After a lifetime of Ma's blunt outbursts, this level of suave was sexy. What's more, Archer didn't do this to me. He could spin me in twelve different directions and I wouldn't know what was up. But he didn't. He didn't do that to anyone outside of his job.

Archer leaned forward like he was hanging on to Chad's every word. "So tell me, Chad, as the guy with the answers, how do you think Cheryl should adjust her plan to keep her in front of the weather curve?"

Chad practically preened at Archer's words. He adopted an expression of all-knowing wisdom. "Well, let's review the Grangers' policy."

I should have been angry. Chad should have been talking to me, but it was like I wasn't there. He shouldn't have been showing Archer Ma's information at all. My husband wasn't on the policy. Though, technically, I wasn't either.

But relief cooled the blood that had been heated all day at the thought of this appointment. Someone else was dealing with this shit.

I barely paid attention. I knew the changes I wanted to make with our policy; the trouble was getting Ma to approve it. Chad's next client came in, an older man wearing a flannel shirt in the middle of summer and a white-and-black cap with the refinery's logo on it. A farmer from somewhere in the county. He probably didn't have to play games with Chad. But Chad was going to tell this guy about having a Barron in the office. I could bet on it. Just like I knew no other Barrons did business with Chad.

Archer wrapped up the appointment as smoothly as he'd started it and held the door open for me. I stepped onto the sidewalk, letting the warm air chase off the chill of the air-conditioned office.

"I think that went well," he murmured after the door closed behind him.

I snorted and strode to the pickup. "That was quite the spectacle." Another thought struck me, and my stomach twisted. I should've considered it before. "When the town starts talking about us, Ma's going to lose her shit."

"She had to know it'd get out."

"Doesn't matter." Ma had been quiet with me all week. Whenever I was out of her sight, she thought I was with Archer. Yesterday she'd asked if I was asking for a divorce. I'd told her we were talking and left it at that.

"If I'm going to be here for another three weeks, maybe I should get to know her."

"Yeah," I said with no inflection. Pushing him on Ma would make her ignore him more. She'd lump him in with the rest of the Barrons.

"Want to grab lunch?" Archer was eyeing the diner a couple doors down. He put a warm hand on the small of my back. "It'll be fine. Cat's outta the bag, might as well commit."

I stared up at him and his square jaw. There were worse things than to admit I was married to a handsome man who made my mouth water, whether he wore a suit and tie or blue jeans and cowboy boots. A successful man with a respectable job, Archer had never been the reason I didn't tell anyone I was married. It was telling them I'd had yet another failed relationship with a Barron. The whispers of "What did she think would happen?" I'd been through all of that once. I didn't want to do it again.

But the truth was running wild in the insurance office behind us. Archer had seen the real me, yet he was staying another three weeks. I was getting to know the real him, and I wanted him to stay for those three weeks.

So I'd have to deal with Ma later. "All right."

He pushed open the door to the diner. The tinkling of silverware on plates resonated throughout the place.

I stepped inside, my heart lurching into my throat. The age in the diner trended older. Mostly farmers and some of the professionals who worked in the businesses downtown and didn't give me more than a second glance—until their gazes landed on Archer.

I moved through the café, avoiding eye contact, until a deep voice laced with accusation stopped me. "Laney, who's your friend?"

I inwardly grimaced. Holden Barron. His dirty-blond hair was brushed to the side, and he had an arm slung across the back of the booth with a half-empty glass of water in front of him.

Holden was Archer's cousin, and from the suspicious look in his eye, I assumed Cameron had told him about Archer and Holden knew this was him. His real question was what was Archer doing with me.

"I feel like you have a good guess," I said as Archer stopped next to me, his hand settled once again on the small of my back. I was tempted to lean into the heat and strength of his touch, but we were in the middle of the aisle and a waitress would be bustling past us any second. "Archer, this is your cousin Holden. Kira's boy."

Holden slid out of the booth and straightened, as tall and broad as Archer. I felt my husband tense more than saw it. No one would look at his affable smile and think he was uptight about anything. Archer stuck a hand out. His go-to good-guy move. "Nice to meet you."

Holden clasped his hand. "Well, this isn't what I was expecting when I stopped for lunch." His gaze jumped between the two of us.

I took a deep breath. This was it. "Archer and I are... married."

Holden gawked at me. "Since when?"

"Our third anniversary is coming up soon," Archer answered casually.

Holden sputtered. "Three years? What the hell, Laney?" He cleared his throat and glanced around. The café was silent. Even Jocelyn, the waitress who'd worked here for decades, wasn't doing a damn thing other than watching us. "Why don't you join me? I haven't gotten my food yet." He woodenly folded himself into his spot.

I dumped myself into the booth and scooted over until my shoulder was smashed against the wall. Archer did the same, not stopping until we were hip to hip. The only way out was to crawl over him, but the secret was out. Now I had to weather the reactions. Was Archer ready?

"Seriously, Laney," Holden hissed. "You couldn't keep your claws in Derek, so you went to Texas—"

"Don't ever talk to my wife like that," Archer growled. I was as bad as Chad, wanting to preen under Archer's defense of my character.

Holden snapped his mouth shut and inspected his cousin. "You're okay with it?"

I held up a finger, and Archer paused as he was about to speak, letting me go first. "One—and actually there's only one—my marriage is none of your business, Holden. Got it?" He gritted out a curt nod because he'd always been more reasonable than the rest of his family. "But I'll grant you it wasn't a coincidence we met. I heard about a job fair and saw his name listed with one of the companies involved. I went out of pure curiosity. If it had been you, after growing up here, would you have skipped it?"

I glanced at Archer. His gaze was speculative, but my admission didn't seem to bother him otherwise.

"Depends on why you went to Texas after graduation." He quirked a brow as if to ask, *another coincidence?*

So much for it being none of his business. I was letting it all out, partly because Archer needed to hear it too. "It was as far away from Coal Haven as I could get, but also affordable. Look, I didn't plan on meeting any of the long-lost

Barrons and then having one of them talk to me. It's not like I'm buddies with any of you."

He nodded like *you got me there.* "You've been back for a while." He switched his attention to Archer. "Why are we only seeing you now?"

"As you probably know, she's not the type to put up with bullshit, and I'm learning that I was dishing it out."

I appreciated Archer taking the blame, but communication goes both ways and he was working on limited information. We both had been.

Holden thought about it for a moment, then nodded. I could've sagged with relief. I didn't owe Holden an explanation, but I hated for Archer to meet his family full of secrets.

Holden's food was delivered, and Jocelyn studied Archer. She'd seen a lot in her day, but this had to liven a dull week for her. "We'll get your usual, Laney," she said without taking her gaze off Archer. She'd probably served his dad when he'd been a teenager. "What can I get you, hon?"

My chest squeezed. I'd ordered the same thing at this diner since I'd been eight and decided I liked the Denver omelet and hash browns. Was Archer going to ask for poached eggs or nitrate-free sausage? Was this where he realized our worlds didn't mesh?

"Two cakes with eggs over easy and links if you have them, please."

I stared at him. Since when did he eat pancakes? Normal ones made with white flour? And sausage that was more flavor than it was actual pork? Introducing him to local fare like knoephla soup was one thing. Cheap diner food would make Briony gag. I doubted Wilson would even enter the building.

"Sure thing." She patted his shoulder. "Welcome to town."

"Thank you, ma'am."

Holden arched a brow toward me. I lifted a shoulder. Jocelyn was Jocelyn. She was never called ma'am. We'd all learned her name by the time we could talk.

Archer focused on Holden. "So. What's my aunt like? The rest of my cousins?"

The men launched into easy small talk. The volume kicked up as everyone went about their business. The rest of town, including Archer's extended family, would know about us by the end of the day. If his friends had planted the idea of annulment in Archer's head, what would his uncles tell him?

* * *

Archer

After we ate, I told Holden when he asked that he could plan a family gathering so I could meet everyone. It had been clear Delaney and Holden weren't friends, but other than his initial hostility, he had seemed as ambivalent around her as she was around him.

She'd been more comfortable around the cousin she claimed she wasn't friends with than she had been around my friends. There'd been no tension, no shyness, no strained smiles.

I had to sit with that information for a while.

She was driving back to her place so I could retrieve the tractor, but she made a turn I didn't recognize. In the corner of the pasture was a trailer house with an acre fenced off around it. The yard was empty, with nothing but another old pickup sitting outside the door.

The vehicle was familiar. It had been parked outside the

garage at her parents' place. "Is this where your brother lives?"

She nodded and turned into a driveway that used to be an approach. Cows grazed the pasture surrounding the yard. "Yes. Ma and Papa moved this out here after Kane graduated." As if she sensed my next question, she added, "He didn't shoot himself in the house. Papa scrapped the pickup he did it in."

"I'm a little surprised he's still okay with staying here." Tough decisions a family never thought they'd have to make, and she'd done it while assuming her marriage was freshly over.

"I am too, but he was okay with it as long as staying here didn't mean he was going back to his old way of life. There was nothing good about what happened, but his choice of location helped keep Ma from claiming it was an accident cleaning his gun." She pulled in next to the pickup. "Living out here was better for him than being at home. After he recovered, he stayed at the house for a while. Then I helped him get set up with online college classes. It's been going really well."

"What's he going to school for?"

"Computer science." Pride rang in her voice. "He wanted something versatile with technology that has nothing to do with agriculture."

I understood better than the rest of Kane's family why he'd been so full of despair. If I'd had no choice but to work the ranch I'd grown up on, I didn't know where my head would've gone. The Grangers were probably better than the owner Dad had worked for, but there were days when it had been like a prison without bars. I had envied the cattle we took to the sales barn. They had gotten away.

Kane pushed open the front door and came outside. When his dark-blue gaze landed on me, I had the urge to prove myself in a way I hadn't done since I won the Truitt scholarship my senior year of high school.

Delaney got out, and I followed her lead.

"You're the brother-in-law I didn't know I had?" Kane said as he came down the metal stairs from his front door. He dropped the tailgate of his pickup and scooted a butt cheek on it as if he was more comfortable entertaining guests in his yard instead of his house.

"Guilty." I lowered Delaney's tailgate. "Though Delaney told me about you."

"I can imagine," he said with a rueful grin aimed at his sister. "Delaney, huh? It's like you're always in trouble."

She scowled. "Only he gets away with it." She hopped up beside me and swung her legs. "We were driving by, and I thought I'd stop in and officially introduce you two."

Kane and I nodded at each other. An easy silence fell between us.

He tilted his face to the sky. "I'm applying for jobs."

Delaney quit kicking her legs. "Really? Where?"

"Fargo."

"Oh."

I glanced between them and tried to recall the state's geography from when I'd planned my drive here. Coal Haven was past the sign outside Mandan that read, "Where the West Begins." Fargo was a few hours away on the eastern border.

"Any hits?" Delaney asked. From her tone, I could tell the information had come as a shock, but she was supportive.

"Not yet. One more semester and I'll have my two-year degree." He must've busted ass in his online classes. "But I could work full-time."

"Full-time work and a full load of classes?" she asked cautiously.

"I like being busy. Better than having too much time to think." He gave her a knowing look. "Although now I know what to do with my thinking time and I don't fear it. I like being challenged."

I got that too. I had a feeling Kane and I would get along better than Delaney had assumed. But three years ago, she had been the one who hadn't gotten along with her brother, more out of resentment.

She swung her legs. "Want me to be with you when you tell Ma?"

"No." Kane sounded resigned. "I'll do it when I have a job. No need to work her up until then."

They didn't have to tell me Cheryl wouldn't like it. I had a feeling any change upset Cheryl.

"So what about you two?" Kane asked.

Like with Holden, I let my wife take the lead. How she'd answered Holden gave me hope. She had been curious about me before she'd even met me. It had to be proof there was a strong connection between us and that was why neither of us could let go.

Her legs quit swinging. "We're talking." An honest answer. One I was good with.

"Ma giving you shit?"

I knew Delaney's answer before she said it. "Ma isn't really talking to me."

"Sounds 'bout right." Kane gazed at the pastures, at the cows that didn't care who was around. "You know I don't want this place, but she's not going to give it to a Barron, even if you're that Barron."

"She might come around." Her tone said she didn't think so.

"Is it that big of a deal?" I asked.

Kane and Delaney nodded in sync.

"Ma doesn't want anything to do with the Barrons."

Kane's soft chuckle was sad. "After we saw how Cameron treated his own kid? And the town still reveres him? Nah, she wants him far away from her land, and you're too close."

That kid was Liam. I hadn't met him, but I couldn't imagine disowning a kid as soon as he was born.

"Cameron doesn't have that kind of power anymore," Delaney offered. "With Liam back and married to Kennedy? The dynamics have shifted."

"They might've shifted, but not for Ma. Keeping the Diamond UU out of the Barrons' hands has been the only power she's had."

Shit. I'd gone from a place where my last name was laughed at to a place where it was feared, even hated.

Kane ran a hand through his blond hair. Briony would chide him about getting it trimmed or learning how to style it. She'd have words to say about his Hanes T-shirt and ripped jeans.

Good thing she wasn't here.

I wasn't protective of Kane because he was Delaney's brother and she worried about him. My urge to keep people like my friends away from him stemmed from how I had felt when Wilson and Briony critiqued my appearance.

My scholarship had given me the opportunity to go to a university in Dallas, the same private university Wilson and Briony had attended. Mr. Truitt had set me up with Wilson, and when he'd met Briony, she'd gotten to know me. Then she'd taken to helping me, advising me on hairstyles, clothing styles, posture—anything that erased the kid I had been.

Your neighbors aren't cattle anymore, Archer. You can quit dressing like it.

I'd lapped up their critiques like a dog that'd run for miles in the Texas heat. With Mama gone and Dad not invested in my well-being, I'd been starved for advice. And to get it from the Truitts? The man who'd awarded me a scholarship that had helped me get a degree? The father of the son I admired because he had everything I'd grown up without? It'd been refreshing.

So why was looking back on those times filling me with irritation rather than gratitude?

Nothing had been wrong with my clothing. It had covered my body well enough so I could spend my money on textbooks. But then Wilson had told me about the paid internship with his father, and there'd been nothing I wouldn't do.

Buy brand-name jeans? Fine, I'd take out an extra loan. And it'd paid off—all of it had been paid off within the first few years at NT Land Agency. I didn't have regrets. I shouldn't have regrets. But I was glad Kane had someone like Delaney by his side. I wished I had realized how good that was before now.

Eight

LANEY

I had told Archer I could pick him up at the motel this morning. The gooseneck had a flat tire I was bringing in for repair.

I parked next to the Audi that hadn't seen a car wash since we'd gone to Dickinson three days ago. I wondered how he'd react to getting mud on it if it ever rained again.

At his door, I paused with my hand raised. The door might have been made of metal, but the frame around it was thin with poor insulation. There was no desk, and Archer was probably working at the table by the door.

"Yes, Mr. Truitt. I understand."

I dropped my hand. I didn't want to disrupt a work call. As much as I disliked the Truitts, I wasn't petty enough to mess around with his job.

"I sent the reports." A pause. "No, I understand. It's not like that." I spun around to go back to the pickup, but the next thing he said stopped me. "Because I trust her. I haven't been with anyone else either. Our marriage isn't superficial."

He said it with more insistence than he should've needed, but I would've done the same. After what we'd learned about each other during the last week, we understood that our first year together had been shallow. We'd skimmed the surface of who the other was, but that he was defending me on the phone to Norville, a man he admired without question? What he thought of me wasn't superficial.

I wasn't surprised that Norville thought I was fucking around. He was on his third wife, and he'd never waited until the last one walked out before he moved on.

"I won't let you down, Mr. Truitt. I'll get the reports sent by three p.m. today—No, I already touched base with the Hassan account. He has everything he needs, and his wife is reviewing it."

I stepped back. I had no idea how long this would take.

"Understood. Thanks. Bye." The door opened. He must've seen my pickup. "Wanna come in for a sec?"

I didn't. Closed doors. Privacy. The last time I was in this room, we'd kissed. I wasn't sure I was ready for that with him again. But I entered. The stress lining his face and the various electronics strewn over the table made me certain he wasn't ready to leave.

"Norville's on your ass?" I took a seat in a chair, but he sat on the bed.

"Wilson just told him I was taking another three weeks." Archer's gaze darkened. "I should've talked to him personally, but Wilson's technically my direct boss."

In name only. Norville kept that company in his iron grip.

"You need to stay and work?" Disappointment sank my mood. After being away from him for so long, I was quickly becoming accustomed to seeing him every day and spending time with him.

"For a while, yes." Rare irritation flashed in his eyes. I'd seen him frustrated, but not when it came to Norville. The man was like a god in Archer's eyes. Allan Barron must've been bad if Norville was the good guy. "I want to make sure I've got everything ready to close the Hassan deal since they're buying a twelve-million-dollar property." His lips quirked. "It's only three hundred acres."

My eyes widened. "Twelve million for three hundred acres?" That was less than a sixth of the size of Diamond UU. There was a listing outside of Mandan that was larger, and it was selling for four million.

Archer grinned. "Texas, baby."

I shook my head. "Crazy. Maybe if I offered Ma five million, she'd actually let me have it."

Million. Crazy.

His smile fell. "You really love your place."

"It's a family legacy." Did I love it? I loved the work I did. I liked being useful. I liked the life I'd had to leave before. I was loyal. That wasn't the same as love, but I wasn't going to inspect my feelings any deeper right now. I slapped my hands on my legs and rose. "I'll let you work."

He stood. "Can I come by later?"

I nodded, but as I turned to go, he cupped my elbow and drew me close with no more pressure than a simple touch of his hand. "I've been dying to do this again," he murmured.

The need in his tone kept me from putting distance between us. Because it echoed what I'd been thinking. How I went to bed every night knowing he was mere miles away instead of eleven hundred and stared at the ceiling, wishing I could be beside him.

When his lips touched mine, I realized what a bad idea

this was. I didn't have the will to pull away. I didn't have the desire to make it stop when his hold tightened, his kiss deepened, and he spun us until my back was to the bed.

Then he lifted me. I wasn't shocked out of the kiss; I anchored myself around him as he crawled over the bed and laid us down.

My legs were around his hips, and his hard erection was back between my thighs after way too long. A small rock of his hips and I groaned, arching into him.

Oh, God, it had been too long.

He took my hat off and tossed it aside. Without breaking the contact our mouths had on each other, he tugged my shirt free. When his fingers hit my skin, I whimpered.

His fingertips had a delicious roughness to them that I had dismissed before, but I knew now it was from hard work.

The bras I wore these days were nothing like the lacy scraps from when we first married. Between the heat and riding a horse whenever I wanted, what I had on was closer to a sports bra. They were cheaper and took a lot more tough living before they fell apart. I also didn't care if they got grungy. It was sad when my nice bras turned dingy.

Today, I hated it. Archer's fingers bumped into my bra like it was a metal chastity belt. But he was persistent—and good with his hands. He didn't stop tunneling under the fabric until he was cupping a breast.

I arched into him, loving the rough scrape of his skin across mine, the way he teased my nipple to a deliciously painful peak.

I was rocking against him like we were naked and not fully dressed in denim and cotton jersey.

With a growl, he abandoned my nipple to skate his hand down my torso. If he thought the sports bra was unforgiving, my jeans were really unyielding. My legs were spread, pulling the fabric snug against me, and I was squished between him and the bed.

But he didn't give up. Lifting himself, he created enough space between us to undo the button and unzip me. Then his hand was on bare skin again.

When his fingertip hit my clit, I cried into his mouth. And like he knew the motel walls were too thin to suppress sound, he didn't let me go.

I rode his finger, desperate to get relief, demanding that my body be filled by him after being empty for so long. I whimpered again, and he adjusted his angle to slide a finger through my heat and into me.

Another groan was swallowed by my husband. I was climbing fast, roaring toward my peak. My climax slammed into me, shaking me from head to toe.

There was a knock on the door. "Housekeeping."

Archer jerked his head up, but he didn't let up. I didn't have time to panic that I was doing way more than kissing my husband. He was stringing my orgasm out.

"We're good." His voice was rough.

I clamped my mouth against his shoulder to keep from crying and moaning. There was nothing wrong with people knowing I was having sex with my husband in his motel room, but I wanted to keep this moment between us. I wanted privacy.

A muffled "Thanks" came through the door, and Archer lowered his head, murmuring against my ear, "We're so damn good."

I was shaking under him, my body clenching and releasing around his finger. He let me ride it out, holding me.

I realized I was biting him and snapped my head away.

"Oh my God," I gasped, trying to catch my breath. "I'm so sorry."

His smug expression matched the satisfied gleam in his eye but didn't diminish the raging need. "Don't be."

I was sorry for biting him. That'd leave a mark. I was also sorry I'd let him do that. I didn't need a reminder of what it was like with him. That'd cloud my thinking. I couldn't think clearly when I was touching him.

He was watching me, so I saw when he read what was on my mind. He withdrew his hand and pushed to the side. We were still close enough to be touching, but he propped his head on his other hand.

"You regret what we did?"

I rolled into him; I couldn't help it. "I should regret it." I let my hand drift across his hard chest. I'd have loved to see him without his shirt again. It used to be a daily occurrence. "It doesn't clear anything up, though."

I trailed my fingers down his abdomen. He had to be hurting. It only seemed fair to return the favor.

He folded his warm hand around mine. "You don't need to." He gave me a hint of a smile laced with regret. "If you touch that thing, I won't want to quit, and I don't think we're ready for that."

He was right. I was letting lust drive my decisions again. That hadn't worked before, and my heart had been broken.

I pressed a kiss to the corner of his mouth. "You've got to keep Norville off your back, and I have to act like this flush is from the heat when I take the tire in. Papa's fishing buddy works there, and it would be weird."

He rolled off the bed and held out a hand. I accepted it and tried to ignore the large bulge in his pants. I liked that bulge. I had enjoyed it a lot. But his job was on the line, and as easy as it would be to stay in bed and distract him from it,

I wanted him to choose me over his work because he loved me, not because I seduced him.

I needed to know that when his next big client came along, he wasn't going to leave me behind. I wanted to be someone's first choice, especially when it came to my husband.

* * *

Archer

I didn't get done by three like I'd planned. I had stayed and combed through all my leads, new listings, old listings, and cleaned up my email to ensure I hadn't missed a thing.

Irritation toward my boss and mentor was unfamiliar, but it burned hot. Mr. Truitt had acted similarly when I'd gone to Vegas with Delaney.

Looking back, he'd been harder on me during the year after I was married. He'd claimed it was so I could make partner. He had faith in me and he'd known I had potential since he'd met me. But over the last year and a half, the talk of making partner had faded as I had toiled away to attract another client like Jaycee Henry or at least gather enough in sales that would've matched what she would've brought in.

Had I made progress and Mr. Truitt worried I'd put it at risk again?

Something about that thought didn't sit right. He'd been my champion. He'd guided me. So why would he want my career to stagnate?

But I couldn't forget the night Delaney left me. One moment I was chatting with Ms. Henry and had a good feeling she'd agree to work with me. Mr. Truitt had sought her out, invited her into the office and introduced her to me.

She was an older woman, divorced, with two adult children. She had been the CEO of a Fortune 100 company, and while Mr. Truitt had seemed to raise her hackles, she and I had a good rapport.

And then Delaney had tried to get my attention, and when my friends had intervened, she'd snapped at them. Not the impression I wanted to leave with Ms. Henry when she was supposed to trust me with helping her buy a hundred-and-fifty-million-dollar property.

The irony that Ms. Henry might've been one of the most sympathetic in the room had I taken the time to hear Delaney out wasn't lost on me. I'd fucked up.

Balancing my job and my marriage shouldn't have been hard. Perhaps I'd been wrong to look toward Norville Truitt when it came to work-slash-life balance. I wouldn't have been surprised if the third Mrs. Truitt filed for divorce in the next few years. Wilson wasn't much different, but he hadn't cheated on Briony yet.

I shut down my laptop, tablet, and grabbed only my phone. I left everything else behind as I drove to Diamond UU. Every time I moved, the pinch from Delaney's bite on my shoulder reminded me what it was like to feel her come around my fingers.

I shifted in my seat. I had to think about something else. I concentrated on the scenery.

Cows and calves grazed quietly in the pastures. The corn was waist high, and sunflower faces were tipped to the sun. I wanted to enjoy the scenery more, but like every other time I drove to Diamond UU, I reverted to the habit I'd gotten into as a kid—wondering what it would be like to drive up on all this and know it was mine. To know I had a say in how it was taken care of and I didn't have to depend on some ignorant jackass to know what the hell to do.

One of the things I did in my job that maybe a lot of

other land brokers didn't was to offer personalized advice. If the buyers weren't going to run and manage their ranches, I encouraged them to review reports and to really listen to the people with the expertise. It was my way to give back to kids like me who were growing up under ranch managers and had nowhere else to go and no other skills but roping and riding and keeping cattle alive.

I pulled into the yard, but Delaney's pickup wasn't parked in its normal spot by the barn. Was she fixing fence? As a kid, I never thought there'd be a point in my life when I missed fixing fence. But I'd miss doing it with my wife.

Cheryl wandered out of the house, her little dog at her heels. My mother-in-law's stern glare followed me as I got out of my car and headed toward them. Portia barked but didn't charge me and run at my heels like I'd seen her do with the delivery driver the other day. In my years visiting land for sale, most of them farms and ranches, I'd learned how to approach strange dogs, or more importantly, how not to.

Portia was most comfortable when I pretended she didn't exist. She didn't trust treats from anyone who wasn't Cheryl, but since I avoided direct eye contact with her and let her get used to my scent and my behavior, she didn't go berserk when I was around anymore.

I think the dog liked me better than Delaney's mom did.

"Evenin'. Delaney around?"

"She ran to the vet for some supplies."

I would've asked what supplies, but I got the sense Cheryl didn't want to talk to me more than she had to. "Is there anything I can do while she's gone?"

"You can turn your fancy car around and drive back to Texas."

So that was how it was going to be. Firmly, I said, "That's not going to happen yet."

"Exactly. *Yet.* You think you can get Laney to go back with you?"

I thought there wasn't much here for her. Could I offer her more in Dallas? "I think I'm not ready to give up on our marriage."

Cheryl swaggered closer to me. It didn't matter that I was several inches taller than she was, she stared me down like a bull with a grudge. "You're going to hurt her worse than he did."

"Derek?"

She ran her tongue across her teeth. Portia yapped as if she sensed the hostility rolling off Cheryl. "There ain't a soul in town who won't tell you what a good kid he was. And he was, most of the time. I'm sure he was a good husband. But he was a shitty boyfriend to Laney. He let his family railroad him into treating her like she was nothing, like she had no worth."

"I'm not Derek."

"But you're a Barron." She said it like it was worse. Maybe it was. I didn't know. "You've already acted just like them. And when they get to you, they'll tell you the same things they told Derek, and you'll listen. Because if there's one thing I know about Barrons, it's that they think they're better than everyone else, especially if that person's a Granger."

In the week and a half I'd been here, I'd heard enough about how people felt about those who had my last name. I hadn't grown up here. I wasn't raised with them. But from what I'd seen, I wondered if the Barrons were just an easy way to dodge blame. Couldn't take responsibility if it was all their fault.

If Cheryl wanted to point fingers at people who'd made Delaney feel like shit, she needed to face a mirror. "And what about you?"

Cheryl looked at me like I was a steaming pile of cow shit. "What about me?"

"You said that Derek didn't make Delaney feel like a priority. That he let his family's opinions affect how he treated her." I ran a hand over my head. The sun was beating down on my dark hair. I should find a ball cap or a cowboy hat to wear. "Yet, you gave her nothing and gave Kane everything. It couldn't have been Derek that drove her away from Coal Haven. They'd been broken up for a year, correct?"

Cheryl's lips puckered as if she tasted my words and they were more sour than any lemon in the world.

"And now?" I pressed. "She's your daughter, but you hate that she shares my last name, and you're using it as a justification to continue treating her like crap. How's that better than how my relatives acted?"

"You don't know what you're talking about. You know nothing about what it's like living like this—"

"You have it pretty damn nice compared to how I grew up," I snapped, and she recoiled. Great. I was not going to lose my temper with my mother-in-law.

She recovered and snorted. "I doubt it. I heard the payout Allan got was more than this whole place is worth."

It had been a nice payday. Dad sold his portion back to his siblings and left town. And the property he bought in north Texas had been beautiful. But he hadn't researched the difference in grazing needs between here and Texas. He'd overgrazed pastures, didn't prepare for the weather or what was required when six months of the year weren't winter, and spent more money on the place than the equipment we had needed to do the work. The land had recovered, but our family's finances hadn't. He'd tried to go bigger, to make more money, and it had collapsed.

"Doesn't mean he held on to it. I'm sure if I looked

through your books, I'd find them as dismal as when the bank came to take away everything we owned."

"My books are fine." Her hostility drained away. "Allan lost it all?"

"All of it. Think he wanted to come home and tell Uncle Cameron that?" It wasn't exactly a highlight of my life. The stress Dad and Mama had been under. Their fights. The way she grew weaker over the years until she finally went to the doctor. Then it'd been too late. "Unless you have something you'd like me to do around here, I can wait for Delaney at the motel."

"Ain't nothing around here for you." Her hostility was lower than when I had arrived. She'd heard what I said, and it had resonated. Maybe she'd see me as a person and not a last name.

I nodded and went back to my car, hating how wrong Cheryl was. Between Delaney and the family I had yet to meet, I had more here than I had in Texas.

Nine

ARCHER

I tracked a hawk soaring overhead—wait. That bird was huge. "Is that a bald eagle?"

Delaney didn't turn and gawk like I expected her to. "Yeah, they come through once in a while. I was going to get a few more barn kittens, but I'm going to wait. Otherwise I'd just have to name them Snack One and Snack Two."

I watched the eagle as it flew farther across the pasture. It was the first time I'd seen a bald eagle in the wild, doing its thing. Dang, that was impressive.

It'd been two days since I'd faced off with Cheryl. Delaney hadn't asked me about it when she met me at the motel so we could go eat at Rattler's, and I didn't mention it. She had enough baggage with her mother that already included me, so I wasn't going to add to it.

I'd be doing enough by going to the Barron family gathering tonight.

Holden had decided to grill and invite me—and everyone else. Only family, he'd said. I wasn't sure how to interpret that, but from the way he'd initially talked to Delaney, I wasn't sure I wanted to know.

Regardless, she was my wife, and I didn't give a shit who had a problem with that. I'd asked her to attend with me this morning when I showed up to rake the hay I'd cut earlier into windrows to eventually be baled. That job was done, and I'd found her by the white barn, filling up the water truck to take to the tanks in the pasture.

Her gaze swept over my jeans and the gray T-shirt that already had a couple of tears around the hem. "You need to go get ready for tonight."

"I'd really like you to come." We'd spent enough nights apart, but knowing she'd be with me would ease the thread of anxiety that'd been nagging me since the invitation.

"Still no."

"Did you think about it at all?" I understood her apprehension. But I didn't think avoiding my relatives like my dad had done for decades was the answer either. "I know it'll be awkward, but I'll be with you."

She swung her feet off the end of her perch on the back of the truck. The water truck was nothing more than an old flatbed with a large plastic cylinder of water. Since she didn't have a more efficient way to fill it, she stuck a hose in the top and turned the water on full force. Took nearly an hour to fill. Her empty lunch bag was next to her. I'd seen Cheryl go inside to soak up the cool air, but not Delaney. She stayed away from the house as much as possible, especially if her mother was there.

Had she gotten the habit from her father? He was gone by the time I arrived and didn't return until after I went to the motel for the night. It didn't faze Delaney. It had been a stroke of luck that I had caught him when I arrived.

Delaney packed her garbage into her lunch bag. "You saw how quickly Holden lost his cool with me. He's the easygoing one of the bunch."

"He seemed to accept us."

"Archer, you couldn't pay me enough to step foot on their property, especially not when your uncles and aunt will be there. All three at once?" She shuddered. "I won't even ride Target in the ditch by Bruce's."

"I don't want to feel like I'm hiding you."

"And if you wanted what was best for me, you'd want me to stay far away."

Dammit. I was thinking of myself. The last time she was at an important gathering with me, I'd destroyed what we had. "I'm sorry. I admit to feelin' a little anxious myself."

Her expression softened. "You'll be fine. You're one of them."

I didn't feel like one of them.

I wasn't in a hurry to go, but she was right, I had to clean up. The drive would take the longest. Holden lived on his mom's land. Delaney had described his place as "rustic and shit."

I wasn't as curious about the house or all the land they owned as I was about the people. Maybe a little about how they lived—with everything I hadn't had as a kid.

Yet when Delaney left, all that luxury surrounding me had been empty. Pointless. Having a chef cook for me was no longer about doing it just because I could. It was because I didn't have time. The housekeeper didn't need more than an hour a week, and she took her time, trying to earn her hourly rate. I wasn't home to make a mess, so there wasn't much to do.

"Have fun." Delaney hopped down from the flatbed and switched the water off. She wasn't acting as hostile as when she'd talked about the Truitts, but her shoulders were tense, her mouth set, and her movements curt.

Was this dinner with my family increasing her trepidation about us? That I'd meet them and suddenly think that whatever they said about her meant I should end the marriage and immediately return to Texas?

"If you change your mind…"

The brim of her cap shaded her eyes as she shut the water off. "I'm meeting Liam and Kennedy at Rattler's."

"Good." I'd miss spending the evening with her. After making her come in my motel room, I wanted to touch her all the time. I snuck light kisses here and there, usually when we were concealed by the pickup or in the barn. Somewhere that wasn't so private that we'd move too fast, but also not quite public. I pressed my lips close to the edge of her hat. Her hair tickled my lips. "Can I call you when I'm done?"

She met my gaze from under the brim. "Yeah. Hope it goes well."

I left with the sincerity of her words. She wanted me to get along with my family. But in her mind, did that mean I wouldn't get along with her?

When I reached my motel room, I ran through the shower and put on a clean pair of jeans and one of the spare polo shirts I'd packed. Ignoring my nerves and wishing my wife was in the car with me, I drove using the directions Delaney had given me.

The countryside was the same. Rolling green hills. Fields full of corn, soybeans, sorghum, and sunflowers, their heads lowering as the sun sank in the sky. Black, brown, and white cows roaming the pastures.

I approached a farmyard with a giant red-and-white rectangular shop, a large matching old-style barn that looked plucked out of a poster, and two smaller shops. A white two-story farmhouse sat closest to the road. It was well maintained for its age, with a porch that ran from one end to the other. My mother would've loved an old house like that.

Delaney's directions streamed through my brain. *Go about a half-mile past Kira's white house with her red-and-white matchy-matchy outbuilding, and the next house on your left is Holden's place.*

His house was indeed rustic and shit. Smaller than the large farmhouse of my aunt's, he'd built a place resembling a cabin. Log frame with rock accents, it was cozy and inviting. The front door opened directly off the walk, and the roof rose to a peak that wasn't a full two stories. It was a good size for a small family. I had asked if Holden had a girlfriend.

Holden is as commitment-phobic as Mr. Truitt, only he's not a cheater. That would require a relationship.

Mr. Truitt was committed to making money. Perhaps it was the same with Holden. Keeping a cattle ranch and farm profitable wasn't easy.

I pulled into an open spot in front of a smaller version of the barn at Aunt Kira's place. The vehicles surrounding my sedan were all pickups. Different models, different colors, but they had one thing in common: they were expensive. Dad had driven an old pickup my entire life. Delaney drove an old pickup. Her dad had a newer truck, a salvage title he'd purchased and fixed up, but he drove a car that got better gas mileage when he commuted.

These pickups were dusty. They were used. But they were new, the kinds with all the bells and whistles. It should have put me at ease. If Wilson and his father drove pickups, this is what they'd choose. But the knot in my gut tightened. This first impression was that they were much different than my in-laws.

Holden stepped out of the house and crossed the yard, his gait relaxed. His worn jeans and faded green Mountain

Dew T-shirt put me at ease. Wilson's uptightness about style didn't have a place here.

Holden grinned. "Hey. You found it."

"Delaney helped."

Holden's expression flickered, and he glanced over my shoulder, his gaze sweeping over my vehicle.

I answered his unspoken question. "She couldn't make it."

Holden's smirk wasn't mean spirited. "I'm sure she's heartbroken. Come on in."

We didn't get a chance to get close to the house. A lanky woman with a shrewd gaze and expertly dyed brown hair with blonde highlights came out. She had lighter eyes than Holden, but their resemblance was undeniable.

She stuck out her hand. "I'm Kira."

"Nice to meet you." I wasn't prepared for her crushing grip. Kira was no nonsense. Like Cheryl, but more aggressive and less defensive.

Delaney had given me the rundown on everyone who would likely be here, but only after I prodded her. *Kira's been through a couple of long-term boyfriends, but she's never gotten married. Holden has a different dad than Nora. Neither one is the man Kira's currently dating.*

Cameron came out and gave me a nod. He was followed by another man who resembled him; the guy in the pickup I had suspected was Uncle Bruce when I was mowing the ditches. He wasn't as tall as Cameron, and his gaze wasn't as calculating as his brother's and sister's. Solemn seemed to be his default expression. The open interest on his face and Aunt Kira's ready introduction lowered my apprehension. Whatever had happened between them and my dad wasn't spilling over to me.

"You must be Uncle Bruce." I switched my outstretched hand to him, hoping he didn't crush my bones like my aunt.

I wasn't ready for the way his eyes misted over and he clasped my hands with both of his. "I really appreciate you coming here, Archer. It's great to meet you."

Hearing stories of a cousin who died was different than being on the fringes of it. I didn't know how Uncle Bruce would've greeted me before, but he seemed delighted to add to his family after such a heartbreaking loss.

He clapped me on the back and steered me into the house. "I can't wait to hear everything about Texas." He leaned closer, his tone wry. "Everything Allan will let you tell us."

I chuckled at the good-natured joke, but his words narrowed my suspicion that the issues that drove Dad away were solely between him and Uncle Cameron. In the house, two more aunts and my cousins were waiting. My cousins appeared to be adults, but the two girls looked like they were barely out of college.

"You won't meet my oldest, Evander," Bruce said, his hand still on my shoulder. "He's in the Army, but he mentioned moving back home after his time is up."

Evander's almost as much of a mystery as your father. He's a few years older than I am, but he and Derek were never super close. Evander was expected to work, and Derek got to do what he wanted. So, after graduation, Evander left and never returned. But the rumor is he might come back home.

A woman with graying dirty-blonde hair combed away from her face floated forward, her smile warm and her arms outstretched. As she wrapped me in a hug, Bruce said, "This is my wife, Willow. You let us know if you need anything while you're here."

Her embrace made emotion clog my throat as memories surfaced of Mama playfully chasing me and Ansen around the kitchen until she caught us in a bear hug.

"So pleased you reached out," Willow said as she pulled

away. I thought for a moment she might pat my head like I was five. I wouldn't have minded—Mama had given hugs like her.

I hadn't expected being here to make me miss my family more than I ever had.

A guy pushed off the island he was leaning on. The only other male cousin I had was Stetson. The oldest of us all. Also the tallest and widest. He was a mountain, but his smile was congenial as he shook my hand.

"Stetson?" I guessed.

His eyes crinkled at the corners. "The one and only."

Holden's sister, Nora, with golden curls and cornflower-blue eyes was introduced next. *Nora's a sweet little thing. Nothing like Kira, but she's young yet. She could surprise us all.*

Stetson's sister, Isla, was the next introduction. She wasn't much older than Nora.

Stetson and Isla seem like polar opposites. Stetson is the center of attention and pretends to be a big teddy bear, but his smile fades as soon as the person he's talking to turns his back. Not sure what that's about, but there's more to him than what he shows the rest of town. As for Isla, well, she reminds me of those smiling virgins in Pride & Prejudice *remakes. People don't realize there's more going on in her head than what she shows them, like Stetson.*

Isla pushed her flaxen hair off her face and tied it back. "I hope you don't mind if I greet and run. The farmers market is going tonight and I'm the director, but I wanted to make sure I got to meet you first."

She darted out the door as Uncle Cameron scowled. Didn't he like Isla putting her responsibilities first? The only person I hadn't been introduced to sidled next to Uncle Cameron and slid her hand up his arm as if to mollify him. My aunt Naomi.

She glanced at me, her gaze calculating. She radiated as much authority as her husband, and there was less curiosity in her gaze when she looked at me. She was assessing me.

I dipped my head. "You must be Aunt Naomi."

"Yes. Nice to meet you." Her voice was warm despite the chilly atmosphere around her.

Naomi is a... People call Naomi a bitch, but she earns the title and, honestly, I think she wears it with pride. I'd admire her if she and Cameron didn't stomp on people to get what they wanted.

All of Delaney's observations had seemed logical, but this was spot on.

Uncle Cameron shoved a hand into a pocket. He was in jeans today, ones that hadn't been through a round of working cattle. His pinstriped button-down shirt would've been nice enough to be considered Sunday best when I was growing up.

All eyes were on me as he spoke. "You and Laney Granger? Care to share what that's about?"

* * *

Laney

I finished off my seltzer and ignored the crowd at Rattler's. There were a few more stares than normal, but so far, no one had said anything. Archer had been here two weeks. Plenty of time for the news to have made its rounds.

"How do you think it's going?" Kennedy's eyes were wide. She'd been to plenty of Barron family meals. I had been a couple of times before Bruce had explicitly told Derek that I wasn't family, therefore I wouldn't be welcome anymore. But after the first time, I hadn't wanted to go back. The second time had been out of spite, and I'd made out with Derek in Cameron and Naomi's bedroom. So there.

"I'm sure they're telling him what a bad idea I am. Or they're ignoring I exist in their world." *Hey, Laney, I can't bring you this time. Family only.* Derek's words should've stung more than they had, but it wasn't like I'd gone home and felt like family any more than I had at a Barron family function.

The fate of an oopsie child. Ma hadn't planned on me, but she hadn't been able to afford a permanent prevention and Papa had refused to have a blade anywhere near his scrotum. I'd heard it all before.

Well, this unplanned pregnancy was saving Ma's ass nearly twenty-eight years later. I'd save it again when she couldn't work anymore and I took over Diamond UU.

The server delivered our food. I had ordered the chicken fettuccini. Remington's partner in the restaurant made a killer sauce for his pasta. The town just called it Shawn's pasta whenever anyone asked what they'd ordered. But tonight, my appetite had vanished. I ordered based off my history—I ordered the same thing at every place. Once I found something I liked, I stuck with it. At least food couldn't decide it was done with me.

Liam dug into his steak. "The only reason they hate your family is because your grandparents didn't sell out to your hubby's grandparents, right? And your mom didn't sell, and neither will you."

"Yes." Hubby. That sounded so normal. Like living in separate states was normal. Like giving a wave at the end of the day before my husband drove to his motel room was normal. And dancing with anticipation before his arrival every morning was normal. Actually, that was normal. The sun had risen and set around him. I couldn't wait to be with him each day, and it turned out that hadn't changed.

"So you never met Archer's dad or his brother?" Liam swirled a piece of rib eye through steak sauce.

I shook my head. "He doesn't talk to his dad, and Ansen's like a big shot horse trainer and gets hired by rich people all over the country. They aren't close." But I thought Archer would like to be. He couldn't hide the hint of longing in his expression whenever he mentioned them.

"Not talking to family seems to be a Barron thing." He shoved the steak into his mouth.

"Right? Archer was so shocked I didn't tell anyone we were married, like he didn't realize that neither had he." But then he considered the Truitts as close as family when they were nothing but users.

The sympathy in Kennedy's gaze didn't set me on edge like it would from other people. "Relationships can be messy."

"Who knows how long we'll be able to say we're in a relationship? Our relationship's messy across two states."

Liam lifted his hazel gaze off his plate. "From the way he's bonding with all your haying equipment, it doesn't look like he's going anywhere soon."

I shrugged as if I didn't experience a jolt every time I saw him on one of our tractors. "He seems to enjoy the work."

Kennedy settled a gaze on me that was wiser than I cared to admit. "The work isn't what's keeping him here."

"No, but his boss isn't going to give him any more time off." After the phone call the other day, I was confident his boss was likely to be even more of a dick. If Mr. Truitt pressed Archer to cut his time in Coal Haven short, would he do it? What would I do? I'd have to think about it eventually. "Enough about my mess of a marriage. Tell me how the boys are doing in T-ball and who they're getting for a teacher next year."

My distraction technique worked. I heard all about summer sports, Eli's speech improvements, and the new shoes the boys were forbidden to wear until the first day of school. This was nice territory. I would never quit being Aunt Laney, but I wasn't sure how long I could call myself a wife.

Ten

ARCHER

After Uncle Cameron had gone for the jugular when I arrived, I glossed over how I met Delaney, our separation, and my time in Coal Haven.

I hadn't expected Holden to swoop in for the rescue, but he'd stepped in, boasting about his Traeger grill and smoker. We were on his back patio pad. It overlooked the pastures, making a scenic view out of the sliding door. Once we reached the grill, he popped the top of a cold bottle of beer and handed it to me. He had an open beer by the grill, and this crowd seemed like the type to question why someone wasn't drinking. I politely accepted the drink and took a small sip.

This was nothing like the cheap shit Dad used to buy.

Holden flipped open the top of the grill. Rectangles of foil were on the higher rack. "You grill?"

"Not for a long time."

"All five-star restaurants now?" He nodded as Stetson

stepped out, followed by my uncles. Did the guys always separate from the women? I couldn't picture Delaney being comfortable in a room with Naomi. She'd made the right call.

"I, uh, have a personal chef."

Even Uncle Cameron's brows ticked up.

I took a bigger drink. "I work long hours."

The others nodded like it sounded sane, but they still didn't get it.

"What is it you do for work?" Cameron asked as Aunt Kira stepped out with us. She seemed like she'd rather be outside, not just with us. A restless energy emanated from her.

I explained my position with Mr. Truitt. I told them about the scholarship, followed by the internship, and my job. Uncle Bruce asked about some of the deals I'd been a part of, but he hadn't heard of any of them.

What an odd notion. I brought in commissions that were tens of millions of dollars. It was expected, but I still hustled to make partner. My world had become my job. And on the other side of the country, my uncle hadn't heard of any of the deals, and he was only interested because it was what I did for a living.

Kira sprawled on the stone bench that ran along the edge of the concrete pad. Her booted feet were crossed like her arms as she regarded me. No wealthy landowners I'd worked with were like her. "You needed a scholarship and an internship to pay for college?"

I nodded, realizing my mistake too late. Dad's business was his business. It had been my life, but this was more intrusive than telling my wife about how I'd grown up.

"What happened to all the money we paid Allan?" Cameron asked in a menacingly calm tone. Bruce studied his beer, and Holden and Stetson watched as if they were more interested in my reaction than my answer.

"You'll have to discuss that with him." I didn't drop eye contact with my uncle and took another drink.

Kira laughed, a hard sound that didn't fit the peaceful surroundings. "Guess we'll have to wait another thirty-two years for that."

Cameron didn't flinch. He reminded me of Mr. Truitt. A man used to compliant people surrounding him. A man who realized that reaction was as important as action. "I'm sorry about your mother."

"Thank you." He'd known about me and Ansen. He knew about Mama, but he didn't know Dad had lost everything. Was he nosy or did he care? "How did you know?"

"That would be me," Uncle Bruce said, looking sheepish. "Your mama used to send us Christmas cards." He glanced between his brother and sister. "She and Willow were pen pals of sorts, talking about raising sons and stuff. I, uh, I found her obituary when Christmas came and went that year without a card."

I nodded, fighting back a swell of nostalgia and sadness. Mama probably hadn't said a thing to Dad. "She was pretty special."

"And her family?" Uncle Cameron asked.

I hated to give my reply. "We don't talk."

My uncle nodded like he expected the answer. "Not a surprise."

"What's that mean?" I'd spent so long being upset with Dad, but my instant defense of him didn't feel odd. It came naturally. Dad hadn't made an easy choice, but he'd fought for it.

"Allan was a proud man." He tipped his head. "A lot like Laney's mom. Too proud to know what's good for them."

Stetson closed his eyes, and regret crossed Holden's expression.

"I don't believe Cheryl is part of this conversation."

"I'm still getting over the shock. Laney is a lot like her, after all. Proud. Leaving when she couldn't get the Diamond UU. Coming back only when things between you two went south. And not showing tonight."

The defensiveness that surged for Dad switched to my wife. I recognized bait when I heard it. I took a moment to study my uncle. When Dad had told us he didn't talk to his side of the family, and then Mama's side cut us off, I had assumed the common denominator was Dad. He must have been at fault.

But at the moment, I could walk away and never talk to Cameron again. I couldn't say that for the rest of the family. What had it been like growing up with this guy? And trying to run Barron Ranch with him?

Holden had turned to manage the grill. Stetson was glaring at his dad, and the disappointment in Bruce's eyes was directed at his brother. A faint smile played over Kira's mouth. Did she enjoy the drama?

"I understand there've been issues in the past between you and them. But I'm not interested in any of that. If Cheryl wants to hold it against me, so be it. If you want to hold my marriage against me, so be it. I love my wife, and I'm here to work things out with her. Anyone who interferes with that is free to go fuck themselves."

Bruce's eyes flared. Kira chuckled softly. Stetson and Holden exchanged a shocked look. People must not talk to Cameron like that, not to his face.

I hadn't meant to say those words, but I didn't regret them. Cameron seemed like the type that trampled people who didn't stand their ground. He was a predator, roaming the pastures, looking for the weak calves.

I wasn't a calf, and I wasn't the ignorant kid of his little brother. And I didn't come here to play his games.

I set the beer down. Another shitty memory to attribute to the drink. "Holden, thank you for the invite, but I don't have much time in Coal Haven. I need to make it count."

"I understand, man. See you around?"

I nodded, appreciating that the loaded look he gave me said he understood more than what I said. I walked around the house. I'd like to have told my cousins and aunts good-bye, but Cameron could explain it since he thought he knew everything.

I got into my car and calmly drove away, not giving Cameron the satisfaction of knowing he'd riled me more than he had. I now had a lot clearer picture of why Dad had chosen to stay and face the reckoning over going home. And, for once, I was grateful for his choice.

* * *

Laney

Liam and Kennedy were splitting a s'mores dessert Remington had created. It was a chocolate lava cake crusted in graham crackers, with a torched marshmallow on top. To cement the sugar shock, chocolate sauce was drizzled over the top. They'd offered me a spoon, but it was a little too close to feeling like a third wheel.

Besides, it'd take longer for two of them to polish the dessert off. These two weren't the type to hang out at the bar. They had each other to go home to. I had a quiet office to avoid while I wondered how Archer's meet and greet was going.

Kennedy put her spoon down. "You're really nervous about how it's going, aren't you?"

"Am I that bad?"

She smiled. "I understand the nerves. Bruce used to make me feel that way about Liam." She rolled her eyes to the ceiling and frowned. "Wait. I guess it was the other way around. They were warning me off him."

"You understand how Archer feels."

"Yeah... I'm not any help."

I laughed. "No, that's exactly what I need."

Kennedy took a sip from her straw and her gaze shifted to the door. Her eyes widened.

Liam's gaze flicked up, and he put his loaded fork back down on the plate.

"He's here," Kennedy said under her breath.

A wave of heat crashed into me before I even looked. A tall, dark, and brooding man stopped at the end of the booth. "Sorry for the interruption." His tone was polite but loaded. "Can I join you?"

I scooted over. His family event had started before I met Liam and Kennedy, and I'd been at Rattler's with my friends for an hour. Didn't seem like enough time to get to know an entire side of a family he'd never met. Dread started welling up. I had wanted the night to go well for him, had hoped it wouldn't affect things between us. But I didn't think it'd go poorly enough that he'd leave early.

Archer slid in next to me, not stopping again until he was touching me. Bourbon and citrus enveloped me. He adopted a smile, his mask sliding into place quickly and thoroughly, and he stuck a hand out. "Hi, I'm Archer."

Liam gave Archer's hand an easy squeeze. "Liam. Your cousin, I guess. This is my wife, Kennedy."

Archer gave Kennedy another boardroom smile. "Nice to meet you both. Delaney talks about you a lot."

"Did you eat?" Enough with the niceties. Curiosity was murdering me. What had happened? Did the whole crew break early? Archer was upset, but was it about the mysterious family rift or me or something else entirely?

"I had a bite," was all he said. The teenaged server stopped by.

Archer looked at my White Claw can like he was about to say he'd have what I was having but changed his mind. "Water, please."

When the server left, I said, "I can drive if you want to have a beer." He could walk to get his car in the morning. Nothing in Coal Haven was farther than walking distance.

"I don't drink beer."

I'd seen him have one when we'd met a client for supper. "You don't like it?"

"I just don't drink it." He flung a casual arm that was anything but relaxed behind me. Tension radiated from the man. "When I'm selling a forty-million-dollar piece of land, clients feel better if I drink, have something they expect a guy in a suit to have, or a drink that makes me just like them."

There was something he wasn't saying, but I wasn't going to press him. I was close to Liam and Kennedy; he wasn't.

I inspected him. "How'd it go? Really? If you don't want to talk about it here, I understand. Just know that Liam and Kennedy probably understand even more."

His expression remained passive. "Weird. Just... really weird. A whole houseful of strangers and a couple of people who spoke as if..." He shook his head.

Liam pushed his plate away. The last bite wasn't as interesting to him as my husband was. "Let me guess. You got introduced to everyone. They maybe showed you their spread, told you how much of the county they owned, then they—Cameron most likely—asked you about Laney. Told you it would be in your best interest—he probably hinted it would be in everyone else's best interest as well—for you to pursue the divorce or the annulment or whatever."

"Close enough." Archer glanced at me like he wanted to see how I was handling the conversation. I hadn't expected it to go any differently.

"I've gotten that talk a time or two." Kennedy elbowed Liam.

Liam shot her an adorable grin, and a spear of envy stabbed my chest. The two were a united front. Kennedy had been warned away from being Liam's friend in high school, but she smiled and nodded her way through ignoring that advice. And when they'd started dating last year, the shit had hit the fan. Yet here they were. Bruce still adored her. He was even nicer to Liam. Cameron was a different story, but it didn't matter. He couldn't touch Liam and Kennedy's relationship, and that probably rubbed him raw under the collar.

Could Archer and I be like that? He was here. That meant something.

Archer peppered Liam with questions about his work at the mine outside of Washburn. The subject turned to growing up in Coal Haven and then to Derek. The three of us regaled Archer with stories about his late cousin. It was the first time I'd walked down memory lane about my ex, and to do it with Kennedy and Liam was special. We'd mentioned Derek, but we hadn't dived into the past like this. We each had our memories and several of them overlapped. And through Kennedy, I was able to hear about Derek's college years and their marriage.

I'd missed so much. On purpose. Back then, I'd had no idea that these two people would be cornerstones of my life. I had assumed they'd dismiss me like everyone else, but really, being here right now, was because of Derek. A parting gift that meant so much more than being able to think about our high school relationship without resentment.

After Liam told Archer how a four-wheeler really ended up in the river, his smile faded and his stare was directed at the door. "I hate to make this about me, but if your choice of wife doesn't make your family happy, sitting here with me is going to piss them off. Stetson just walked in."

My heart dropped. The family dinner had been tenser than Archer let on. I gave him a squeeze back. I understood being on the outs with the Barrons of Coal Haven.

"He'll probably sit in the bar like he usually does," Kennedy murmured.

Stetson was friends with Remington. And women interested in either one knew to find them at the big table in the bar.

"Nope," Liam said under his breath and shifted. Kennedy's arm moved like she was rubbing Liam's leg to reassure him.

Stetson cast a big shadow over the table. His T-shirt was tight enough to look sprayed on. His jeans weren't his usual tattered pair he wore around town, and he'd combed his wavy hair instead of stuffing a ball cap on his head.

His deep brown gaze touched on me, over to Liam and Kennedy, and to my husband. "Archer."

"Stetson. Look, if you're here to reaffirm the message of who I should or shouldn't acquaint myself with, I'll have to politely ask you to keep walking."

My breath stalled. This was how I wanted Archer to act around his friends. I wanted him to demand better—for himself and for me. I wanted to go back in time and do it myself.

Stetson's eyes narrowed, but I didn't sense hostility. He was thinking about Archer's request. He finally nodded.

"My dad said it should be up to us whether we're going to continue the silent treatment. I reckon I've been told enough who I should and shouldn't talk to." His gaze flicked to Liam. "Figure it's time I decide for myself."

"Appreciate it." Archer gestured to the space in the booth next to him. "Care to join us?"

The corner of Stetson's mouth kicked up. "Ain't no one ready for that level of drama. Just wanted to stop and say no hard feelings you lit outta there before dessert. Holden's idea of dessert is to grill more shit anyway. Have a good evening." He knocked at the edge of the table before he walked away.

Kennedy spoke first. "That was monumental."

Liam nodded, his stunned expression still in place. "If Stetson rebels against Cameron, it's subtle. More like who can out-stubborn the other. This was close to outward defiance."

"I'm glad that went well." Archer's smile was the one he wore when he was working. "I've heard all about y'all as kids, but I hear you have twins."

Kennedy dug out her phone to show him pictures. My friends might've realized that Archer was avoiding any more talk about his family or how the night went. They'd probably known when I'd done it too. But we laughed over stories of the twins, and when the evening was over, Archer gave me a lingering kiss good night and left in his car. I went home by myself, wishing I was crawling into bed with him instead. Nothing about this night felt settled. I thought I was getting to know Archer, but tonight I'd seen the layers he kept hidden from me.

* * *

Archer

. . .

I stared at the ceiling of my motel room. Every so often, the drone of an engine broke through the quiet. I couldn't sleep.

Liam, Kennedy, and Delaney had stayed at Rattler's until after ten. I'd stayed the entire time, and it shouldn't have come as a surprise, but I'd had fun. Liam's irreverent humor reminded me of Ansen. My brother and I hadn't been close the last few years.

Why, again?

Then the night had wrapped up. Delaney went home, and I came back to the room. Alone.

I grabbed my phone. There'd been too many nights I'd lain awake wishing I could talk to my wife. I wasn't doing that when we were at least in the same zip code.

She answered with a soft, "Hey."

"Sorry to bother you. Were you asleep?"

Rustling came over the line. "No. Let me just step outside before Ma pounds on the wall." I heard the door open and close, then she said, "Is something wrong?"

"I had fun with you tonight."

"Good. Spending time with my friends is one of my favorite things. Other than riding Target." A distant moo came over the line. "Why'd you really call?"

I let out a slow exhale, wishing she was with me in the dark, tucked into my side. If she were curled next to me, we probably wouldn't be talking, and I needed to talk. Thoughts and worries swirled in my head, and they'd rob me of sleep.

Yet, I started with an innocuous topic. "Aunt Naomi was exactly as you said. Cold and distant."

A soft snicker came over the line. "Ant."

"What?"

"Nothing. Just that you say 'Ant Naomi.' I'd say 'Awnt

Naomi,' but I wouldn't or she'd stare at me and I'd turn to stone."

I chuckled, but it faded. "Uncle Cameron asked about you. I didn't tell him more than what we told Holden." I thought back to the awkward explanation with a roomful of eyes on me. People I'd just met who knew my business. "Am I like him?"

On paper, I should have been thrilled. Uncle Cameron was exactly who I had wanted to be—who I'd wanted my dad to be. Not only had Cameron successfully run the Barron Ranch, he was also the CEO at the refinery. He'd started there before I was born and had worked his way up. My uncle was stern, confident, and I doubted there was a person who had railroaded him on this earth.

He was Dad's opposite.

"What makes you ask that?"

"We both cut Dad out of our lives and seem to be better for it." What would I have done in Dad's place? What if I'm better because of what Dad did?

"What happened?"

"At Holden's? Or with my dad?"

"Both."

"It's been easy to blame Dad," I began as I stared at the ceiling. Liam had hit the right tone when he'd guessed how my night went. "He thought, as the second oldest, he should've run the Barron Ranch. Cameron was going to have a full-time job and a family."

"But Cameron wasn't going to give up control?"

That would've been the easy answer. I had told her Dad was a ranch manager growing up. Now he was a hired hand for whomever didn't fire him. I hadn't told her about that before. "I think he knew Dad was shit at running anything. The siblings paid Dad for his share, and Dad had sunk it into a place in Texas. Over seven hundred acres, a breathtaking vista, a lodge, and enough space for two boys to cause all sorts of trouble and not get caught."

I had to stop. Delaney didn't respond. Seven hundred acres had gotten reduced to an abandoned hunting cabin.

"I don't like to drink beer because it reminds me of when he'd sit at the table, empty cans all over, and try to figure out the books. Then he'd stomp and yell, and he and Mama would argue."

"He's an alcoholic?" She was surprised but understanding.

"Truthfully, I don't know. Eventually, we didn't even have money for beer. And that's all I can remember when I have a beer."

"And that's why you don't really drink."

"Probably."

"You're not like Cameron," she said.

I needed to hear it, but the shitty feeling didn't go away. "I cut Dad out of my life." And I'd done it so I could do better. Just like his siblings had done to him.

"Sometimes you have to."

But Delaney hadn't. Cameron's statement had hit home. Dad and Cheryl had a lot in common. They were stubborn and prideful and made ego-based decisions that hurt themselves and those they loved.

"You're not like Cameron," she said again, with more confidence than I felt. "You don't make others feel like shit for what they don't have, and you won't destroy them to get what you want."

And that was what had bothered me. "After he made sure I knew you'd dated my cousin, he pointed out all the land in the Barron family. He used Diamond UU as a comparison."

"Oh," she said like it was suddenly clear. "So he was

more like Wilson, in that he couched his insults in supposedly helpful information."

Only Cameron hadn't been insulting me. He'd been subtly pointing out how the Grangers' property fell short of anything Barron. From the oil wells on the land to the vast acreage to the age of the buildings and shops, Uncle Cameron hadn't hidden his pride for all things Barron or his disdain for all things Granger.

The rest of what Delaney said got through my head. "What do you mean 'like Wilson'?"

"Insults couched in info? Like when he said your company's insurance will pay for breast augmentation in certain circumstances."

"Why the fuck would he say that?" Wilson didn't need to be paying any attention to my wife's boobs.

"Same reason Briony would make the stylist comment. They didn't think I was good enough for you, and they wanted to pick someone they could further control you with."

"Why didn't you tell me?"

"I dunno. Maybe I was afraid you wouldn't see anything wrong with it, and I was a little ashamed they had to mention it in the first place."

"You have absolutely nothing to be ashamed of. I like your style—and your tits." If I didn't want another eighteen months of her not talking to me, I had to listen, but she needed to be comfortable telling me. "Why would they want to control me?"

"So you won't leave the company. You make them money."

"Wanting me to work for them might be more about trust."

"It's about image with them. You have the looks. You

have the brains. You bring in the dollars. I feel like that's more important to them than who you are. Norville should be begging you to be partner. Unlike Wilson, you would've earned it."

I could see her point. The Truitts were concerned about image.

Archer, you can't meet a client selling a two-hundred-million-dollar piece of property in your used car. Seriously. Use our driver. Our cut of a two-hundred-million deal was significant. I couldn't risk it on my pride.

Dallas was a big city, and the size of the land deals in Texas and surrounding states made it a competitive market. We had to stand out any way possible.

"In the weeks before I left," she continued, "you were pushing me to drive something newer, to go for the management position when I couldn't stand my job in the first place, and we only went to cocktail and martini bars. I didn't think that was coming from you."

I thought back to those days and the casual chats with my friends when we weren't talking about work. I hated to think my friends had purposely been eroding my relationship. I couldn't imagine what the reason would be.

Norville should be begging you to be partner.

"Maybe..." Her breath hitched like she wasn't sure she should say what was coming next. "Maybe you need to ask yourself an honest question. Did you quit talking to your dad and your brother before or after you met Norville Truitt?"

"No, I'd already left home." But my answer fit as well as a pair of overalls on a horse. I couldn't hide from the answer to that question. I didn't want to be like my uncle.

In my dark motel room, I took a stark look at myself. I didn't talk to my dad. My brother wasn't really in my life.

My wife had left. A judgment I had once made toward Dad was turned around. There was a common denominator, and it was me.

LANEY

"Holy shi-it, you've started something, girl." Ma tossed the bag of cattle mineral onto the pallet in the shed. I'd backed the pickup to the door so we could unload. She took a drag off her vape pen and blew out a gusty cloud of strawberry-scented smoke. "Jocelyn at the diner asked if Archer quit talking to his daddy like his daddy did to his siblings. Then old Earl, you know, Elsie's grandpa?" She described Earl each time by referencing an old high school frenemy. Elsie had left for college and came back once every five years with her three kids. She might have been a delightful adult, but it wasn't like Elsie and I talked any more.

"Yes, I know who Earl is." The drone of the riding lawn mower was muffled as Archer rumbled behind the house. Papa had commented on how he was missing good fishing weather. Archer had hopped on the John Deere, and Papa had grabbed his pole and tackle box and sped away.

"Well, he says that Stetson and Cameron are having some kind of standoff. That Stetson's all buddy-buddy with your hubby, and his daddy ain't having it."

It'd been two days since Stetson had stopped by our table at Rattler's. "No one knows anything, Ma."

"They know you and Archer are married, but he's staying at the motel. Imagine all the reasons they're coming up with." She shrugged. "Whatever. Kane never had the town gossiping about him like that."

She knew full well Kane had given the town enough gossip. She might have wanted to forget the attempted suicide, but that didn't change reality.

I yanked a bag of mineral from the back of the pickup and hauled it to the pallet. I'd gone to town early to load up. I hadn't expected Ma to help me. Did she want to talk to me about something other than what Earl had said?

Did I want her to talk to me about something? By the time Ma chewed over a topic, she'd lost her patience and her tact.

"When are you moving back to Dallas?"

I stayed at the edge of the pallet, thankful I had dropped my load before she sprang that question on me. I might've stumbled and twisted an ankle. "What do you mean?"

"I mean, you and your hubby seem to be getting on just fine. It's not like he can move into the house with you."

I folded my arms and braced my legs. Those were not the reasons why Ma had asked.

Ma took a drag off her pen. "Kane told me yesterday that he wants to move."

"Oh." He hadn't mentioned when he was going to tell her. I had planned on going with him to his next therapy appointment, but he'd messaged me and said he wanted to get used to going alone. Had he gotten a job sooner than expected?

I shook my head. He was doing what he needed to do for himself, and he didn't need me to do it. Good for him. "What does me going back to Dallas have to do with Kane moving?"

Ma swung her arm out to where Archer was on the mower. "With you and him here, what's Kane got to do?"

"Kane doesn't want *to do* anything." I tried not to look at Ma like she was speaking a made-up language, but damn. Kane hadn't touched anything ranch-related since that night. The therapist supported his decision. No one expected Kane to go back to the job that had made him miserable.

Why couldn't Ma accept that her precious firstborn boy did not want to carry on the legacy of the Diamond UU, nor should he be expected to? Why couldn't Ma accept that I wanted to?

"He just needs a little more time, and with you and city boy over there doing all the work, Kane doesn't feel needed."

"Maybe Kane is finally at peace with leaving," I said more gently than I intended.

"He'll come around. Ain't nothing in Fargo for him."

Other than a multitude of jobs and social outlets he hadn't had access to his entire life, no. Nothing there for him.

"Ma, going to school is what helped him recover. Now he wants a job. Not this."

"He recovered just fine. He's bored, that's all, not being able to ranch."

I ground my teeth together as I stared at her. How could she be so willfully oblivious? Kane's head trauma had kept him from helping around the ranch for a while, but it'd been a year and a half. I'd run as much interference as possible to keep him from feeling chained to Coal Haven. I'd taken over his ranch duties. I'd buffered him from Ma and her ingrained expectations. I'd arranged our finances so he could start school and take a double load.

He wanted to move so he could meet new people and find a job he enjoyed. I wanted to find him, give him a big hug, and let him know I'd help him with anything. And I had the feeling he didn't need me to. He was venturing out on his own without me. Without Ma.

I needed to channel Ma and be firmer with her. "He doesn't want this for a career. He couldn't have made that much clearer."

"We all go through that phase." How badly could she minimize this? Ma ignored my incredulous stare and clucked her tongue. "Of course, we don't all—" Her throat worked, and her eyes misted over.

I'd never seen Ma cry. By the time I had arrived home after I learned Kane was hurt, Ma had returned to her formidable self.

She cleared her throat. "This ain't an easy life, Laney. Even when we're raised in it, years like this make us feel pretty damn helpless. It's our experience that gets us through. The 'this too shall pass' shit. Kane didn't have that experience. He'll see. It'll be fine."

"He won't," I spat out. "Because he won't be here. I get it. You got stuck with me. You had your son; you had your successor. I was the surprise that ended up being nothing but baggage. But guess what? I'm here, and I want to do this. Kane doesn't. So unless you want to drive him back into his depression, you'll encourage him to follow his dreams, and you'll even help him move. Then you'll burn down that trailer house to show him he has your utmost support and always will. At least one of us should have that from you."

Ma blinked. She blinked again.

My chest was heaving. I hadn't realized my volume increased as I went. I adjusted the bill of my cap, pulling it down.

After several moments of silence, Ma finally said, "Shit, Laney." Her throat worked again. "I wouldn't expect you to understand."

"You obviously aren't trying to either."

"Don't be acting all high and mighty now that you're one of them."

"Oh my God, Ma. My marriage has nothing to do with Kane or this ranch."

"And it never will."

I drew back. "What?"

"Figure it out." Ma started to saunter away. "Since you're so much smarter than me."

I stared after her. The back of the pickup was still loaded with bags of mineral.

Figure it out.

I was so over the Barron last name and all the baggage that came with it. I was Laney Granger. I'd married a man named Archer. Why couldn't it be that simple?

* * *

Archer

Cheryl stormed toward the barn. I looped the lawn mower around and craned my neck to look for Delaney. She was inside the shed, watching her mom walk away. The intensity of her glare could rival the sun.

I finished the row I was mowing and ambled the mower toward the shop. Delaney yanked a bag out of the pickup, her wiry muscles bulging as she carried it into the shed. She'd do them all, one by one, and then grab a sandwich to eat while filling the water truck. Delaney's expression was full of all the thunderclouds the land needed in the sky.

I killed the engine and hopped off. Jumping in, I grabbed a bag, my core muscles firing up. This wasn't gym equipment. I wasn't pulling a weight sled or doing planks. This was *work*. I found where she was stacking the mineral.

Dust filtered through the shed as we worked, grunting and breathing hard. By the time we stacked the last bag on the pallet, her expression had relaxed into resignation.

"Wanna talk 'bout it?" I asked.

She sniffed and brushed the back of her hand against her cheek. "Just Ma being Ma." She slammed the tailgate up and propped an elbow on it. "Kane told her he's moving, so she's blaming me."

"Why?" Cheryl had to see it was what he wanted.

She rolled her eyes and shook her head, but I caught the glint of moisture wicking over her eyes. "Just Ma being Ma."

I crowded closer, dropping a hand to her waist. She needed support, whether she wanted it or not. "Why, Delaney?" I asked quietly.

"Not only wasn't I planned, but she thinks Kane's leaving because I'm here and he's not needed. She won't admit that everything she planned for him is everything he doesn't want." She sniffled. "And then I had to go and become a Barron, and she's apparently pissed about that."

"Well, that explains why I wasn't invited over for tater tot hotdish." Delaney hadn't thought I knew what it was, but Dad had made it when we were kids. Mama was born and raised in Texas, but she'd been fascinated with his love of the casserole.

She scrubbed her face, leaving streaks of dirt behind. "Ugh. Moping doesn't get the cows fed, and I have to figure out how the hell we're going to do that the rest of summer and all through the winter."

"The hay we cut won't be enough." I stated the obvious.

She shook her head and gazed at the pastures. "No. We have, like, two-thirds of the bales we usually get. Not enough rain, and I don't think we'll get enough for another cutting. Buying bales is going to be expensive as fuck, and I think Ma is denying how bad of a spot we're in with this too. Probably thinks if it gets bad enough, Kane will come to the rescue." She gazed at me, her blue eyes full of desperation. "I've got to take care of this so he feels free to move."

I'd been thinking about the hay issue. Hay was no different than any other resource. When supply went down, cost went up, and this was an area where I could help. I had a lot of contacts in the farm and ranch world. "I might know some guys."

She chewed the inside of her cheek before she said, "Transport will still be expensive."

"Ah, honey, remember? Everything's negotiable."

The corner of her mouth ticked up. "I think the way you worked over my insurance agent, Chad might drive across the country to pick up hay for you."

"Tell me what you need and I'll make it happen."

"I know you can." That wasn't an appreciative tone.

"What brought this on?" She was about to brush my question off, but I slid my hand back around her waist. "I'm not upset, Delaney. We're talking. This is what I'm here for."

"Exactly. And when we're done talking, then what?"

Then I'd bring my wife back home. She loved this life, but she wouldn't admit she was miserable working with her mother. After talking to her the other night, I agreed that I didn't have to cut Dad out of my life. But I had accepted it was perfectly reasonable that I didn't have to stay and tank my life with him.

She leaned against the pickup and folded her arms, a look dangerously close to defeat on her face. "I missed this place the entire time I was gone. I missed waking up in the morning and walking outside to hear mooing. I even missed spring calving. I was sick of manicured lawns and strategically planned parks."

"I missed it too." And I had. I hadn't admitted it to myself until now, but I'd known. I missed running out the door and the only traffic I had to watch out for was our dog. Mama had named him Rembrandt "because he had an artist's soul." Our dog had loved people almost as much as he loved circling his cows. Not like Portia.

"Do you still?" she asked. "Miss this life? Or is this like a dude ranch for you? Work it for a while, have a little fun, discover yourself, and then leave."

The answer came easily. "We were working for someone else. It wasn't my dream, and now I buy and sell that dream for others. This, with you, means a lot more than that ever did. I wouldn't be here if you weren't important to me."

Her shoulders sagged like she was disappointed with my answer. What had her mother said to her?

She might love this place. It was her home. But I wasn't sure it loved her back. Not like I did. I also wasn't sure she was ready to see that, and she wouldn't return with me if she thought her home was in trouble. "How 'bout you show me those numbers and I'll see what I can do?"

* * *

Running numbers next to Delaney shouldn't be sexy. But it was. When we were first married, Delaney had been sexy as hell, with softer edges and a subdued personality, but she'd been easy to talk to. I could ramble for an hour about my work, but she'd never brushed it off. Never changed the subject. Never gave me the sense she was about to drop dead with boredom. Summing it up to the fact she had been raised on a ranch was only part of the equation.

Delaney could rattle off the number of cattle she had, how many she planned to sell and how much she expected to earn, where that money would go, and how much feed, silage, and hay it would take to get them through the rest of the year until they could pray for rain and hay again.

"We'll dilute the hay we have with silage; it'll help, and our hay won't go to waste. They're out there grazing pastures full of the damn bugs, and we haven't seen many issues. Other than they aren't putting on the weight they need because of the drought."

I scribbled some data down. "One of my old clients moved his family to Nebraska. I could give him a call. He might have some leads."

Delaney's eyes brightened. "Nebraska would be better than Oklahoma."

The transport costs had her worried. The cost of mileage, the extra paperwork involved in hauling across state lines, the added cost of decent hay in a shortage. The work I'd been doing in Dallas that had consumed me could be used to help my wife.

"All we're doing is getting information. But the people I'm contacting are like you. They've done this for a living. They know what bad years are like. They'll be good to work with."

She nodded and met my gaze. I held it, just enjoying being in a quiet room with her. Whatever had bothered her at the shed had taken a back seat to obtaining enough food to get her herd through the fall and winter. A tiny crease formed between her brows as she calculated bales and how long they could last.

I liked working with her. I liked seeing glimpses of her ass when she dug tools out of the truck. And the memory of what had happened in the motel room kept me rooted to the fact she and I were napalm together. But I missed having her next to me outside of the bedroom too.

I missed the nights when I didn't have business dinners and wasn't out of town for work. We closed the world out of the condo, cuddled on the couch, and streamed movies. Some nights she'd fall asleep, and I'd carry her to bed. I'd get in next to her while her soft floral scent curled into my nose.

The motel had become my purgatory. I had to sleep by myself and listen to the cars coming in off the highway. Teenagers revving their engines at all hours, reminding me of how Ansen and I used to raise country-boy hell. We might not have had a lot of friends, and he was several years younger than me, but he'd wanted to see how fast the old truck of Dad's could go. We'd hooted and hollered at the dust cloud I'd kicked up.

The longer I was in Coal Haven, the more those memories surfaced.

Delaney peeked at her phone for the time. "Kane wants to talk to me. Ma must've told him she told me and is probably making him feel terrible for leaving."

"I'm glad he has your support."

"Thanks."

Her tone was guarded, so I pressed. "But you still feel guilty?"

"I resented him for so long. The golden boy who got everything. I didn't realize..."

I splayed my hand on her thigh and gave her a reassuring rub. Hadn't I just been thinking about how differently I'd been viewing my childhood as an adult? "Don't hold being a kid against yourself."

"I don't know what I would've done differently." She leaned closer until our heads were tipped together. "Not gone so far away for college? Come home more?"

"Do you really think it would've helped?" I asked gently.

She slumped and leaned her head against my shoulder. "No. It took being away to make me realize this is really what I want. It wasn't jealousy from seeing Kane getting it."

I had the life I'd dreamed of when I was a kid. She had the life she had dreamed of. Too bad they were so far apart.

"I'm not surrounded by buildings and people," she continued. "I can ride Target instead of going for a run. I hate running."

I chuckled and rubbed my hands up and down her legs. We hadn't gotten to do much with just the two of us since our trip to Dickinson. "I do run and ride a bike, but I haven't been for a long ride in a long time."

"You need to fix that problem."

"Any ideas?"

I thought she'd suggest an evening ride if it cooled off enough, but she thought for a moment. "This weekend. We'll take Target and Papa's horse, Bolt, and go to Medora."

"The Badlands, right?" She nodded, and I sifted through my memories. "Dad actually talked about Medora." Family rides and camping when he was a kid. He used to tell stories around the table when Mama was alive. More good memories I'd forgotten about.

"It's getting harder to find horse-friendly trails, you know, since mountain bikes don't shit like a half-ton animal, but there are still some good ones." Her blue gems twinkled and her mouth quirked. "We can even camp. Papa will cover for me for a weekend, as long as he can still sneak away to fish at least once."

"Do you have a trailer with a camper?" I hadn't seen anything but an old white trailer that would be cozy for two horses. They either hired out when they had to transport large numbers of cattle, or they used the nicer pickup with the gooseneck trailer. The gooseneck didn't have a space for sleeping.

"Nope."

"An RV?"

Her smile widened. "Also, no."

It'd been years since I'd stayed in anything less than a five-star hotel. She thought I'd balk at staying in a tent. Little did she know that Ansen and I would camp in the bed of Dad's pickup under the stars. We'd run to the creek and hunt for snakes. Bonus points if we spotted a venomous one.

Mama used to bring us lemonade and brownies. Sometimes, we hadn't been able to last the entire night. We'd been so young we'd scared ourselves silly. When we were older, we would've done fine, but by then, Mama was gone. It was like we'd made an unspoken agreement that the memories were too raw to try it again.

They weren't raw anymore. Just bittersweet. A little more bitter since I had no idea what my brother was doing these days.

I'd take care of that issue when I returned to Dallas. I had two weeks to win my wife back, to show her I could somehow give her what she wanted, and to get her to seriously consider that what she wanted wasn't in Coal Haven.

On a slightly less important note, our sleeping arrangements could be closer together. I leaned into my touch and her thigh flexed under my hand. "The real question is whether you're packing one tent or two."

Alarm widened her eyes, and I laughed. Instead of being insulted that she hadn't realized tent camping meant closer quarters than my motel room, I wasn't. I'd noticed the beat of heat in her eyes and the flush that crept up her neck as she realized exactly that.

"We have only a tent that sleeps four."

My grin remained in place. Still a small space.

Her eyes narrowed. "But separate sleeping bags."

"Sure." I'd give her that. I wanted her good and ready when I got between those toned legs again.

Twelve

LANEY

I pushed the shopping cart through the store. It was late evening, and we were grabbing supplies for our camping trip. Archer wandered next to me, garnering attention from everyone we passed. It was partly because of who he was, but also because he was hot. His shirt hugged his defined chest, and he'd bought a distressed denim–colored ball cap.

When he'd showed up wearing that thing, I'd nearly dragged him into the barn and mounted him. I wouldn't have cared where the straw had gotten. But I had refrained.

He looked approachable, doable. The way the cap revealed the definition of his face was just unfair. And he looked more like a Barron than ever.

I couldn't believe I'd suggested it. A weekend of camping.

The longer Archer was away from his life in Dallas, the harder I was falling for him. Did I think camping was some larger test? Like, if he lost his shit dealing with nothing but me and a horse in the heat, I'd finally know the last couple of weeks had been fake?

Would that be better or worse?

"Why lemonade and brownies?" I asked. There was a burn ban in the state with the drought. We couldn't have a campfire, so all our food had to be cooler-friendly and eaten cold.

He selected some bananas. "Mama used to bring them out to me and Ansen when we tried to camp in the yard."

"Tried?" Had he been camping family vacation–style? We were struggling ranchers, but Papa had still planned excursions. We'd taken the horses to Medora for a couple of nights. We'd dragged tents to Lake Tschida and Lake Sakakawea, each about an hour away. One year, Papa had even bought a used RV and gotten it running well enough to drive three and a half hours to Devils Lake. The Lake Region was a fertile area, thanks to the state's largest natural lake. We'd been so miserable being eaten by mosquitos he'd sold the RV as soon as we returned. *No point in fishing there again if I lose half my blood.* "Is this your first camping trip? Like real camping trip?"

He nodded and studied the apples.

"Okay, lemonade and brownies. What else?" Food wasn't the only thing I planned. I wanted to make this fun for Archer. The reverent way he'd asked for lemonade and brownies told me a lot. The memories were important, and I couldn't taint them with a shitty camping trip.

"Sandwiches?"

"Anything but bologna and white bread."

We loaded up on lunch meat, whole grain bread I probably wouldn't like better than Ma's stuff, Pop-Tarts—I'd never thought I'd see the day Mr. Personal Chef selected strawberry Pop-Tarts—and juice and water.

He adjusted his cap. "Think that's good for the weekend?"

"It'll be fine. There's a gas station and a few restaurants there."

We turned out of the beverage aisle. I stopped the cart before I mowed down Holden. Stetson was with him, holding a package of chicken.

"Archer." Stetson's gaze went from him to what was in the cart. "Jesus, Laney, what the hell you feeding him?"

Holden's expression was just as aghast. "You do realize what all those cattle you raise are for?"

"Ha ha," I said sarcastically. "I'm taking him camping this weekend."

"Hazen Bay?" Stetson asked. This was the most he'd talked directly to me in my life.

"Medora," Archer answered, his arm coming around me in a move that was natural, closer to how we usually interacted in public. "With horses."

"Been forever since I've done that," Holden said, his expression wistful. "What are you two doing tonight?"

"Packing." Most of that would be done in the morning. I had found the tent and loaded the feed pails, a square bale, and tack for the horses already.

"We'll grab another pack," Stetson said, lifting the pack of chicken. "Come on over to Holden's. He's grilling."

I blinked at the two men. Archer waited for me to answer. He would've said no if he had a strong instinct to, but he'd told me their reactions to Cameron. Archer could go just to get to know them better. I was a different story. These two didn't seem hostile toward me, but if any of their parents were around...

"It would be just us four," Holden said. Had the trepidation been written across our faces? "You bring a side dish.

Then Stetson won't bitch about how I make nothing but meat."

Stetson rolled his eyes. "You don't."

Holden shrugged, unabashed.

It was that exchange that swayed me. These two men weren't like Archer's friends in Dallas. They were arrogant, and they were guilty of excluding the people their parents told them to, but they'd grown up. Wilson and his wife got off on making me feel like crap; they liked their control over Archer.

Archer's cousins liked grilling, and they didn't seem to mind me. We weren't teenagers anymore. And Cameron wouldn't be there.

I leaned into Archer's side for support. "We can bring a salad."

"I'm grabbing a dessert too." Stetson pulled a pack of cookies off the shelf without looking too hard at what he'd gotten.

Holden held up a bag of peaches. "I've got dessert handled."

Stetson huffed. "Something you don't have to grill."

"Challenge accepted." Holden's grin was sly. "I can grill cookies."

"Fine," Stetson conceded. "But I'm getting whipped cream. The spray kind."

Holden glanced at us. "Come on over when you're done."

They wandered off, grumbling to each other about the sweets. I'd gotten a glimpse into the real them, and I wanted to laugh. The guys had been so far above me my entire life. Stetson had been a football star, and when he and Holden had been on the same team, Coal Haven had gone to state. They were the guys who girls sighed after as teens, and they were the county's most eligible bachelors as adults. Never had I thought I'd witness them bicker about whether grilled peaches were a proper dessert.

"Sure you're okay with this?" Archer asked. "Give me a sign and we'll leave when you need to."

I grabbed a pack of fudge-striped cookies to throw into our supplies. "No. I think this will be different."

It had taken several months to keep from feeling like an outsider when it came to my hometown. And the town was starting to embrace my husband. Would that change anything?

* * *

Archer

Holden had grilled his peaches—which were fucking amazing with whipped cream piled on top. We were sprawled in lawn chairs on his front porch, the pinks and purples of the setting sun painting the horizon.

After we'd eaten, Stetson had made the mistake of asking me what I do. I'd glossed over my job the other night when the rest of our family was here, but Stetson wasn't asking for a fluff answer.

But twenty minutes later, I thought I should shut up. The wind had died down, and the night was pleasant, if still warm, but perfect as long as we weren't working. I finished up telling them about the different reports I gathered and how detailed I decided to get about the weather cycles over a certain property.

"So, anyway. That's what I do." I prepared for an awkward pause, a reaction like the playful eye roll Briony gave when I slipped and geeked out about my job. It wasn't my job per se that got me excited. Reports were reports. It was digging into the personality of the land. The way I was born and raised seeped into everything I researched.

Mineral rights had given my great-grandparents and grandparents wealth, and I dealt with them in Texas. Water rights were another issue. Oil didn't mean a damn thing if the property owners couldn't get access to a water supply.

Stetson took a swig of his beer, a thoughtful look on his face. "Dan Anderson could use a guy like you."

Surprise lit Delaney's eyes. "Dan's selling?"

Holden nodded. "They don't have any kids to take over. Which is a damn shame. Those eggs of Alice's are phenomenal."

"I used to ride to his draw all the time," she said wistfully. "It's so peaceful." She spoke to me. "Dan's place is across from Bruce's place."

Holden grinned like this draw was a secret only they knew about. "Evander and I used to go there too. Dan chased us out twice, thinking we were partying." He snorted. "Those were the only two times we weren't up to no good."

Stetson opened the package of cookies, the plastic crinkling. "They're moving so Alice can be somewhere warm. Arthritis or something. I hope they get as much for that place as possible. I wouldn't be surprised if that property is all they have for retirement."

A steady list of everything I'd do and the questions I would ask this Dan ran through my mind. I couldn't shut it off. I had told Delaney I was working my dream job, but I wasn't talking about the Truitts or the paycheck. I liked all things land.

Land was a finite resource. Wars were fought over it. People stole it and died for it. What was done with it determined our survival, so I took my job seriously. I'd seen how poor stewardship destroyed families like mine. I wanted to position the right buyers at the right time. I wanted to make sure people like Dan and Alice were taken care of after they'd dedicated their lives to growing food for countless others.

"So." Holden gestured between me and Delaney with his beer. "What's with you two?" Stetson slapped his shoulder, but Holden held his hands up like he was innocent, his longneck dangling from a couple of fingers. "The whole town is wondering. What's the point of being family if I can't be nosy?"

"We're still working it out," I replied. I thought I'd hate the intrusive question but found it a relief to address. Delaney and I didn't fucking know and now they knew that.

"It's complicated," Delaney said quietly.

I nodded, hating the answer. Being with Delaney was simple. Figuring out where to be with her was starting to be the hard part.

Holden ran a finger down the condensation of his glass bottle. "If I didn't know how complicated relationships were, I'd be in one."

"It's why I'm out of one," Stetson said in a way that told me there was a hell of a story there.

Holden scoffed. "You're out of one because she was batshit."

"She wasn't batshit when I started dating her," Stetson shot back.

"Right." How could one word hold so much sarcasm? "That's why none of us warned you."

Stetson's jaw clenched, but he ignored Holden. "Whatever's going on, don't let our family fuck it up. Yours either,

Delaney. I'm betting your mom wasn't happy to learn you married him."

"She was thrilled," Delaney said sweetly. "Monogrammed towels are arriving next week."

Stetson sputtered out a laugh. "I'll bet your momma raced right out to engrave 'Barron' on everything." His expression turned somber. "How's Kane doing?"

Kane had to be close to Stetson's age, maybe a couple years older. I doubted they were friends, but they'd been around each other their entire lives.

"Good," Delaney answered in a way that told all of us she was fine talking about her brother. He really was doing well, and she didn't mind sharing it. "He's moving to Fargo."

"He's out completely, then?" Holden asked and Delaney nodded. He waited like she was going to tell him she was taking over Diamond UU. But that wasn't going to happen —and I didn't know if it ever would. Holden must've sensed the answer to his question was loaded. "He'll do great in Fargo."

"I think so too," she said confidently. "And I'm glad others think so."

Tonight had shown me how far out of her element Delaney had been in the city. From her marketing job where she designed campaigns for items like ketchup, then going home to a small apartment before she'd moved into the condo, to how she used to sit quietly at the table with me, Wilson, and Briony, as if she were afraid to speak.

But with my cousins, guys I knew hadn't gone out of their way to include her, she tossed back drinks, teased them about the sizes of their pickups, and joked about how it was a good thing Holden was grilling chicken because her ma might smell Barron beef on her.

Getting her back to Dallas hadn't been an easy prospect before. Right now, I was questioning whether it was something I should even be considering. I wanted what was best for her, but what if it meant leaving the stable future I'd worked so hard to build?

Thirteen

LANEY

Of course Archer would take to camping and trail riding all day like a fish to a fresh bowl of water.

Archer and Bolt got along as if they'd grown up together but hadn't seen each other until a ten-year reunion. Bolt was a nine-year-old gelding. While the horse was still in his prime, Papa was not. Ma sometimes rode Bolt, used him to get the occasional roaming cow back into the pasture, but other than asking Bolt for the occasional spin, the pace was easy. Bolt had pent-up energy and loved expending it. I often raced him to Liam's and back when he was being a little asshole to the other horses. Kane used to use him more often, but he'd stayed off the horses since his injury. He hadn't said, but I thought he didn't want to give Ma false hope.

"I can't believe how pretty it is." I glanced behind me. Archer gawked around him, unashamed of looking like a rugged cowboy. To be fair, he couldn't ditch that look right now if he tried. He'd produced a tan Stetson hat from the trunk of his car when he'd arrived at my place.

Archer was scanning our surroundings, abject awe on his face. We were crossing between two buttes. The trail ran alongside one, the sheer face of the butte rising almost vertically above us. The ground sloped down, less steep, but enough that you had to put full trust into your horse. We were surrounded by dirt, rock, and prickly brush.

"I mean, look at those colors."

I nodded but didn't respond. He'd been gushing about the scenery the entire trip. From how the scraggly brush managed to grow in the shale faces of the buttes to the various shades in each layer of rock in the exposed canyon. When we'd driven here, I'd been glad I drove. If it'd been him, we'd have veered off the interstate going through Painted Canyon.

Each time I saw Painted Canyon, I acknowledged how stunningly unique and beautiful it was. But it was like experiencing it for the first time again with Archer. Exposed canyon for miles. Shades of pinks and purples, even grayish blue, layered in the sides, dotted by green brush. Put that against the clear blue sky and it was breathtaking. One of the words Archer used.

Riding through the state park on a horse wasn't the same visual experience. We were down in it. Buttes towered above us. They were more than hills with a ton of character, but it was pretty, all the same. And technically challenging for a ride.

Target knew the drill. Bolt kept wanting to edge past us and be in the lead, but Archer kept him under control, like he'd grown up on a horse, which he had. As if he needed to be sexier.

He'd willingly walked away from the life, while I'd been

pushed away. And he had that other existence waiting for him in another state.

I shouldn't be getting grumpy on such a beautiful day. I should be elated. I was in Medora on a horse again. I hadn't done this since before I left for college.

But this day was only showing me we paired well together, and not just in the bedroom. Unfortunately, I wanted to make my home in North Dakota, and the way I lived here was what he hadn't wanted in Texas.

This ride was supposed to be relaxing, but all I could think about was why in the world he wouldn't want to stay. He enjoyed ranch work. Yes, he loved his job, but were the small-scale farms and ranches in North Dakota that much of a downgrade?

The answer I came back to was that I wasn't enough. Again.

I twisted in the saddle. "Ready to head back?"

When his gaze switched to me, I was captured by the pure joy in it. I'd seen a lot of expressions on Archer. He'd tried to remain in perfect control of his emotions—bad for business otherwise—but I'd been his wife.

I'd seen him upset, irritated, calm, content, and even happy. I knew what he looked like when he came inside me, or when his head was tipped back and my mouth was around him. I knew those expressions. But joy? No. Not even when we'd said our vows. He'd been satisfied, his eyes full of promise when sealing our nuptials, but not joyful. Not elated.

"We're riding again in the morning, right?"

I snickered. "If your ass can take it."

"My ass is ready," he growled, as if I was the one who might be sore in the morning for completely different reasons.

I had no business thinking about those reasons on a

horse with my hot husband riding next to me. "I may have even mentioned to Kennedy and Aspen we'd be camping. We might get company for the evening."

I had no shame about telling my friends to come out. It took my mind off sharing a tent with a guy I told myself repeatedly I couldn't think clearly around when we touched.

What had I been thinking? Two nights in a tent. Forget the sexy times. Having my irresistible husband right next to me after I'd sweated all day and smelled like horse?

Way to win him over, Laney.

"Liam too?" he asked.

I didn't miss the hope in his voice. I wasn't sure how he'd react to my next bit of news. Turning back to eye the trail, I spoke loudly enough for my voice to carry over the creaking saddles and swishing of the horses' tails. "Yes. And the boys."

He laughed. "Good thing we bought way too much lunchmeat and those cookies." Once we were on ground where the horses didn't have to concentrate so much, Archer started the conversation again. "Did you expect me to be a dick about Liam's kids?"

"I worried you'd be upset I invited my friends on your first major camping trip." Would he figure out I was afraid to spend the entire weekend with just him? But also, I liked hanging out with him and with people I also enjoyed being around.

"I like seeing you have a good time, Delaney. They're all an extension of you."

He could say the most perfect things. Like when he declared he liked my style and my tits. That was my kind of romance.

We navigated to the valley, and he finally gave Bolt enough slack to walk next to Target. "So, if it's not the company, then what? You've been quiet for over half the ride."

I chewed the inside of my cheek. "Nothing has changed your mind." Being with me wasn't enough to do it.

He swayed with Bolt's movements. A relaxed, experienced rider. The skills had come back like he hadn't shunned this part of him for over a decade. "I don't know what the answer is. I won't lie and say I'm not worried. Everything I worked for is in Dallas. I owe Mr. Truitt everything."

The blinders around his boss were still firmly in place. "If Norville really was the father figure you want him to be, wouldn't he want you to be happy?"

"It's not that easy."

I swiped at a fly with more force than needed. "Then what is it?"

"I know you think he's a sleaze." Archer gave me a flat look.

What would it take for him to see that Norville only cared about Archer because Archer earned enough money that Norville and Wilson could jack around? It wasn't Archer flying to Cabo. It wasn't Archer buying a third home in Florida. And it certainly wasn't Archer getting transported by helicopter or private jet when he had to travel for work.

"He's pragmatic." Archer continued his defense of his boss. "In his mind, we've been apart longer than we've been together, and he's protective of me."

"So protective he's been giving you more work?"

"I left for a month with little to no notice."

I sighed and closed my eyes, letting the gentle side to side of Target's gait lull the simmering anger to a dull ache. "We aren't going to come to an agreement about this."

"You don't have to like Mr. Truitt," he said with a touch

of resignation. "I'm just asking you to understand that he was there for me in ways my dad never was."

We didn't talk for a few moments, the only sounds the snuffles of the horses and the bugs buzzing in the dirt and the brush.

What if Derek's mom had taken me into her thin arms and treated me like the daughter she never had? When Ma had been in her prime, telling me I'd better think about my future because *there ain't nothing in Coal Haven for you*, would I have started to think Willow hung the moon and stars when all she'd been after was a free ranch hand?

Willow might be the wrong comparison. What if I had been naive enough to get in with Naomi? How differently would I have turned out?

I hoped I'd be savvier than that. But eighteen-year-old me had been severely short of support, and both Willow and Naomi had attained lives I had thought were unattainable. "I can understand."

He gave a nod. "That's enough for now."

* * *

Archer

We rode into camp. The trees were scattered around clearings and large enough to provide decent shade. I hadn't expected trees this large with the dry, rocky soil, but the campground was near the Little Missouri River. This place wasn't for RVs. There were some tents and a few camper/trailer combos. The site was loosely split into areas where groups could camp together, and each section included a small corral for the horses. A water shed was on one end, providing rudimentary showers and water spigots for the horses. Sitting around a campfire for the evening would've been nice, but we'd have to do without hot food unless we went to town.

I rose from the saddle a few inches, pressing down on the stirrups and leaning forward, easing protesting muscles. I hadn't ridden for more than an hour in years. Sometimes I hopped on with my clients, especially if I had the sense a seller needed me to understand I wasn't selling a product, I was selling a large chunk of their life.

Bolt wanted to take the lead until the very end, but I made him patiently wait as Delaney swung off Target and looped her lead rope around a corral gate. We took off the saddles and brushed the horses down. While she put them into the pens and stored our gear, I hauled fresh water.

I was wiping my hands off, enjoying the musky smell of horse sweat, when I caught Delaney eyeing the little camp we'd set up. When we had arrived, she'd settled the horses, and I had put up the green-and-black dome tent that fit our duffel bags and bedding.

I couldn't wait for tonight. The hard ground would be worth having her sleep close to me again. But she stared at the thing like it was a fighting octagon and I was the number one–ranked competitor.

I was looking forward to quality time. She was dreading it. I couldn't have that. "I can, uh, sleep in the cab of the pickup."

She jolted like she'd forgotten I was there. "No, it's fine. It'll be fine."

I lifted a brow. She sounded like she was convincing herself. "I don't know. After a five-hour ride, I might want the padded seats."

Her soft chuckle was what I wanted to hear.

Vehicles were constantly coming and going from the campground, but a pickup pulled up behind her dad's pickup and trailer. Liam waved from behind the wheel. Excitement I hadn't felt in a long time welled up, like I was a kid and friends had stopped over. I hadn't known what that was like, but I did now.

"Kennedy!" Delaney trotted to them, her ponytail swinging and her hips swaying. I couldn't take my eyes off her.

Liam slipped out of the pickup the same time both back doors opened and two little boys shot out.

"Target!" one cried. "Eli, it's Target."

"Bolt!" Eli chased the other boy, who must be Owen. "I get to pet Bolt first."

Liam was grinning when he caught my eye. "Did she warn you she invited all of us?"

"The more the merrier." I meant it. How much I meant it surprised me. Until I'd come to Coal Haven, my social time functioned as casual business. Forget jeans or cookies and chips. And definitely not kids.

Ansen and I would've lived for a camping trip with friends like this.

Yeah, I needed to give my brother a call.

Delaney and Kennedy were chatting and digging chairs out of the back of the pickup. Liam and I jumped in to help them arrange the chairs around the firepit that would stay unlit for the season.

Kennedy pushed a few stray strands of dark hair off her face. "I made a bunch of summer sausage sandwiches."

I clapped my hands together. "Sounds perfect. Y'all hungry? I brought supplies too."

"We can pool our stuff," Delaney said, "and make a potluck." Her gaze strayed to another car pulling in behind

Liam's truck, and a gorgeous grin spread across her face. She was even more unreserved around her own group of carefully cultivated friends.

My wife whooped when two women got out of the car. One had her hair pulled back; it could have been the sun, but parts of it looked red. She wore jeans faded from use and work outside rather than as a fashion choice and a pink T-shirt that said, "Titrate or Die." Delaney had said Lyric was the one who worked in a lab. Titrate sounded labby. That must mean the other woman in jean shorts and a baby-blue tank top with thin straps was Aspen. She was frowning at her choice of sandals as footwear.

Delaney noticed. "Don't step in horse shit and you'll be fine. It's not as if we're going for a night hike."

The woman broke out in a grin. "I've never felt so city in my life."

Delaney gestured to her as she grinned at me. "Ms. Kansas City there is Aspen. She teaches at the elementary school with Kennedy. And this is our hometown girl, returned to work her science magic in the lab at the clinic, Lyric."

I shook both their hands. Each met my handshake with a sturdy grip and a cursory inspection. I hadn't won them over by just being here. Good. Delaney needed friends like this.

I knew where I stood with everyone in Coal Haven. Delaney's mother. Her friends. My family. There wasn't a deal hanging off this social interaction like there often were with Mr. Truitt's dinner parties. The only reason I had to impress anyone here was because they mattered to Delaney; therefore, they mattered to me.

"Full disclosure," Lyric said as she rounded to the trunk and took out folding camp chairs. "I'm best friends with your cousin Isla, and I am obligated to gossip with her about you."

She wasn't kidding. Her frankness was refreshing.

"I'll try to give you plenty of good things to say."

She quirked a brow as if to say *we'll see.*

Aspen lifted one of the chairs from Lyric's fingers. "And as a teacher, I'm obligated to play coy when parents try to get gossip out of me. I'll forever act clueless." She tipped her head to where Liam stood with his arm draped over Kennedy's shoulders. "Those two gave me a lot of practice."

Kennedy chuckled. "That was mostly with the other teachers."

We surrounded the cold firepit and pulled the coolers together. The rest of us helped Liam and Kennedy juggle paper plates, juice boxes, and sandwich-making supplies for the boys.

"Aunt Laney, can we ride Target?" The boy I thought was Owen bounced up and down, with liquid squirting from the straw of the juice box he held.

This was the first I'd heard she was close enough to Kennedy to be called aunt.

Delaney balanced her plate on her lap and stacked lunchmeat on her bun. "I can lead you around on her after we eat."

Eli sucked down his juice until it squelched at the bottom. "I get to go first." The boys started arguing while Liam tried to break in.

"How about I lead one of you on Bolt?" I offered. "If Aunt Delaney thinks he'll behave."

Owen crinkled his nose. "Who's Dee Laney?"

"Me," my wife answered. "Just like your dad is nicknamed Liam, I'm nicknamed Laney. I think Bolt will be fine. He had a long ride, and it's just around the campsite."

While I internally beamed at Delaney's confidence in

me, they went quiet and stared at me until Owen said, "I get to go on Bolt first."

Eli's expression flashed his disagreement. "No, I get to ride Bolt first." More arguing ensued.

I shot Delaney a rueful glance. "I only meant to help."

"It wouldn't matter," Liam said around a mouthful of sandwich. "Parenting more than one kid is nothing but refereeing."

"Same with teaching," Aspen added, then leaned over her chair to my wife. "Hey, Laney, did you get any pictures from your ride today?"

Delaney dug out her phone, and the ladies went through photos. She got animated and talked with her free hand while periodically steadying the paper plate on her lap. Lyric jumped up and hovered between their chairs so she could see too. Then Kennedy scooted her chair closer.

The huddle of women with Delaney at the center summoned another memory. Before Mama died, we used to meet up with her cousins and their kids. She'd had a big family. They'd all resented Dad for meeting Mama in Guthrie. She'd been there for a horse auction, met Dad, and they fell in love. She didn't return to El Paso, then he'd moved farther north and east, and she'd gone with him. Mama had told us once that her family resented him for taking her so far away. Too far to easily drive, too short to fly. Mama died so young, her family had heaped more blame on Dad for their lost time with her, and they'd cleaved Ansen and me out with him. But for a few summers before Mama was too sick to travel, we had big get-togethers with lawn games, barbecues, and music.

God, I'd forgotten those.

If I had thought of those family reunions any time before now, it would've been just another loss. Just another thing I would never get back, thanks to our way of life.

My throat grew thick as I watched Liam juggle a thousand questions from his kids. Would Delaney realize that if she came with me, we'd still get to visit and plan camping trips? Or would I have to make a choice between this kind of life or my job?

I was no longer sure what I would pick.

Fourteen

LANEY

I was stuffed into my sleeping bag with nothing but my head peeking out. I had used the shower station to clean the dust and sweat off me. When I returned, Archer had left to wash up.

I was waiting for my husband to return as if I were a Renaissance virgin on her wedding night. Irritated, I unzipped the top half of my sleeping bag. I was wearing a pink-and-black sports bra under a red-and-blue oversized T-shirt I hadn't realized I'd taken from Archer when I left Texas until his brow crinkled as he studied the SMU logo.

Damn. I'd been sleeping in this shirt so long I'd forgotten it wasn't mine in the first place. At least my orange basketball shorts were all my own.

I sat up and sighed. He'd return soon. And he'd take the sleeping bag next to mine, and we'd sleep together for the first time in over a year and a half.

I picked up my phone. I hadn't missed the girls'

knowing glances when they saw the pictures of Archer from our ride. More than one picture. At least I'd managed a few solely of the countryside. But I'd done a lot of supposed selfies that happened to capture the tall, dark rider behind me. The one with his cowboy hat tipped low, looking off to the side so his chiseled profile was perfectly outlined by the sun.

Lyric's words from when I gave her a hug before she left with Aspen wove through my brain. *Just remember that Barron men can be really dense, but not all of them are clueless about what's right in front of them. That one out there is a good example.*

Liam's a different story, I had joked since Liam had been behind me talking to Archer. The two guys had visited all night and had helped the kids on the horses.

She had scowled and rolled her eyes. *Don't get me started on how stubborn Granger women can be. You know who I mean. That guy is smitten. Don't give up on yourself.*

I hadn't. That was why I was here.

And Archer was here too. He'd led Owen and Eli around on Bolt, negotiating their arguments like a seasoned pro.

I hadn't thought about kids until tonight. No one had asked in Texas, and we'd never had "the talk." I had instinctively known that without kids, we'd have a cleaner break when Archer learned I wasn't the woman he thought he'd married. I couldn't help but wonder if it was still like that.

I blew out a gusty sigh. No matter which way we turned, there was an obstacle. I wished our life was like our ride today. A little technical, but nothing that would make us stop.

I heard the horses nicker and a deep voice murmur. A guy talking to horses shouldn't be so sexy, but my body flushed and my pulse raced. I knew what it was like for him to speak softly like that to me in the dark of night.

His steps crunched on the gravel as he approached. He'd kept the cheap pair of flip-flops I had bought him in Dickinson. He didn't bat an eye when he saw the outdoor shower station. It was little more than a bathroom stall with a showerhead next to a building. Obviously, his childhood had been nothing like I'd made it out to be—him and Ansen sitting at a long table wearing cravats while servants waited on them. That was sort of how he lived as an adult, only he'd exchanged the cravats for ties.

The zipper rent through the night, and I watched the flap of the tent fall inside to reveal his powerful outline wearing basketball shorts.

"Need anything before I crawl in?"

Space. Another tent. To pack up and head home, where we'd be under different roofs. "No, I'm good."

He set down a couple bottles of water and stooped inside. The *zherpp* of the zipper echoed like a drumroll in my ears.

"Think it'll get cold tonight?" he asked as he squatted and folded his jeans and shirt. He stayed squatting as he tucked them neatly away, his powerful calves flexing and bunching.

I watched him take out his outfit for tomorrow, this routine so much like our nightly one had been as a married couple. But then we still were a married couple. "Not with as warm as it's been."

"A'right."

My mouth ticked up at the hint of his drawl. He kicked off his footwear and tucked his long legs into his sleeping bag. The tops of his shoulders stuck out, but he turned on his side, hitched himself up on an elbow, and pounded his pillow into the form he liked best.

Longing tugged at my heart. I was tempted to roll over and face him like I used to. We'd talk into the night, which would often lead to sex. Many times, we'd already had sex, and we'd just talk. About our jobs. About where we should go for our next date night and the places we'd already been. About the happenings in the world. It hadn't seemed as superficial then as it did looking back on it now. We'd both kept a part of ourselves out of the relationship in an attempt to stay the person we needed to be at the moment.

Superficial conversations or not, the nights had gotten so long and quiet without him.

I turned toward the other side. I couldn't indulge my fantasies and then get used to the loneliness once again when he left.

"I liked seein' you with your friends," he said quietly.

"I never had that, you know. Friends. Not real ones." I would've been ashamed to admit this to Archer when we were first married. It was natural to tell him now.

"I knew y'all weren't super close, but you didn't consider them friends until recently?"

"No, not even Liam. He was just the kid next door."

"I grew up in a small town. You'd think I wouldn't be surprised."

I stared at the wall of the tent. "It makes sense, though. Relationships are complicated, especially between hormonal kids from all different backgrounds. There's no other school in town, no private school, no religious school. Coal Haven can't be divided along district lines that would separate the haves from the have-nots. We're all bundled together, year after year after year. Then I started dating Derek, and it was a welcome relief from having to invite Becky Sanderson to a bonfire, where I had to watch her try to make out with someone else's boyfriend—sometimes mine."

"I wouldn't have made out with Becky Sanderson."

As if those were the magic words, I rolled over. "She was very persuasive. Making out with her usually meant feeling her boobs, and she had more than me, so after Derek dumped me, I got stuck with guys like Chad."

"Fuck guys like Chad—and by the way, I think you can get better service at another agency."

"Everyone but the Barrons use them."

"Who says that? Them or real people?"

I frowned. It was usually Chad dropping names, but he'd been a braggart in high school. I, of all people, should know he hadn't lived up to the hype. "Damn."

Archer's soft chuckle traveled between us. "I'll be happy to dump that asshole for you."

"No, that's something I want to do myself—after I find a company with lower rates and higher respect."

I couldn't see much of him in the darkness of the tent. The sun had set. No light was getting in through the vents of the tent we'd kept open.

"Can I scoot my bag closer?"

I froze, like a little rabbit on a trail with a horse bearing down.

"Delaney," he said softly. "I just want to hold you."

My mouth went dry, but I managed to croak, "You know what usually happens when we cuddle." The heat in the tent intensified, so instead of being the rabbit scared that a horse was going to trample it, I was worried I'd get gobbled up by the big bad wolf. "You're a bad influence."

Humor dampened the searing heat. "I'm not."

"You so are. You lured a young girl to Vegas and made her marry you."

He pretended to think. "Hmm, was that before that same girl stripped me down in the honeymoon suite and had her way with me?"

"She would do no such thing."

"She could and she did." He wiggled his sleeping bag closer. The crinkle of tent fabric filled the air, as his proximity made me want to unzip my bag and crawl in with him. The guy was a furnace on a normal day. He went nuclear when he was turned on.

"I think about our wedding day a lot," he murmured. His warm hand cupped my cheek.

I arched into him. "Me too."

"You wore that little white dress, and all I could think about was how fucking lucky I was."

My eyelids fluttered shut as if I could block out the hurt that followed. "You didn't know me—"

"Bullshit." When I opened my eyes, shocked at the vehemence in his tone, he continued. "There was something between us then, and there's something even stronger between us now."

"But—"

This time, he silenced me with a thumb on my lips. He pressed closer and dropped his head toward mine. Energy coursed through my body as his lips touched mine.

It'd been way too long since we made out in his hotel room. An infinity since we'd been together, since I'd felt his weight on me, since we were skin to skin.

As he deepened the kiss, plundering my mouth with his tongue, the mint of our toothpaste mingling, I wasn't hit by memories or yearning. I was in the moment. This was me and him. Us.

I clutched his shoulders. The T-shirt material bunched in my fingers, and I worked the unwelcome material up. It was blocking me from his chest.

His tongue twined with mine, licking, tasting, devouring. I wanted that on the rest of my body. The more I wiggled, the more the sleeping bag was pushed down. With a tug and a pull, Archer lifted me free of the downy material and rolled me onto his chest.

I stretched over him. There was way too much clothing around him. His shirt was gathered around his shoulders. His sleeping bag was between us. I still wore way too much clothing, and he had his shorts on. But I was on top of him, and for a moment, it was enough.

The moment passed. I stuffed the top of his bag down and splayed my hands on his hard pecs. Finally, I got to touch him. His heart hammered under my fingers, and I ground into him. He might not have felt my efforts, but I needed to do something to answer the ache between my legs.

A hard ridge buried under goose down and cotton pressed up.

I let out a frustrated growl. I wasn't close enough. I wanted more.

Archer answered by tunneling his hand between us. He stopped at my shirt and broke our kiss to slip it off. I did the same with his.

"Fucking bra." His big hands cupped each breast and kneaded the fabric-covered flesh. I lifted my torso to give him more room.

I agreed. Fucking bra. But what he was doing was better than the nothing I'd had for the last year and a half.

The sports bra fit too well for him to pull the fabric down and bare more skin, so he continued farther, sweeping his hand down my belly and slipping beneath my shorts.

The bra had served to keep me from flashing the world my nipples on the way back from the shower. The shorts had been something easy to get on while I was damp and that would cover my parts from public view.

"God, Delaney. No underwear? This whole time?" With his other hand, he gripped behind my head and brought me down for a searing kiss. Just as he was licking me, he slipped a finger through my heat and slid through the wetness until he landed on my clit.

A ragged moan echoed deep in my chest. My hips bucked and then ground into his hand. He held me, one hand on the back of my neck and one working my clit like the expert he was. I stuck my ass in the air and encouraged him. I needed him inside me, but the position we were in made it hard for him to adjust the angle of his hand.

I whimpered, writhing in his grip. He held the kiss so I wouldn't moan his name and alert the entire campground to what we were doing. A rhythmic metallic banging resonated from somewhere outside the tent. A horse snorted and stomped.

The rough pad of his finger stroked me. Almost there.

I met his tongue stroke for stroke. I was so close to coming in his arms, staggered by how badly I wanted this. How badly I wanted this man. How lonely I'd been without him.

The metallic banging got louder. I broke the kiss, panting and staring at him in the dark.

"Someone's horses are having issues," he murmured.

We stared at each other for another heartbeat. A horse whinnied, followed by more banging.

"Shit," we both said at the same time. I scrambled off him, trying to find my shirt. The one I grabbed wasn't mine, but I yanked it over my head anyway. Archer was out of the tent with his boots on before my head cleared the fabric. I stuffed my feet into my boots and clambered after him, praying the horses were okay, but also hoping the situation was important enough to make me stop and think about what I was doing. Because if I had to crawl into that tent with Archer again, I would be naked in thirty seconds flat. Maybe I should be the one to sleep in the pickup.

* * *

Archer

"I can't believe he did this." I squatted and wrapped my arms around Bolt's thick neck.

Why Bolt chose sunset for a dust bath, I didn't know. But he'd managed to wedge his head under the corral and get good and stuck. He was on his side while Target peered over from her corral, and they nickered back and forth. In the beam of our flashlights, we could see Bolt try to roll up only for his neck to get held down by the gate. He didn't realize he could curl his head in and wiggle out. He needed to be guided.

I held him down as Delaney lifted the corral panel. It wasn't more than an inch, if that, but it was enough for me to help the furry fool change the angle he'd been trying to free himself from.

As soon as Bolt's snout jerked free, I jumped back. He rolled up and lifted himself to standing. I pressed into the corner to keep from getting a hoof to the gut or headbutted as he turned and shifted.

Delaney kept repeating, "It's okay. You're fine," in a calm and even tone to prevent a panic attack in a full-grown horse.

He shifted side to side, but he calmed down and nosed Target. Bolt chuffed back and forth with his friend.

Light slashed between me and the horse as Delaney aimed the flashlight toward Bolt. "Is he okay?"

My wife asking about Bolt first, and relief that it was a minor hiccup in an otherwise relaxing weekend, made me grin. "He's fine. But he won't win any awards for smartest horse in the campground."

"I hope this makes him rethink where he's going to do his next dust bath."

I scaled the panel and hopped down on the other side. Delaney kept the flashlight, highlighting the way back to the tent. Back to where I'd had her quaking in my arms, ready to come for me between one breath and the next.

Her steps grew slower as we neared the dark outline of the tent. Damn. She was having second thoughts.

"Let me get a bottle of water to wash ourselves off." Thankfully, no injuries to two-legged animals or four also meant there'd been no blood. Other than the faint smell of horse, we'd gathered nothing but dust.

I snagged a water from the cooler.

Delaney's boots crunched behind me, but she didn't approach me. She waited by the camp chair set up outside the tent. "At least we didn't wake the entire camp."

There wasn't much seclusion at this campsite, but we'd gotten to Bolt quickly enough. "Nah. He was more confused and disgruntled than terrified. That might've brought some others around." If horses could get embarrassed, that was more like what Bolt would be feeling. He was probably as relieved as us that he didn't wake a bunch of strangers.

"I was more confused and disgruntled. Leave it to Bolt to get himself into a pickle like that."

I chuckled, then hissed as I splashed ice-cold water over my chest and arms.

Delaney snickered, so I flicked the bottle her way. Water sprayed out and hit her. She yelped, then cut off the sound. "Stop it," she hissed, while trying not to giggle.

"Just helping you rinse off." I did it again.

"I swear, Archer. I'm going to dump the whole cooler on your head if you don't stop."

A cooler of half-melted ice wouldn't be enough to douse

the fire my wife had ignited before Bolt interrupted. I handed the bottle to her and waited for her to rinse her hands off.

She set the bottle down, and by the time she'd straightened, I had stepped closer. "Now where were we?" I murmured.

Darkness cloaked us. The tent blocked us from the rest of the camp, and there was nothing but Badlands pasture at our back.

"Making a bad decision. Maybe we should—"

I claimed her mouth. The cold of my quick wash had faded. The adrenaline of the horse rescue coursed through my veins.

She laid her chilly hands on my chest, and I tensed, but it wasn't enough to break me away from her.

She pulled back a sufficient amount to whisper against my lips. "We shouldn't do this."

"Why not?"

"I don't know. It seems like something a responsible adult would say."

"I want to taste my wife again. How is that wrong?" I couldn't make out her features as she stared at me in the dark. I'd kill to see her in the daylight. Shorts. Cowboy boots. Rumpled hair.

I could usher her into the tent, but I guided her to the chair.

"Archer…"

Her hesitance gave me pause. I waited. Was she going to tell me to stop? Would I suffer the worst case of blue balls in male genitalia history? Would this be the time she told me never to touch her again?

She whipped her shirt off. "God, I missed you."

My grin had to be a mile wide as I swooped her up in my arms and captured her mouth for another kiss. She easily wrapped her legs around my waist; the collar areas of her boots dug into my back, but I didn't fucking care. I had my wife in my arms.

I pushed my tongue into her mouth, too desperate to be suave, but she met me stroke for stroke. I'd have to put her down to fumble with the zipper of the tent door. But there was the chair. And my mouth watered to taste her.

I cautiously set Delaney down in the chair as I dropped to my knees at her feet. Grass tickled my skin and small rocks dug into my kneecaps. Again, I didn't fucking care.

She might've taken her shirt off, but I wasn't getting too far through that sports bra she wore. If I could see her better, I'd try to get to her pretty pink nipples, suck one into my mouth and enjoy the way she squirmed in my arms.

Later. In the tent, I'd rip the material over her breasts and free the tits that had been haunting my dreams.

I curled my fingers around the waistband of her shorts.

"Out here?" she whispered.

"Honey, if I don't get my mouth on that hot little clit of yours and feel you coming against my face, I don't think I'm going to make it as far as the tent." The logic was backward. I didn't think I'd survive much beyond her exploding against my lips, but the urge to give her another orgasm was so strong, so consuming, that the thought of her world exploding and narrowing down to only me drove me like a stallion in a field of brood mares.

"I—I guess it's dark enough." She lifted her hips, and I yanked her shorts off the rest of the way.

I settled her boots over my shoulders. Finally. I lowered my head, not needing one ray of light to know where I had to touch.

At the first lick, she bucked off the chair, a cry ripping from her. I heard the slap of her hands over her mouth, but I didn't let up.

Her taste was back on my tongue and all was right in the world. This woman had tied me in knots the first time I saw her. The rest of the world ceased to exist as soon as she'd sauntered into my life, acting like she didn't give a shit about my business or the amount of my commissions.

Other men might be insulted that she'd known about my family, that she wasn't as ignorant as she'd pretended. Maybe I would've been one of those guys. Maybe I would've gotten pissed had I learned she'd grown up dating a cousin and knew the dollar signs that followed the Barron name around. That would've been before I almost lost her.

Another squeak escaped her. Since her hands were now clenched around the armrests of the folding camp chair, I imagined her biting her lip. She let out a low moan that didn't reach farther than the circle she and I made.

One day, we would do this when she could be really fucking loud.

"Archer," she breathed, and her hips rocked into my face.

As long as I got to hear my name on her lips, I didn't care how quiet we had to be. I settled into my kneeling position and devoured her. I didn't play around. She liked when I made tight circles with my tongue, so I did just that. She loved when I pushed two fingers inside of her instead of fucking around with one. And as much as she liked when I had my head between her toned thighs, she liked my dick inside her better.

We'd get there.

Her muscles clenched around my head, and her breathing grew more ragged. She was so damn close.

I threaded two fingers inside her tight heat, giving her something to ride. I barely had my digits in all the way when she shattered. Heat flooded my face, and she shook around me, releasing hard gasps and tiny whines.

I wanted to enjoy this moment, but my erection demanded to be released from the mesh shorts that used to be loose and baggy. I carefully set her feet on the ground and ripped open the zipper of the tent. I couldn't see a damn thing, but the desire pounding inside me practically gave me night vision.

I couldn't see Delaney, but I grasped her hand. There was a second where I wondered if she'd resist, but she rose and stepped through the tent flap first.

Fifteen

LANEY

God, this was heaven.

My boots were off. My sports bra too. I was completely naked and so was my husband. I hadn't needed thirty seconds to strip since I'd been mostly naked before I entered the tent. We tumbled onto the sleeping bags, and Archer had my knees hooked over his shoulders as he drove into me. I pressed my hands against his hard chest as he stroked in and out.

The way he filled me, how well he knew my body and what got me off instantly versus what would let him play awhile, centered me. The misery of all those nights alone seemed justified.

We fit together.

I couldn't believe he hadn't been with anyone else. He said he hadn't dabbled in the dating pool, but a part of me had been too afraid to believe it. Archer was too sexy, too much of a catch to go without. In the motel, he'd been able to get me off with no relief for himself. But the way he lost control tonight settled my nerves. He wasn't a man who was quick in the sack.

Tonight, he was unhinged. He swung his hips, pounding into me. I'd be across the tent if his hard grip on my hips didn't keep me anchored in place.

His pace increased—the force was punishing in all the best ways—until he kicked his head back. I wished I could see the way his face tightened, his teeth clenched, as he kept from shouting my name all over the campground.

Heat flooded my insides as his erection pulsed and released. For the first time in a long time, I didn't feel so lost. So alone.

For tonight, I was enough.

He sagged over me, his head hanging. I eased my legs down until I cradled him. He was still inside me, but he wrapped his arms around me and buried his head in my neck.

"I love you, Delaney."

I tensed, my mouth open to reply, but unsure of what to say.

He lifted his head. "There's no pressure. I need you to know that no matter what, I love you."

No matter what. But a lot mattered. There were aspects of our life that had more say over our marriage than love. Geography and NT Land Agency were the two biggest.

I pushed my hand through his thick hair and said it anyway. It was the truth. "I love you too."

He turned his head into my touch.

He braced himself on his elbows and gazed down at me. "I can't tell you how happy I am to hear that."

I couldn't tell him how scared I was to admit it. I'd never quit loving him. I'd tried. So damn hard. All those tears on my pillow when another day went by and he hadn't called.

The tossing and turning because the wall of heat next to me was missing. I had tried to despise him, but I'd failed.

Then he'd showed up. Asking for an annulment. The final nail in the coffin.

But he'd stayed. And he'd integrated himself into a life I had been sure he wouldn't understand. He fit so damn well it hurt.

He started moving again. His erection hadn't flagged like it normally would've.

He captured my mouth again, thrusting slowly in and out, like we had all the time in the world. In this tent, in the middle of nowhere, we were exempt from all the constraints of time.

"Delaney?"

I arched my back. What he was doing had reignited all the nerve endings that had been incinerated on the chair outside of the tent. "Yeah?"

"I should've asked you earlier, but are you still on birth control?" He pumped into me, and I planted my heels to meet his increasing force.

"Yeah. I never had the IUD removed." A baby would complicate an already complicated relationship.

"Good." He spoke like he had no idea how wild he was driving me, but this was Archer. He knew. It probably chafed him that I hadn't come a second time when he'd exploded through his first climax. "So damn good. I'm going to fuck you all night long and come over and over again in your tight little body."

I groaned, unwittingly clenching around him. "For such a gentleman, you talk dirty."

His chuckle vibrated right through my body. He dipped his head and captured a nipple.

I bit my lip to hold back a cry. I'd had no idea nipples could be so sensitive until the first time I'd been with

Archer. It was like he'd programmed them to instantly respond only to him.

"I fucking missed these," he growled.

I stuffed my fingers into his hair and rolled my hips, encouraging him to continue stroking us to another spectacular orgasm.

"You mean the world to me, you know that?" He licked across a nipple, and a shiver racked my body. He did the same on the other side, taking turns until I was a shaking, quivering mess. "There's nothing I won't do for you."

Except give up his life in Texas. And it was unfair of me to ask when I wouldn't give up my life here. Archer was an optimistic idealist. I was a realist. I'd known that as soon as I met him. I couldn't shake the last eighteen months or the year before that, when Archer had showed me everything I thought I couldn't have.

So, I gave myself tonight. I could pretend for one night that our marriage would end in something other than a severing of our vows.

* * *

Archer

When Delaney slept, she was all in.

I lay on my side and watched her. It'd be creepy if I wasn't married to her.

Her mouth was partially open, her hair fanned around her and tangled on itself, and her cheeks still had a freshly fucked glow.

So much sex.

I'd topped my record. The last orgasm was damn near painful, but I had flung myself into it. As long as I could still get Delaney to climax, I was coming too. The force between us last night and into the early hours of the morning had been powerful. Like two comets hurtling into each other.

She had her arms flung out. The position was how she must've landed after she'd pushed herself off me, muttered a satisfied "I can't take any more," and passed out. I had just dragged her into my arms before I succumbed to exhaustion.

How long had it been since I'd ridden all day, set up camp, and had sex all night long?

Never. By the time I had met Delaney, I'd been twenty-seven. All my schooling was done, and I was immersed in the world of commissions and making partner.

After I'd gotten married, it had been time to propel myself to the next level. I had a wife. Maybe we'd talk about starting a family. Did she want kids? I had wanted to have a more secure future when we first married. I wasn't going to let my kids grow up hearing about money issues and witnessing all we owned get taken away. But now I had diverse stock, a retirement plan, savings, and a nice place to live. Delaney wouldn't suffer alongside me like Mama had with Dad.

Delaney sighed, then stretched, her eyes still closed. She had tossed on the green T-shirt she'd worn the night before. Her sports bra was probably underneath one of us. The sleeping bags were tangled, but we'd generated so much heat last night we had only needed them for padding.

Her eyelids drifted open, and a little line pinched between her brows. "Were you watching me sleep?"

"It was adorable."

A scowl mixed with good humor. "I'm not adorable."

"Sometimes you are. When you're not killing-me sexy." We shared a smile, but hers faded quickly.

I thought I'd have to pry, but she spoke. "Now what?"

"Now, we go for a long ride and have another night of quiet tent sex."

She wanted to talk more. It was in the furrow of her brow. The concern welling in her eyes. The fear underneath it all. If she asked the hard questions, I wouldn't have answers. We'd talk ourselves in circles. I didn't want a repeat of how I grew up, but her idea of the American Dream wasn't a two-million-dollar condo or downtown Dallas.

Her expression softened. "You haven't seen Medora yet."

I grinned to hide my relief. "But first I need to know why all the commercials on the radio are in a Southern accent."

She laughed, then shot me a playful scowl. "It's where the West begins."

"The West. Not the South."

She giggled and trailed her fingers along my chest. "They have ice cream and a candy store."

"I'm in."

She laughed again and rolled to her stomach. "Or we could be lazy, go for a ride, go to town, cool off with ice cream, and then go to the musical."

I didn't give a shit about musicals. I wanted to get back to us alone in the tent with me inside her, but if she wanted to go, I'd be right next to her. "I like the sound of that."

A buzzing made me frown until I realized it was my phone. By the time I dug it out of my pants, I had a missed call from Mr. Truitt. "Shit. I'll be right back."

I stepped into my pants and stooped out of the tent. I zipped it shut so Delaney could dress as I called my boss back.

"Archer." Disapproval rang through his greeting.

"Sorry I didn't get to the phone in time."

"Listen, I talked to Vonda last night, and she hadn't seen the crop rotation reports yet."

"I emailed them, Mr. Truitt." I had stayed up after leaving Holden's and worked until after two in the morning to get it done before we left town. I know I hadn't been too tired to forget. "Maybe they landed in her spam folder."

"You'd have been able to discuss them personally if you'd been able to meet us at the Gallery last night."

"I'm sorry. I sent all the information she needs." Vonda had a life. She probably hadn't literally seen the emails yet, but they were in her inbox.

"They like hearing it, Archer. Our clients aren't coughing up millions of dollars to read reports all night. Give her a damn call. If Wilson has to do another thing for Vonda's account, he might as well collect the commission."

I tipped my head back and quietly inhaled a steadying breath. If Wilson was more ambitious, I might worry about him swooping in on my payday. As it was, Mr. Truitt had a point. He always did. Vonda Montgomery was an investment adviser, taking a cryptocurrency windfall and sinking it into something more evergreen and tangible. She was excited and knew nothing about agriculture life, but she was about to become the proud owner of cotton, corn, and sorghum fields. Born and raised in Chicago, she had big dreams of giving back to the world in a way she'd never thought possible. Having space to live and work, where before she'd only had an eight-hundred-square-foot apartment in the city.

She'd also done a shitload of research and didn't need me mansplaining the reports to her. But Mr. Truitt was from a different generation. If nothing else, I should call and make sure he hadn't alienated her.

"I'll give her a call."

"You do that." There was a pregnant pause. Tension

crawled up my gut and across my shoulders. "I took a chance on you, Archer."

"I know you did, sir." Whenever he said this, it was to stress that I wasn't performing as expected. The last time I'd heard it was after the client dinner when Delaney left me.

"You're like a son to me."

But I wasn't a son. Wilson was probably sleeping in and wouldn't face any repercussions from unanswered calls. "I understand."

His tone softened. "I know you do. You've come so far. You can do whatever you want in the world, Archer. I don't want to see it all vanish."

"Thank you for that, Mr. Truitt." Usually when he said he believed in me, I hung on to every word. I had needed the confidence. When he said it this time, it was like he knew where my wound was and prodded it to keep me going in the direction he wanted.

When he hung up, I didn't call Vonda. It was fucking Saturday. But I'd send her a message and ask if she wanted to discuss any questions over the weekend.

Delaney ducked out of the tent to put her boots on. I hated to let reality intrude on our vacation. "As long as we're staying in, mind if I dig my laptop out?"

She didn't look up at me. "You might have to drive somewhere to get a better signal for your hotspot."

"You mind?" She wouldn't have offered if she did. Right? And if she did mind, what would I do? The answer should be clear, but it wasn't.

"No," she said in a neutral tone. "I'll take care of the horses while you do that."

I wasn't leaving her with the work. "I'll help, and then I'll see what I have for a signal."

She straightened, then tapped her boots against the

ground to get her pant legs to sit around them. "You don't have to. Norville's still pissy. His golden boy is defying him for a woman."

The urge to disagree with her wasn't as strong as before either. "He's worried I'm leaving a client hanging."

"He should know better."

"He does. It's just how he is."

She closed the distance between us and gave me a quick kiss on the lips. "What would have happened if you had given your dad the same grace you give Norville?"

She strode away, leaving me to ruminate over what she'd said.

* * *

Laney

Archer dropped me off in town and went to find a better signal. The heat beat down on the sidewalk, so I found the ice cream shop I'd remembered. I waited in line for twenty minutes before I finally made it to the front to order a creamy mint chip cone. I thought of messaging Archer to ask what he wanted, but ice cream wouldn't last long in this heat.

I walked out of the shop and put my sunglasses back on. The ice cream was perfect. I'd been roaming town for an hour. How much longer would Archer be? I wanted to show him the candy shop where they made taffy for us to see. And the unique souvenirs full of toys our parents would've played with as kids—things like cheap plastic dolls and silver six-shooters with orange handles.

I wandered through town, all the way down to the zip

line. I squinted at the couple going up the line, their legs swinging out of their bucket seats. What was that view like?

I licked my cone. Why didn't I go on it? I wanted to experience it, and I was in Medora. I hadn't been here since I was in high school. The zip line might not be around if I didn't get here for another ten years.

I found the booth to buy tickets. My phone buzzed while I was standing in line.

How's it going? I won't be much longer.

I snapped a picture of the couple zooming down the line to the starting point and sent it. **I'm going on a ride.**

He called.

I answered. "Gonna talk me out of it?"

"You haven't gone yet?"

"No, I had to finish my ice cream. I'm in line to buy tickets."

He groaned. "Ice cream sounds good right now."

"It was." Norville was being a hard-ass to make a point. Archer knew it. I knew it. I didn't have to lay out what my husband was missing. But dammit, the afternoon would've been a lot more fun with him. If it was legitimate work, I'd understand. But Norville liked to make a mountain out of pinto beans to feel like a big man.

"Get two tickets," he said. "I'll meet you at the start."

I smiled as I hung up. I reached the counter. Damn. There were waiver forms.

I messaged him. **I can't get tickets. You have to sign a waiver.**

He didn't respond. Was he on his way? I hovered by the ticket stand. Watched the mini-golfers from a distance. People streamed past me.

This wasn't like Archer. He'd never stood me up in Dallas. He worked a lot. He'd put the Truitts' needs and feelings over mine. I wasn't sure what to think. Was this a sign of what it would be like if we got back together? Norville flexing to remind Archer of what he thought my husband's priorities should be, and my husband striving to please him?

A woman heading my way craned her neck to look behind me, an appreciative look on her face. Then she nudged her friend.

Curiosity made me look over my shoulder. A tall man wove through the crowd, his intense gaze on me from under the brim of his distressed-denim hat.

My grin was as instant as my relief. "I wasn't sure you got my message." I wasn't sure he hadn't ignored me.

"Sorry." He gave me a quick kiss. "I was driving, and then it took me so long to find a parking spot, I forgot to respond."

I should've had more confidence. I twined my fingers through his, and we got our tickets. There wasn't a long line, but I described the shops I'd been to.

He nodded and listened. We buckled in, and the bucket seats climbed higher and higher. The view spread out before us. The western-style strip mall. The landscape with the bushy trees and hundreds of tourists. The traffic coming to and from town.

"This is cool," he breathed and grabbed my hand again. "Thanks for waiting for me."

"I'm glad you could come."

The ride stopped at the highest peak. His thumb stroked the back of my hand. "Show me everything in town you think I missed out on, then we'll grab supper. And tonight..." He gave me a searing-hot look and my breathing stuttered as our seats lurched forward for the swift ride down to the start. "We're going back for ice cream, and I'm going to lick up every last drop."

Oh... He wasn't talking about the cone. If I'd wanted to

wipe out my earlier concerns about how his job might inter-
fere with us, that would do it. It wasn't a long-term solution,
but I was willing to accept it for the rest of the weekend.

Sixteen

LANEY

Archer directed a semitruck to the haystack. Round bales were stacked like a pyramid on the trailer, two bales wide on the bottom and one row over the top. The driver got out and unhooked all the bindings that had kept the bales from tumbling out during the transport here from Nebraska.

I couldn't believe that with a few calls, Archer had found good quality, affordable hay. Since returning after Kane's injury, I'd built up what we had to make sure we had at least a year's supply, but Ma wasn't as good at math. She survived by ballparking, and while that might work most years—not well, and definitely not the way to optimize return—it was shit during dry years like this with the added problem of a new pest.

The truck unloaded the hay with one tip of its trailer. Ma had bowed out of the delivery. She didn't say, but it was either because she couldn't run the skid steer with the hayfork since the stack was neatly unloaded in one shot or because this was Archer's doing.

She grumbled something about bringing in the hay that we *didn't have to pay an arm and a goddamn leg for* and left on a cloud of strawberry-scented vapor. There were still round bales in the ditches and in the field we hayed, but I didn't want to stack it until the semis were done off-loading all the supply we'd ordered. The trucks needed the room.

I signed the invoices and waved the driver off. Another delivery was coming tomorrow, and one a day after that, and then my ladies would be nicely fed throughout the fall and winter. The sky was overcast, and we had a respite from the brutal heat we'd had most of the summer. There was relief all around.

I hopped into the old Ranger my dad had rescued from an auction and fixed up. Archer climbed in beside me. Kane and I used to argue about who got to drive the Ranger, but Archer never dove for the driver's seat. I couldn't tell if it was because he didn't have the urge to be in control at all times, if he was cognizant of not stepping on my toes, or if he wasn't invested in the ranch like I was. I bumped through the field and along the pasture until we reached the yard.

"I can make you a sandwich," I said when I pulled up next to the white barn we kept the Ranger in. He'd never said anything about the bologna sandwiches on white bread other than he didn't want to eat my parents' groceries. Ma wasn't paying him, but I didn't press. "We have leftover lunchmeat."

Ma had not hesitated to eat the leftover food Archer and I had brought back from Medora.

"I'll have to pass." He gave me a regretful smile. "I need to go back to the motel and do some work."

"Sure." I covered my disappointment as he leaned in and

kissed me. He was juggling being with me and his normal job—even though he was technically using vacation time.

He got out and paused with his hand on the roll bar. "Have you given any more thought to staying with me in the motel?"

He'd asked that question when we'd returned a few days ago. After a sex-filled weekend, the natural transition had seemed to be that I would stay in the motel with him. But when he'd asked, I'd paused. He'd given me a kiss and told me to think about it.

I had. A lot.

"It's not that I don't want to. It's easier to be out here for chores and in case..." Who was I fooling? "It'll be easier for me when you go back to Dallas."

"And you're so sure that'll be the end of our marriage?"

It sounded like an honest question and not a challenge. So, I answered honestly. "I don't want it to be."

I didn't think Norville would allow Archer's attention to be split across the country. Archer and I hadn't discussed long-distance options, like we both knew it'd create more issues than it'd solve.

He'd have to commute. Norville would hemorrhage at the idea. I could fly in and visit, maybe during the summer when calving was over or before we had to move and work cattle in the fall.

He didn't push off the Ranger and storm away. "Want to meet for dinner?"

He might have been upset with my decision, but he didn't show it. He still wanted to make time to be with me.

Breakfast, lunch, or dinner, I wanted to be with him all the time. I could drive to town, meet him. We'd eat at Rattler's. Then I'd be wondering what happened after we ate. Would I go into his motel room with him? And once we were done having sex, would I stay or would I go?

He didn't have much more time in Coal Haven, and I wanted to make it count. He'd met my family and my friends, and we'd worked and played together. But there was one place I wanted to show him. "Why don't we brave Dan Anderson's wrath and ride to his draw tonight?"

The corner of Archer's mouth kicked up. "We could always ask him."

"Where's the fun in that?"

He chuckled. "I'll bring food."

"Let me know when you're on your way, and I'll get the horses ready."

"It's a date." He went to his car.

I bit my lip to keep from grinning like it was Christmas morning. How could I still be looking forward to a date when we'd been spending so much time together?

I got out of the Ranger as he drove away and walked to the house. I let the smile break through, not even dreading a bologna sandwich, when Ma banged out the front door. Portia trotted out after her.

She glowered at the empty driveway. "How long is he staying?"

"Another week and a half." He had to drive back, or I would've gotten a few more days with him.

"You going with him?"

If Archer asked, I wouldn't be able to answer him. But I knew what I would do when the time came. "Probably not."

She cleared her throat. "Why?"

"Because I'm helping you."

She sank onto the front step. "There ain't anything for you here, Laney."

I was so tired of hearing that. There were things here for me—because I had worked for them. I was about to launch into a diatribe about how I had carved out a nice life in Coal Haven, no thanks to her, when I noticed how her shoulders sagged. The dark circles under her eyes amplified her resigned expression.

When we would have this talk before, Ma would be defensive. We'd argue. Nothing would change. What if this wasn't one of those times?

"This is my home," I said, a pit forming in my stomach.

"You're sleeping on an air mattress while your husband is planning to leave town. I'll give it to him—he stuck it out longer than I thought he would. And what he did with the hay... Maybe I should tell him I appreciate it." She took a puff off her pen as Portia trotted to the backyard. Even the dog sensed the heaviness of the conversation. "You might as well stick with him as long as it lasts."

At least she didn't sound confident that the end of Archer and me was imminent. "The Diamond UU is my home."

I didn't get an eye roll. She didn't let out a frustrated sound. She scrubbed her face with her free hand. "I know you love this place; I really do. But you gotta let it go."

"Let it go to who, Ma? Kane's moving. He told you how he felt."

She met my gaze. "It's still his."

I stared at her. Her words rang in my head. "But..."

"Laney. This place has always been his. I know we couldn't give you much to go to college, but you got to go."

I'd worked three jobs to pay for tuition and put a roof over my head, but she knew that. I lifted my hands out to the sides and let them drop, slapping the tops of my thighs. "Am I being selfish, Ma? Greedy? Is that what you think?"

"No, you ain't." She sniffed and blew out a hard breath. "I know how much you love this place. I wish I loved it as much as you, but I was pushed into it just like Kane. Only child and all that."

Kane wasn't an only child, but I didn't point that out.

Discussions that didn't dissolve in Ma walking off or us yelling at each other were rare. I didn't know if I'd make progress with her, but I might get a definitive answer. So, I waited to hear what else she had to say.

"Being a Barron doesn't even sound as bad as it did before." She squinted at me. "Do you know Naomi walked by me the other day and ignored me? No sneer, nothing."

"You're related to royalty now," I said wryly, and she chuckled.

"I felt like a goddamn queen." She sniffed again. Ma didn't have allergies. Was it emotions? "All I have to give is this place, Laney. I've dedicated my life to it, and it almost took my son." She pushed her palm across her nose and sniffled. I didn't dare move. Ma didn't cry, so if she broke down, I'd break down, and we'd both fucking hate it. "I owe him something. I have to give him something for what—"

She pushed out a hard breath and buried her head in her hands. Her vape pen stuck out between two fingers. I stood where I was, wringing my hands together. We'd never been in this position. What should I do?

She lifted her head, her face wan. "Anyway, it's his. Oldest passed down to oldest, the way it's always been. You can talk to him about managing the place. I know he don't want to. I'll stick around. Lord knows it takes two people to run this place, me getting old and all that. He'd pay you."

I shifted my stance. I wasn't sure what to think. Ranch manager of the Diamond UU. A family legacy, in a way. One Kane and I would split. He was moving, so the trailer house would be open. I could build up around it. Have my own barn, a small shop, even my own horse pasture.

I should be happy. I had told Ma this was home. She had made room for me when she hadn't done more than clear the office before.

My small victory felt off. Regardless of who owned

Diamond UU, Kane was moving. Ma wasn't as young as she used to be. Papa had little interest in the place. When he retired, he'd move to full-time hunting and fishing. I was needed at Diamond UU, now more than ever.

I'd gotten my dream, but I was afraid of the price I would be paying for it.

* * *

Archer

Trees grew thick around the higher edges of the draw. I'd had a good idea of what it might look like before we rode out. A minuscule valley since the hills around Coal Haven weren't large.

The draw wasn't small, but it wasn't a deep chasm. It was bone dry this year, and probably during many years, but I could imagine how stunning it was during a time when water trickled through it. It would be a small oasis in a wide-open pasture carved out by trickling water, adding enough moisture that trees grew at all levels, adding shade and definition. The hills were so mellow, it was hard to tell they were there unless you were driving by on the road. Only the trees made it possible to spot.

The ride out had taken forty-five minutes. We'd had to ride past Liam's place, then Bruce's, and across the highway to get to the Andersons'. Bolt's and Target's lead ropes were hooked around a narrow tree while Delaney and I perched in the grass not far away. Another tree provided a canopy from the punishing sun. We wouldn't be here long, but I sensed the specialness of the place.

Before I met Delaney at her place, I'd stopped at Rattler's for some fried pickles and prime rib sandwiches.

Food that would be good cold. Maybe not the pickles, but I was willing to risk it. I didn't think the soup we'd had my first week in town would travel well.

Our food was gone, and the garbage was stuffed into Target's saddlebag.

I planted my hands in the grass behind me. Delaney scooted away, then laid her head on my lap with her legs curled at her side. "It's so peaceful. All you hear are the birds and the bugs and the wind."

We didn't talk for several minutes. Just enjoyed our surroundings and being together. I didn't find this sort of peace often. I couldn't remember when the environment around me was ever so calm.

"I hope the next owner appreciates this spot," Delaney murmured. I brushed my hand over her hair, grateful she was talking. Ever since I'd arrived for the ride, she'd been quieter than usual.

"From what y'all said, Dan might warn the new owners to put security cameras up or buzz the place with a camera on a drone."

She chuckled. "I don't think Dan knows about drones with cameras. He was in the hardware store the other day complaining that his real estate agent kept wanting to send him documents to sign digitally. He had to get an email account just for the papers."

"How do you make it this far into the century without email?"

"I bet when he and Alice move to Arizona, they'll be all decked out with smartphones and loving life. Stetson said he thought they could ask more, but they still own a section and a half. Even with a sixty-year-old house, they should get two million."

I frowned, doing a quick calculation. "I could get them three."

"Even with a sixty-year-old house?"

"I could get that for them with no house."

She aimed her grin my way.

"Sorry, was that cocky?"

"No. Confident. And sexy." She fell quiet for a moment and stared at the slopes and shadows of the draw. "When I was younger, I wished Dan realized that all the kids around here thought this was our secret place and we would never throw a party here. When Liam, Derek, and I were younger, like before Derek and I started dating, we'd ride here and hang out. It was the only place we felt like we could just be. Liam wasn't Cameron's personal shame. Derek wasn't hounded about who he spent his time with, and I didn't have to prove myself to anyone."

I listened. Any response would have been inane. In Dallas, a park would be her best option. Some of the properties I'd been on had gorgeous draws, but they lacked this sense of peace.

I traced a finger over her forehead and down her cheek. Her eyes drifted shut. I continued stroking her face, swooping down her nose, and softly outlining her lips. The stress that had been gathering in her features relaxed away. We had nothing to worry about at the moment, nothing to do other than enjoy being with each other.

A sound droned in the distance.

"Ah, hell. He found us." Delaney stood and brushed off the back of her jeans.

I did the same and wandered past the horses. A four-wheeler approached. I waved and walked out to meet it. I wasn't worried. I'd worked with all kinds of landowners over the years.

Delaney followed. "Are you going to work him over like Chad?"

"No, we're trespassing. I'm going to kiss ass." I adopted

a big grin and waved like I was excited we had a visitor. The older man's scowl lightened, and he killed the engine. I jumped in before he could accuse us of anything. "I'm really sorry. I know we're not supposed to be here, but Delaney said I couldn't go back to Texas until I saw the jewel of the county."

Dan's suspicious expression transitioned into pride. "I didn't realize you thought so highly of it, Laney."

She smiled, barely hiding her relief at not being chased off like she was a twelve-year-old. "I try to limit my visits since it's not my land, but yes, it's one of my favorite spots. I love that it's off the road and private."

Dan bobbed his head. "Alice and I used to love coming here. But she can't get on the four-wheeler anymore." He chuckled. "Or if she gets on, it's the getting off that's hard."

I guessed Dan to be in his seventies. He couldn't hide his worry for his wife, but his smile spoke of fond memories.

"We'll get going," I said. I didn't want to push my luck. "Sorry again to make you come all the way out here."

Dan lifted a shoulder. "Eh, it breaks up the day. As long as you're not up to no good."

"Naw, it's gettin' too hot for that," I said.

He chortled. "Ain't that right. The heat's been good for Alice." His eyes dipped to Delaney's hand. The logic behind her not wearing her ring made sense. There were times while helping at her place I thought it'd be best to put mine in my pocket. Didn't mean the primal part of my brain liked her finger bare. He lifted his gaze to mine. "You said you're going to Texas?"

"I'm from there, yes."

He bobbed his head. "I knew your dad. How is he?"

Unexpected longing cascaded through me. I didn't know the answer, but I pressed the flash of guilt and said, "He's doing good. I'll tell him I ran into you."

"Eh, I'd be surprised if he remembered me. I'm quite a bit older, but Alice used to sell eggs to your grandparents."

Another person talking about family I'd never met was easier than lying about knowing how my dad was doing.

"Well, have a good trip." Dan adjusted in his seat. "Next time you're in town, give me a holler. You two can come out here anytime—until we sell it anyway. Let me get this noisy thing out of here before you untie the horses."

He sped off, and I caught Delaney staring at me.

She was giving me the same look as when she'd said she liked my confidence. "You can charm the pants off anyone."

"Good business isn't always about being shrewd and inflexible. It's about knowing who has the power and how they want to use it. Dan loves this place. Too bad about Alice." Weird that I felt like I knew the couple from a few minutes of conversation.

Delaney let out a wistful sigh. "I guess we'd better go."

Puffy clouds in the sky took turns shading us from the sun as we rode in the ditch past Uncle Bruce's place. The smell of clover surrounded me, and the buzz of grasshoppers nearly drowned out the sound of the horses sifting through the grass. The drone of a different engine cut through the peace.

Delaney looked over her shoulder. "That's Bruce."

I was going to wave, but he slowed and parked on the side of the road. He rushed out of the pickup and rounded the hood. Delaney and I rode toward the road.

"I'm glad I caught you," he called as we neared. "I wanted to make sure to tell you not to be a stranger." He gave my wife a small smile. "You either, Delaney. Willow and I would love to have you both over."

She tried to hide her surprise. "Uh... thanks, Bruce."

He bobbed his head. "You two busy tomorrow night?

You could come over then. I know you're not here long, Archer."

I glanced at Delaney and let her answer. I wanted to get to know Uncle Bruce more, but she had a loaded history with him. Changed or not, he'd given her reason to be guarded. Regardless, I appreciated that he wasn't ignoring her now and was being outright neighborly.

"Sounds good," she answered carefully. "Want us to bring anything?"

"Just yourselves." Bruce paused, glancing between us, a smile on his face. "We're really looking forward to it. Glad I caught you."

His sincerity was staggering. I didn't sense underlying reasons to have us over other than he wanted to visit. There was no deal getting made. There was no hidden agenda to coax me into dissolving my marriage. He and his wife wanted the company, and they wanted to get to know their nephew.

Bruce hopped in his pickup and drove away. Delaney and I turned the horses for home.

She was quiet, stuck in her head, her shoulders rounded.

"That was out of the blue, I take it?"

She popped her head up. "So far out of what I ever imagined. I think he's actually happy to have me over and not just enduring my presence to get you there." She shook her head, and her gaze went distant as if she were lost in the past. "He tried to hold on to control after Derek died. Took care of Kennedy like she was a kid, which I guess she needed for a while. But then he broke down. He's been so different ever since."

Losing someone could do that to a person. Would my dad have understood more than the other siblings? Would they have been able to lean on each other?

Bolt knew where we were going. I relaxed and used the

time to watch my wife. Her body rocked with Target's steps. I took a mental snapshot of this moment. Riding a horse in the middle of a broom grass- and clover-filled ditch, she was radiant. The golden skin on her shoulders glowed. Her ball cap shaded her face, giving her a shyness that reminded me of when we first met.

The ride to her place was as quiet as the ride out. She had something on her mind. Did she have another argument with her mom? Or was she like me and thinking about how the clock was ticking and I'd leave soon, but we hadn't made any decisions yet?

ARCHER

"Come in, come in." Willow ushered Delaney and me into the house. She had a pair of reading glasses on top of her head and a floral apron over her clothing.

My wife entered, her eyes wide as if every corner she looked into held ghosts staring back at her. This had to be trippy for her.

"Laney." Willow yanked Delaney to her and held on for several seconds. "You don't know how glad I am to see you again."

The same wide-eyed stare was directed toward Willow. "Um, thanks."

My aunt patted her shoulder as she broke away. "No worries, dear. I know how weird it must be."

Willow tugged me into her embrace. I accepted it better than Delaney. I doubted Cheryl hugged like this.

"It smells delicious," I said as I stepped back.

"Oh, it's nothing. Just a little hotdish I whipped up."

Delaney clasped her hands in front of her. Her gaze touched on the family portrait that hung on the wall—a much-younger Bruce and Willow with two little boys. The one that must have been Derek reminded me of Ansen at that age. He had a mischievous grin and a lock of hair that stood straight up toward the back of his head. The older brother was more solemn, wearing an expression that made it seem like he'd been dragged, bribed, and threatened into sitting nicely for the photo. That also reminded me of Ansen.

Damn, I needed to call my brother.

Delaney caught me staring and gave me a guilty smile like, *Sorry you're having a meal at my ex-boyfriend's house.* I gave her a smile to let her know this didn't bother me.

Delaney handed a bottle of wine to Willow. "I had to rely on Archer's recommendation since I don't drink wine."

"Oh, look at that. I don't get a chance to drink much wine either." Willow flipped her readers down from the top of her head. She studied the label. "It'll be exciting to try the new stuff. Let me put this in to chill. Right? Is that what we do with wine?"

Delaney shrugged and I nodded.

"Make yourselves comfortable. I'll be right back." Willow whisked the bottle away in the direction the delicious smells were coming from. I exchanged an amused glance with Delaney. Willow was the peacekeeper of the family, and from what I'd heard from Delaney about Bruce and Derek and the whispered rumors that Evander might actually come home, Willow must've had several full-time years of keeping the peace. It was a compliment she left us to do her thing while we took care of ourselves.

Delaney tipped her head toward the living room. I followed her in to the couch. Everyone talked about how the Barrons were so well off, but it wasn't apparent from the house. It might have more square footage than Delaney's parents' place, and it had been updated at some point in the last ten years, but the style wasn't extraordinary. It was comfortable. Homey. No doubt what Willow was going for.

The door opened and Bruce entered. He brushed off his boots on the rug, his gaze seeking us out. "Archer, Laney. I thought I heard you two pull up." He didn't bother checking on Willow. They were probably the type of couple where she shooed him out of the kitchen. The house was her domain; everything outside its walls was his problem.

Dad had thought that was how it worked. I remembered the night Mama had set him straight. *Allan, if you want me to decide what's for dinner for the rest of your life, you'd better help make it once in a while.*

The memory coaxed a smile to my face. Dad could do little more than brown hamburger and throw together random casseroles, but he'd done it once a week until Mama died. Ansen and I would take bets on whether we'd have to eat leftovers the next day or whether Mama would make the remains disappear.

Bruce sat in the recliner across from the couch. "Is this different than you remember, Laney?"

Surprise brightened her eyes like she hadn't expected Bruce to comment like Willow had. "A little. I like what you did with it, with the distressed wood and—" Delaney jumped up as dishes clattered from the kitchen. "I'll go see if she wants a hand."

I held back a smile. Delaney was battling her own memories and sitting with my uncle after years of animosity made helping Willow in the kitchen the better option.

"It'll take a while," he said. "I'm not proud of how I acted before..." He clenched his jaw and averted his gaze. "I can only change moving forward, and Laney's a good kid. Always has been. Kane too."

"I think she's pretty amazing." I shot my uncle a wry grin to lighten the mood. "Kane too."

Bruce chuckled. "We didn't get much chance to talk the other night. Tell me about your brother."

"Ah, I don't know a whole lot. We haven't... We don't..." What should I say? I was getting tired of not knowing how to answer the simplest questions about my dad and my brother.

He doesn't know I'm married.

Honestly, if something happened to him in the last three years, I'm not confident I'd know.

All the memories I've been having the last three weeks have made me feel like a gigantic ass for not reaching out to him.

"Your dad?" Bruce asked, his tone gentle.

I clenched my jaw and lifted a shoulder. All the same things that had run through my mind for my brother fit my dad too. "We're not close."

"Oh." Bruce sat forward and put his elbows on his knees, his fingertips touching each other. "How was Allan last time you saw him. Really? And so you know, whatever you tell me stays between us. Cameron and Kira... If they want to know, they can behave better and ask you themselves."

I debated what to say. Mama wouldn't have sent Christmas cards if Dad had ranted about Bruce. She supported Dad, and she'd trusted Bruce and Willow with updates about the family. I'd do the same. "Dad lost everything before I was ten. The new owner of the ranch let him stay on as manager, and Mama was the lodge housekeeper." After he'd made us move out. "But any profit funneled to them, not us. Then Mama died three years later, and things really went downhill. I blamed Dad. I won the scholarship, and that changed everything.

"Mr. Truitt—he's my current boss and the guy who sponsored the scholarship—was everything Dad wasn't. When I went back home, I think my dad and Ansen thought I had become an arrogant bastard. I think I gave up on Dad and I antagonized my brother. And I can't say they were wrong to quit talking to me."

Bruce stayed quiet for several moments after I stopped speaking. I wasn't sure I wanted him to say anything. Nothing would make it right. Not the mistakes Dad had made, nor how I'd acted toward him and my brother.

"Cameron's the oldest." His brow furrowed as if he had to bolster himself to keep talking. "He had the authority. Our parents put him in charge of everything." He wiggled his hands. "Everything. From the moment we left the womb, I don't remember a time Cameron wasn't the boss of us. Kira and I, we went along with it. But we were younger and there wasn't as much expected of us. But your dad is only a year younger than Cameron. He had to do just as much work, sometimes more, but he never got our parents' attention. Cameron got all the glory, all the rewards."

I got a better sense of Dad's personality. He'd wanted to prove himself, so when he'd failed, he made sure no one saw. He'd kept us isolated. Perhaps he didn't think he deserved rewards, and the rest of us didn't know why.

"They fought." Bruce's chuckle lacked all humor. "Those two fought all the time. And when Dad handed full control over to Cameron? Allan was pissed. I was trained to believe Cameron's word was law. Kira too. So we didn't help. I can't blame your dad. For never coming home. I can't blame him. I just wish things turned out better for you all."

"Me too. But since I've been here, I've remembered a lot more of the good times. And I'm grateful for that."

His smile was so fatherly it damn near ripped my heart

out. "Good. If you don't mind me asking, and tell me to butt out if you need to, but where are you and Delaney going to live?"

I didn't want to lie, but I didn't want to get into it. I lacked answers to a lot of important questions. "We're not sure yet."

"I imagine leaving your job won't be easy, but I wasn't sure if you'd move into Delaney's parents' house or the trailer."

I lifted my brows. "Excuse me?"

Bruce waved a hand. "Oh, I ran into Kane at the grocery store. Willow needed some green beans. Anyway, he said Laney will be ranch manager, and her mom plans to work less. But I can't imagine either of you wants to live in his trailer house."

"Definitely not," I uttered, not sure how else to reply. I was willfully ignorant of Dad's and Ansen's well-being. I was out of the loop with my wife, but not because I wanted to be. Why didn't she discuss this with me? We were trying to work on our marriage, so for her to decide to stay and manage the Diamond UU—when she knew my past—was almost like me going to the condo and finding her gone again. Confusion and betrayal mingled in my brain.

Delaney appeared at the entry of the living room. "Dinner's ready." She grinned at me. "Willow is such a good cook, I bet her food is better than your chef's."

I couldn't force a smile. Because what Bruce said sounded recent, and I'd been around Delaney all damn day, receiving hay shipments. And she hadn't mentioned any new arrangements, ones that would affect our future together.

* * *

Laney

"I'm sorry, all right?" I sat in my pickup in the yard outside the barn. It was the only private place we could discuss what Bruce had said. "I talked with Ma yesterday and it just... It was a shock, and I didn't know what to do."

I had known Archer was upset about something, and it most likely had to do with me. What should've been a pleasant visit with neighbors I'd lived near my entire life had turned into the biggest acting gig of my life. It was like I was out with the Truitts again. Smile here. Say something smart. Cue laughter. My stomach had churned the entire time, which was too bad. Willow made really fucking good hotdishes.

I hoped Bruce and Willow didn't realize that Archer and I were anything but a happy couple. But from the way Archer's eyes had flashed, we were not. I shouldn't have been surprised when Archer told me what he was upset about. It was a small town, and I should've talked to him yesterday.

His hot gaze burned the side of my face as I stared out the windshield. "You mean you know what to do, you just didn't want to tell me."

"Archer, this is my *life*."

"What about me? What about *us*? Don't you think this is a decision we should make together?"

"Oh, you mean like you've been talking to me about where we should live?"

His brows drew together. "We've talked."

"You've said you love your job, it's your dream, Norville's awesome, and you're going back to Dallas." He'd made it clear, but silly me, I'd hung on to hope.

"There was nothing here for you."

"*Everything's* here for me."

"Except me."

"That could change." I thought he would have no rebuttal. He'd said there was nothing here for me, but had he evaluated his life? There was nothing in Dallas for him that he couldn't do here. The Truitts couldn't have that big of a hold on him.

His voice was deceptively even when he said, "You want me to stay here with you and do exactly what destroyed my family?"

My mouth dropped open. No. That wasn't what I was asking. I hadn't seen the correlation between that and how he'd grown up.

But it was exactly what I had expected him to do. I had been so stuck on his unquestioning loyalty toward Norville Truitt that I didn't stop to consider the deeper motivation.

He read my surprise. "Exactly, Delaney. I've done everything to keep from being put in the same position as my dad, but you're doing everything to shove me back into it. We don't own anything; we have to rely on someone else's permission. I like your brother, but I'd be turning everything over to him."

"I would be the manager." It would be my job. Yes, in my family business, but I'd be doing what I was good at. What I enjoyed. And I'd be where I was needed. My marketing education and my short experience made me less qualified than most other applicants. I'd be more lost in Dallas than before. "You can do whatever you want."

"I am doing what I want."

"Then do it here."

He wasn't swayed. "My first three years, I only got clients passed to me because of Mr. Truitt's connections. It took years before I built a good enough reputation that clients sought me out themselves. Now I'm asked for by name. Do you realize how much that means to me?"

"Do you realize how much it means to me not to depend on what other people think?" That was the life I wasn't going back to. Archer had a line he refused to cross; I had mine.

He stared at me for a heartbeat, then shook his head. "This is what you want?"

"My family needs me. I'm not going to just leave them."

He recoiled, hurt and shame flashing in his eyes. "You think that's what I did. Left my dad and brother to suffer while I made a better life for myself."

"I did the same, and I almost lost my brother."

"You can't blame yourself—"

"Not for all of it. But if I'd been home, I might've seen how miserable Kane was. I might've seen the signs, or recognized his depression, or... I don't know. But I can't leave Ma to either do it all or lose it. She could get the ranch into serious financial trouble, and that would blow back on Kane."

He went quiet for a few moments, and my hopes crushed under the weight of the silence. This was why I hadn't said anything. This inevitable conversation.

"What are we doing here, Delaney?" he asked softly. "I've been in Coal Haven for three weeks, but we haven't resolved a thing. If neither of us is willing to bend, then what?"

"I've already bent, Archer. That didn't work out either."

He met my gaze. Did I look as stricken as he did? "Okay. I guess we have another week."

"No matter what, I'm glad you came to Coal Haven." It'd be closure, at the very least. Or maybe at the most?

His jaw tightened as if he wondered the same thing. "Me too." He opened the door of the pickup and slid out. No lingering goodbye kiss, no asking me if I'd changed my mind about sleeping at the motel. "See you in the morning."

"Bye."

I sat in the pickup until he left, knowing that by not answering a goddamn thing, we'd given the best indication of how and when this marriage was going to end.

Eighteen

ARCHER

I pulled into the parking lot and parked in front of my door. I'd grown fond of this room. The little table shoved between the bed and the window was nothing like my office in Dallas.

I worked in one of the high-rises downtown. Had a corner office. Wilson had the corner across from me. My office was done in clean lines, a perfect blend of metal and wood with grains that added a hint of ruggedness. The space reflected me. Slap a suit on me, and all of a sudden, I wasn't some hick kid who hadn't showered in days.

My phone rang, and I picked it up off the seat, hoping to see my wife's face on the screen.

Wilson's name was listed instead. Damn, I hated looking at my phone and wanting it to be her, only to be disappointed.

I hit the answer button and let the sound drift through

the car, as if holding the phone to my ear was too laborious. The talk with Delaney had left me wiped.

"Archer, how's it going, man? Landed yourself a nice milkmaid or something?"

"What? No."

"I'm kidding, I'm kidding. You're like a cow guy and there're cows there— Never mind. Anyway, great news."

"I could use some of that."

If he sensed any turmoil in my voice—like my fucking life was going to be upended and never be the same if Delaney and I divorced—he ignored it. "Listen, you know how the Sheridan Nine is up for sale?"

"I know it." Every land broker in Texas and the surrounding states knew the Sheridan Nine was up for sale. Selling at five hundred million, the commission alone would be well into the eight figures. Talk about a payday. Someone could retire off what they would make from that deal.

"I've heard some Hollywood big shot has been sniffing around, but get this—one of my buddies just called. He's made it big in tech, like *big*, and he's like you—grew up doing that shit, cows and horses and stuff. He wants it."

"He wants it?" I hated to be dubious. Just because the guy had been raised like I had been didn't mean he knew what came with a sale like the Sheridan Nine. "He realizes he's buying the horse- and bull-breeding operations, along with the regular cow-slash-calf side of the ranch?"

Not only were those three separate businesses, but the Sheridan Nine was big business. These were not simple family-run ventures. The Sheridan Nine had several levels of ranch managers and hundreds of people on staff, and it spread out over three counties. I didn't mention the wildlife and regulated hunting programs the Sheridan Nine managed.

"He gets it. His wife is, like, some rodeo queen."

"There's rodeo queen, and there's Sheridan Nine." I'd be surprised if the wife had competed on a horse that cost as much as what one of theirs went for at auction. Last year, a twelve-year-old gelding sold for almost a hundred thousand dollars, and he was going to be nothing but a leisure riding horse.

"Are you trying to ruin this deal before it's even started?"

"No." I pinched the bridge of my nose. "No. For five hundred million, I want them to know what they're getting into."

"I said you're the guy. Malik can't wait to talk with you. Thing is, we need to move on this fast."

Dread pooled in my gut. "How fast?"

"How soon can you get back?"

"Wilson—"

"Do you realize how big a payday this would be?" Excitement tinged Wilson's voice. "This would make you partner. Father wouldn't be able to ignore that kind of payday. Father's got that trip to Bali next month, and I don't know shit about cows. You're the guy, Archer. You'll like Malik. This'll be fan-fucking-tastic."

I leaned my head back and closed my eyes. How the hell did I get out of this?

I couldn't. This was my job. If I turned it down, Mr. Truitt would never forgive me. He might be so upset he'd fire me. Then what? Everything I'd worked for was done? I turned my back on my family and damaged my marriage and had nothing to show for it?

Did I risk it?

Three weeks ago, this kind of news would've been, as Wilson said, fan-fucking-tastic. I would've shed the tie, Wilson would've called Briony, and we would've hit the town—in a dignified and professional way, but absolutely we would've celebrated.

The argument with Delaney earlier crowded out all enthusiasm. I'd have to leave early. But after our talk in the pickup, I had driven to the motel wondering if there was any reason to stay.

If I believed in signs, this would be a blue-and-yellow neon one telling me I'd better grab what I'd lost eighteen months ago.

Losing my chance at making partner dulled in comparison to losing my wife.

Why did it have to be a goddamn choice? Why couldn't I have both?

In the end, the question was whether five more days in Coal Haven would make a difference.

A payday of millions of dollars would make a hell of a difference. I had a nicely padded savings account, but this amount of money was life changing. Not just for me, but for my wife.

Leaving felt wrong, but staying didn't feel quite right. This deal might be the answer. "I can drive back in two days."

"Mr. Hollywood could move on it in two days. You need to get back faster. Ditch the car. You'll be able to buy a new one. Get a red-eye or something."

"I don't think they have red-eyes here."

"Well, fucking hitchhike. How bad do you want this?"

"I want it," I said without inflection as my mind raced. If I stalled too much, Mr. Truitt would threaten to turn it over to Wilson. Not a good look for the company, since the prospective buyer had approached Wilson first. "Look, I need time to gather all the information and make a list of what I want to talk to Sheridan Nine's agent about. Why don't I give Malik a call? What's his last name?"

"That's my man." Is he being smug? "Malik is his last name. His first name is Rogers."

I could get started on the reports, since I'd clearly made my decision. I got off the phone with Wilson and stared at the front door of my room for a minute before I called Delaney.

When she answered, I didn't hesitate. "Wilson called. I have to leave in the morning." I used her silence to fill her in on the details and ended with, "So yeah. It's a shitload of money for us."

"Us?" she asked with more hesitancy than I cared for.

"Don't give up on us, okay?"

"You think Norville is going to let you do a deal this big and then somehow split your time between Dallas and Coal Haven?"

"Delaney—"

"No, Archer. Do you think this is a huge coincidence? 'Some Hollywood guy sniffing around'? How long has Sheridan Nine been for sale?"

I clamped down on the defensiveness her question coaxed out. "Five-hundred-million-dollar properties don't move in months."

"Bullshit. The Truitts want the deal; that's no surprise. But they suddenly found a buyer right before they feared you wouldn't return?"

I sighed. "It's not a conspiracy."

"Maybe it's a coincidence. But they're dangling partner again. They're not going to want to share you with anyone. They're getting you back into the office, where you can make them a lot of money."

"Norville's not an evil mastermind. He's just a guy trying to run a successful company."

"Whatever, Archer." Delaney suddenly sounded as tired as I felt. "Have a good trip."

"Is that goodbye?" Acid chewed through my stomach. Was this it?

Wasn't this where we were heading? She'd had the balls to call it.

"Goodbye," she said and hung up.

"Fuck!" I hit the steering wheel. Hit it again. "Fuck."

I wiped a hand over my face and got out. I shut off the Delaney part of my mind. If I thought about her, I would tank this deal, and it wasn't a sure thing in the first place. Because the only thing I could do was prove her wrong. Show her that somehow, I could have it all. The Truitts didn't have the power over me she thought they did.

* * *

Laney

I faced the metal door. I had raced to town, the fear that he might be gone already hot on my heels. A simple goodbye and hanging up on him wasn't enough. It wasn't any more closure than we'd had before.

I knocked and waited, wringing my hands. How was he going to react?

When he opened the door, the dim light from the lamp by the bed illuminated his dark figure. All I could make out was that his hair wasn't in the neat arrangement it usually was.

"Delaney?"

"I'm not here to go with you. I'm not going to beg you to stay. I just... need you right now." I wasn't sure what I was asking or what exactly I was there for. I just knew he hadn't left town yet, and I wanted to be with him as long as possible.

He opened the door farther, and I stepped inside. His little office was set up on the table. He was working. Of course he was.

He closed and locked the door. Without taking his eyes off me, he closed his laptop.

Nerves shook my body. I didn't want to argue. Neither did he. Being alone with him clarified why I had stared at the steering wheel for so long and didn't go into my parents' house.

"I thought we should have a proper goodbye." I was proud my voice didn't shake and I didn't break down in tears. "One we didn't get before."

He closed the distance between us and stroked the back of his finger down my face.

"Say something," I whispered.

"We've said it all." He cupped my face and leaned down to touch his lips to mine.

It was like a switch flipped and we reverted to that day when he'd gotten me on the bed and into my pants.

My back hit the mattress, but our pace slowed. Archer savored me. I ran my hands through his hair, and he took his time kissing me. Lazy strokes of his tongue made me want to demand more but coaxed me into slowing down. The hard length behind his fly pressed between us, but he refused to rush.

He kissed his way down my neck, and I turned my head to give him better access.

"This is probably a bad idea," he said.

"It's all a bad idea."

As if that was the final confirmation he needed that I wasn't going to change my mind, he worked the hem of my shirt up.

"Thank fuck," he growled when he saw I was wearing a

lacy bra and not the unforgiving sports bras I had on while camping.

Cool air hit my nipples a heartbeat before his hot mouth closed on one. I groaned and rolled into him. Between his hard body between my legs and his lips on my skin, I was panting and ready to blow.

We hadn't done anything intimate since our camping trip. With the lack of our own space and the unanswered questions between us, it hadn't felt right. But it was done. We were done. This was being free to just be us, together.

His tongue lapped over my tight peak, and my moan was pure need. He switched sides but didn't leave my wet nipple to get cold. His hand gripped and massaged the other breast.

Drawing back, he finished taking my shirt and bra all the way off. As soon as the material slipped over my head, I tugged his polo up. When his chest was bared to me, I spread both hands across it.

A sad smile that belied the raging need coursing through me touched my lips. "You have a farmer's tan."

He glanced at his arms, where the skin was darker than his shoulders, and softly chuckled. "It's been a while."

I traced the collar line at his neck. My ring finger was still bare, and after this summer, the tan line was gone. There would be no indicator I had ever been married after I signed the annulment papers. And I would. I wasn't going to fight it, and no judge would know that Archer and I had spent three weeks together learning everything we hadn't known about each other before.

God, this was hard. "Archer..."

He planted a firm kiss on my lips. "I know."

Then his hands were at my pants. Impatience drove us both as I kicked my boots off so he could get me completely naked. I wanted to take my time, but I wanted to be so lost in him that sadness couldn't touch me. The way he shucked his pants made me think he felt the same. He ripped the comforter away, so we lay on clean sheets.

Always a considerate partner. In almost all areas.

I let my hands roam his defined body. Hard pecs down to rippled abs. His erection jutted toward me, and I curled my fingers around him.

He watched, his face cut with intensity, as if he were taking mental pictures. I was doing the same.

I kissed the round mole at the joint of his shoulder. Then the tan line close to his collarbone and another on his hard pec. Pushing my fingertips against his chest, I rolled him onto his back. "I want to explore you."

He held his arms away. "Yes, ma'am."

I trailed kisses down his chest. My hair swept over his skin, down his abs, as I made my way to his erection.

He had a beautiful body everywhere. The light was still on. I could be intimidated, but I wasn't. I called my body type rangy, but the way he let me roam, the subtle vibrations under his skin as if the exertion he spent to keep from attacking me made him shake, suffused me with wanton confidence.

I wrapped my fingers around him once again. His cock twitched under my palm, and I gave one pump. Two. That earned a groan from him, and he rolled his hips into my touch.

I lightly pressed a kiss to his tip before I trailed my tongue along his heated flesh.

"Fuck, Delaney. You're killin' me."

I took him into my mouth and hummed. The next groan from him was deeper, more guttural.

I should've done this before now. I'd had three fucking weeks to taste this man as much as I wanted to, but I'd abstained.

What the hell for?

I pulled back and took him in again. Another groan, another roll of his hips. One of his hands buried into my hair, twisting in the strands.

I kicked up the pace, but after a few times, he gently tugged my head away. I released him with a pop. My body was on fire, and I wanted nothing more than to drive him wild. But he flipped me over and draped my legs over his shoulders.

He looked at me from between my thighs, his dark eyes hooded, promise smoldering in those brown irises. "Sorry, I couldn't wait."

I couldn't get a word out before he dipped his head. With one lick, I bowed off the bed. This wasn't like what he did during the camping trip. Now, he took his time. He licked, then backed off. He sucked me into his mouth, then retreated. I was writhing and fisting my hands in the sheets, gasping his name, but it didn't matter.

He played with me. I was his toy, and I was powerless against him. He had spun me around and opened me up like I was a rag doll. And I loved it. God, I couldn't get enough of this man, and tonight was all we had together.

"Archer." I bucked against him, losing the rhythm out of pure desperation to get a release.

Finally, he let me go. I squeezed my eyes shut, and my back came off the sheet. The explosion wasn't a body slam; it rolled over me, encompassing me in a cocoon of ecstasy and warmth and passion. I hung in the cloud for a few blissful beats before I drifted down like a feather in the breeze.

I opened my eyes and blinked back tears.

"Hey." Archer peppered my body with leisurely kisses as he crawled up and lay even with me. "What's wrong?"

"That was just really beautiful." I swiped the back of my wrist across my eyes. I hated being fucking sappy.

"Because you're really beautiful." He ran a hand up my thigh, hitching it higher until he could place his erection at my entrance. "You're everything."

I might've broken down, but he pushed inside, and I was transported to a place where I felt good from head to toe, inside and out. We fell into a steady rhythm. The same tension from before quivered under his skin, but he patiently stroked me toward another peak.

"Archer," I gasped. "I don't want this to end." When I came, he'd come, and then it'd be done. He'd need sleep to drive all day tomorrow, and I'd have to go home. Just because it was easier than staying.

His response was to kiss me. The distraction was what I needed. Energy swirled through my body, gaining in strength and size until I shattered again, only this time it wasn't just me. We came together, his body bunching and tightening over me.

He broke the kiss and buried his head in the crook of my neck as he rocked through the rest of his release. I hugged him with everything I had as tears leaked out.

When he withdrew, he didn't get out of bed. He maneuvered us between the covers and tucked me into his side.

If I wasn't home for chores, Ma would understand. She'd figure out where I was.

His arms around me, I drifted off, sleeping harder than I would've had I spent the night alone. I didn't know what time it was when a soft kiss pressed into my hair.

I might've imagined the words "don't give up on us" before I woke up to the sun trying to break through the crooked mini blinds. I was alone in bed, and his things were gone.

I finally let myself cry.

Nineteen

ARCHER

I scrolled through my phone as I took the elevator up to NT Land Agency. I should have been delighted to be strolling into work. I was going to make partner after working here since I was twenty-three.

I peered at my watch. There were so many reasons I felt like I was dragging an entire herd of cattle behind me as I commuted to work. The drive had taken two days. One really long day where I had nothing to do but watch the road and review what I'd done with my life. Yesterday, the drive hadn't been as long, but I'd spent hours compiling information on Sheridan Nine. I hadn't reached out to anyone. This was a coveted piece of land, and Mr. Hollywood probably thought he had plenty of time. But time would only lower the price.

However, competition might drive the price higher. A few million to these guys wouldn't hurt, but they didn't get rich enough to drop five hundred million on something by being wasteful.

I rolled my neck. Last night I had been back in my king-size bed. The best mattress money could buy didn't help me sleep any better than the full-size mattress I slept on in Coal Haven.

The motel room hadn't had Delaney's clothing in the closet or her toiletries stuffed into a drawer.

Like a lovesick kid, I'd found a half-empty bottle of her lotion and tormented myself with a sniff.

Fuck, I was in bad shape.

The amount of work looming ahead of me didn't help. Normally, I'd be itching to dive into a property that size, gather all the details about the various businesses under Sheridan Nine's umbrella, and start pumping out financial reports, weather reports, and any tidbit of data that would put me over the top and convince the client he had a leg up in the sale. But it wasn't even eight in the morning, and I was ready to leave.

The elevator stopped at the fifth floor, and I suppressed an eye roll. For fuck's sake. I could've driven out to the Grangers' from the motel in the time this elevator took to get to my floor.

On my tablet, I sifted through work emails I hadn't paid enough attention to in the last week. Notes from Ardell in billing. Forwards from my assistant. Two new leads. A tract of land in southeast Oklahoma and a farm for sale in the middle of Nebraska. The Nebraskan farm was highlighted as a motivated seller. Family illness. They needed to sell and get the money as soon as possible. Not the easiest for a farm in the middle of nowhere.

New leads and this type of challenge usually excited me. I loved making money for clients, and this family needed every cent. I could travel, get out of the office, and meet new people, but my mood tanked. I'd rather be with my wife.

All I had to do was finish this deal. I'd make partner and have some flexibility in my career.

The door finally whispered open on the thirty-second floor. I stepped out and beelined down the hallway straight for my office. Chitchat would only bog down my day. I turned the corner. Wilson's door was open, and Mr. Truitt was leaning over his desk, his fingertips pressed into the top. Wilson was reclining in his chair with his hands behind his head.

I had suspected that part of my appeal for Mr. Truitt was that I didn't fill him with the fear I'd jack around until I jeopardized an important assignment. Wilson hadn't—yet. But he insisted on acting like he was so damn good he could afford to be all casual and shit. Mr. I'll Take Care Of Y'all.

When he saw me, Wilson raised his arms into the air. "Hey, Archer. Finally decided to grace us with your presence?"

Mr. Truitt turned, and his scowl softened. "Archer." He waved me in. His gray hair was trimmed short and gelled to the side. He was tanner than when I'd left. He must've been hitting the golf course. "Come in and shut the door. We have a lot to catch up on."

I entered and set my bag down with the multitude of electronics I'd dragged across the country with me next to the chair across from Wilson's desk. Unlike my office, Wilson had selected a trendier theme. Oranges and greens decorated the space like a frozen yogurt shop, along with the same outside-the-box chairs. The one I chose resembled an orange-colored backward ocean wave, kind of like Wilson's hairstyle.

Mr. Truitt sat on the edge of Wilson's desk. He hated

the chairs, but even he'd had to admit they fit for the type of clients his son attracted for urban development.

"Did you get a lot of work done on the trip?"

Not *How was your drive?*

How was your visit?

Did your wife come back with you or is there a good chance you ruined everything by coming back to work?

"Yes," I said simply. I should be listing everything I'd prepared last night in my condo and the two nights before that in my motel room. I blamed the lack of sleep.

Mr. Truitt's neatly trimmed brows lifted. He regarded me with that shrewd gaze of his that instantly earned respect. When I'd first met him after I won the scholarship, I'd noticed all the differences between him and Dad.

Expensive suit, but it hadn't been the suit. It'd been that his clothes were clean and had no holes. Nice. Professional. Dad had looked like a rumpled mess when Mama had dragged us to church.

Mr. Truitt's hair was always trimmed. He had a standing appointment every two weeks. In one year, he likely paid more for his haircuts than Dad had his entire life. Could Mr. Truitt tell that my last haircut had cost twenty bucks? I didn't think so. Why did I use the same hair person as he did?

But more than appearance, it had been the look in Mr. Truitt's eyes. Undiluted confidence. It had been intoxicating for a kid raised by a guy who hadn't known how he was going to afford a few cans of soup.

"Is everything taken care of in North Dakota?" he asked.

Wilson sat forward, the heels of his loafers hitting the floor with a thump.

"I don't know," I answered honestly. "I hope not."

Mr. Truitt pushed off the desk and sat in the chair next

to me. He rarely showed this much sincerity when discussing personal lives. Mr. Truitt lived for business—except when he was having fun. But then he had people like me and Wilson in place so he could jet to any golf course in the world.

"Archer," he said with that rare fatherly tone he used with me. "Don't you think that if staying together was the right thing to do, it wouldn't be this difficult? You were gone for weeks."

Three. I'd been gone for three weeks. Who was to say how long we needed to work on our marriage?

Weary, I pulled out my tablet. "All I know is she's important to me, and I can't just go on with my life. There are a lot of options these days." I'd had nearly twenty hours of travel to think about them.

Bismarck offered straight flights to Dallas. I'd been working remotely for three weeks. I had to visit sites, and I had to meet clients, but with a little planning, there was no reason I couldn't do both. Compelling enough to pack the annulment papers with me instead of leaving them behind for Delaney to sign.

But I was wise enough to know I couldn't bring up those details until I made partner. Mr. Truitt was old-fashioned, and Delaney had accurately determined that he was controlling. Change upset him. It was why his own son put him on edge.

I flipped open the tablet, where it was faster to pull up the documents from our cloud account. "I've compiled quite a bit of history and current information for the Maliks about Sheridan Nine. I'll gather more before we bring them into the office tomorrow."

For all the rush back, Rogers Malik hadn't been able to come in from Houston until late afternoon tomorrow. I tried not to think about the extra day I could've had with my wife.

Mr. Truitt didn't look at the tablet. He watched me, that shrewdness back in place. I countered it with a calm persona. I already had all the proof that I was partner material for NT Land Agency. It was in my work history and in the tablet I held. Sheridan Nine would be the clincher.

I wasn't sure what went through Mr. Truitt's mind when he accepted the tablet, but I couldn't bring myself to care.

* * *

Laney

"Laney, did you hear me?"

Kennedy sat across from me in a booth at Rattler's. I was busted staring out the window. Archer had left two days ago, and I'd been about as worthwhile as a water tank full of holes. When a new laptop had been delivered earlier today, I'd stared at it on the porch for fifteen minutes.

The concern in Kennedy's doe-brown gaze made hot tears prick the backs of my eyelids. "I'm sorry. I missed it."

I'd called her the day after Archer left. When I'd cried myself out and then cried some more. I'd lain in that bed until housekeeping knocked on the door.

He hadn't left a note. He hadn't called or messaged. I'd heard nothing from him. Had he really told me not to give up on us?

It all had seemed like an illusion that had grown stronger when the parking space in front of the door was empty. No charcoal-gray Audi.

Did he make it back okay?

He was probably at work today. It took two solid days of driving, longer with traffic and added stops.

What was I thinking? He was probably in the office, looking stupid hot in a gray suit with matching tie and a dress shirt that would hide his farmer's tan. He'd probably even stopped to get his hair trimmed. It was what Mr. Truitt would do.

I glowered at my water. I hadn't dared to drink. There wasn't enough White Claw on the planet to drown the memory of Archer, but I might be tempted to try.

Kennedy was worried about me. I'd heard it in her voice when she'd invited me out tonight. I suspected Kane had called her and asked her to check in. If I was this pathetic after a few days without him, how was I going to last the month? The year?

At what point would I give up? Or was I doing shitty because I had given up? What if he gave up and moved on and I was here heartbroken? My mind circled back to one more detail.

"He took the annulment papers," I blurted.

Kennedy nodded because she'd heard me say it before—at least two other times.

I stirred the ice in my glass with the straw. "Do you think he'll be back?"

"I don't know. I do think he loves you though."

"I wish it was enough."

"Sometimes we need a bigger push to get out of our own way."

"I just wish I knew what that push was." I sighed and let melancholy blanket me. This sucked. When I'd left him in Dallas, I'd had my brother to worry about. Then Diamond UU.

Now all I could do was wallow in the misery. I took a drink of my water, biting the straw between my teeth.

"I wasn't talking about him," she said tentatively.

"Hmm?" I set the glass down.

"The push. I wasn't necessarily talking about Archer."

"But—"

She held up a hand, closing her eyes like she *just couldn't* with me anymore. I would take it personally, but the woman could silence a class full of fifth graders. I didn't stand a chance. "Laney, you've become one of my favorite people, but that stubbornness and fire I used to dread crossing my path are blocking yours."

"What do you mean? I can't let Diamond UU fail. What would Kane do? And Ma—"

"Have you asked them?" She arched a brow. She damn well knew I hadn't. Tapping a finger between us, she leaned forward as if to further protect our quiet conversation. "It's important to Kane to run his own life, and you're making decisions for him."

"I'm not."

That brow ticked up again. "You are. Same with your ma. Liam leases out the pastures. Kane could do the same if he wanted income from the ranch without doing anything."

"What if Ma runs it into the ground?"

"What if she's hanging on, going out in the heat and the blizzards because you are? Your dad still works. Your mom and Kane could downsize so the Diamond UU is more manageable for her. Or she might want to retire altogether so she can go on all those fishing trips your papa takes. But she and Kane are not going to downsize if the ranch has to support a ranch manager, and they're going to make sure they have a place for you. Your ma's rough around the edges, but she cares about you."

I had thought Ma made me ranch manager as a consolation prize. But what if she and Kane had finally talked?

What if they'd had to figure out a way to support my ass because I refused to fucking leave?

"Oh, God." I'd spent so long wondering why I wasn't enough that I settled for where I was needed instead. But I wasn't needed anymore. Kane had plans. Ma had plans. But they wanted me to be happy, so they were trying to be flexible.

Kennedy held up her hand again like she was putting my panic on pause. "I'm also not saying Archer doesn't need a wake-up call. But you two didn't get anywhere when you both were spinning your wheels. You were like this." She made fists and put her knuckles together. She didn't have to explain it. Archer and I had been like two bumper-to-bumper trucks stuck in the mud, revving to get out, but I was in his way, and he was in mine.

"What do I do?"

Holden picked that moment to walk by. He swung into the booth next to Kennedy. "You ladies need a problem solver?" He frowned at my water, and his eyes narrowed on me. I could picture what he saw. Pale face, wan expression, bloodshot eyes. "Am I interrupting something?"

"Archer left, and I don't know what to do." Holden wasn't the last person I'd thought I would open up to, but he certainly was far down as an option. Yet, he was here. I'd rather have Liam's insight, but he'd stayed with the kids so Kennedy could straighten my shit out.

"You want to stay married to him?" he asked like his solution would depend on my answer. He also asked like he was taking my dilemma seriously. I never would've imagined this.

I nodded.

"Your brother has Diamond UU?"

Damn, news traveled fast in Coal Haven. I nodded again.

"Then buy yourself a ticket and spend three weeks in Dallas."

I chewed the inside of my cheek. It wasn't that easy. "Archer tried that already, and it didn't work."

"Then do it naked."

I coughed out a laugh. "Holden."

Kennedy chuckled and elbowed him.

"Seriously, though." Humor drained from his face, and he looked around. The place wasn't full on a Wednesday evening, and no one was in the booths around us. "Look, I was in a serious relationship once."

I glanced at Kennedy, but she looked as surprised as I felt.

"We went through some shit." His throat worked and overwhelming grief blinked over his face before it was gone. "And I didn't know what to do. She gave up on me, and she had every right to."

"I'm sorry," I whispered. That must've been when he had moved away for college. I didn't know anything about his years away. I wasn't the only secretive one.

"Look, I'm telling you both this because you're family—and you know Barrons don't make that claim about just anybody." He arched a brow at Kennedy, and she gave a knowing nod. Liam had been dropped off that list and still was off it according to some relatives. "And you both can keep a secret. But if that fiasco can help, fuck, anyone, then maybe..." He lifted a shoulder. "If she had come back and tried, if she had grabbed me by the collar and said, 'Listen up, fucker. Get your shit together so we can figure this out,' my life might be a lot different."

He ducked his head to look me in the eyes, like I really had to hear what he said next. "I know I'm the one to blame, but at the same time, I wish she'd showed me she had some faith in me. In us. Neither of us made a move, so she moved on. She's a happily married mom of two, and I fuck around."

That wasn't where I thought his pep talk would go, but it resonated. Archer and I had waited a year and a half for each other. We'd waited for the other to make the first move.

So maybe it was my turn, and I had to make it count.

Twenty

ARCHER

A phone rang in Wilson's office, and I jolted myself out of my trance. My screen had gone blank. How long had I spaced out?

I tapped into the financial report I was looking at. Malik had talked to the bank, and he and his rodeo star were ready to move. I had to admit that on paper, he and his wife seemed like good candidates. I wasn't the one who needed to approve them, but it eased my conscience.

Mrs. Malik had said she wanted to keep it going just like it was. She and Rogers had not only grown up on a farm and ranch, but she had also gone to school for agricultural business, and she currently owned her own financial firm that catered to agricultural industries. I suspected she was the one driving the sale; she'd bring her expertise, and Rogers would add the tech side. They'd be well-rounded owners.

I checked the time. The Maliks weren't going to arrive for another hour yet.

Fuuuuuck.

I had taken my suit coat off and loosened my tie. I'd get myself together before the couple arrived.

Briony was in Wilson's office. The Maliks would meet here, we'd go over the specifications of the sale, answer questions, and then go out for a late lunch. Another client meal. Briony would give the impression we were a family business and add to the charm that would make the Maliks sign on with us.

It was manipulative, as Delaney had pointed out.

Mr. Truitt strode in. His large office was across from mine and Wilson's, and he'd been in all day. The size of this sale must put him on edge. Either that or he wanted to evaluate how I handled pressure. He should know by now, but Mr. Truitt prided himself on his standards.

"Archer, a word." He tossed some papers on the desk.

"What's this?" I notched my tie tighter and straightened it. I read through the top sheet. My name was scattered across it, along with requirements for my job. My world slowed to a stop as the meaning behind the words unfolded. "I don't understand."

He waved a hand. "Oh, it's legal mumbo jumbo. The fine print for a broker in this firm working on a deal the size of Sheridan Nine."

We hadn't discussed the deal. We didn't even know if the Sheridan Nine owners would sell to the Maliks or to Mr. Hollywood.

The burn in my stomach that began when I first read the document morphed into a steady flame. Only this wasn't anxiety. It was something stronger. More visceral.

"What exactly does the fine print say?" Did he expect me to sign without asking questions? I'd comb over the document and then find a lawyer who wasn't associated with the Truitts before I considered getting a pen near this thing.

"It's a noncompete clause of sorts." He spoke as if it was nothing, but the look in his eye was all savvy businessman. A look I used to admire, but now I had the urge to smear it across the floor. "With the size of your commission, you could do a lot."

"Like strike out on my own?"

Norville should be begging you to be partner.

I had thought it was a compliment. But Delaney had seen what I hadn't. They hadn't begged me. The partnership was the carrot they dangled in front of me to keep me at the agency. To keep me from brushing off my suit and hanging out my own shingle in this industry.

"Exactly. You understand, of course."

It wasn't the most cutthroat move I'd witnessed from him. It was his agency. He could afford expensive, knowledgeable lawyers. It gave him a lot of leeway to do what others might consider wrong.

I tapped the middle of the top sheet. "What about the part where I have to agree to stay on for three years in the Dallas office after the deal is complete?"

"Brokering a sale the size of Sheridan Nine will only increase business. We'll be higher profile; we might even have to add staff. It makes sense to have my head guy around."

"Especially if I'm partner."

His expression shuttered. "Especially if you're partner."

I leaned my elbows on the top of my desk. "But if I'm partner, wouldn't that negate the noncompete clause and the three-year term? I mean, my vested interest would be NT Land Agency."

"If you're partner, yes."

"If," I echoed. There it was. Manipulation. Dangling a carrot he didn't plan to feed me. I let out a humorless laugh.

"Find something funny, Archer?"

The laugh continued, acting as a vent for the mushroom cloud of regret, shame, and frustration. "Oh, yes, Norville. So damn funny."

Mr. Truitt's brows slammed down. "Care to enlighten me?"

"My wife was right."

This time, he was the one who leaned forward. "Tell me, what was your little wife right about?"

"You." I pushed my laptop across the desk. I checked the drawers. There was nothing in them but a pack of mints, paper clips, charging cords, staplers—shit I didn't need. Except I popped a mint in and crunched it between my teeth.

"Your wife"—contempt dripped from him—"knows nothing about me. She's not a part of this life."

"Neither am I." I had nothing personal in my office. Not even a picture. I had used the excuse that I could look in my phone when I wanted to see my wife's beautiful face.

How had I deluded myself so thoroughly?

I rose, and he scrambled out of his chair. "Archer, this is a contract. We can negotiate."

I pressed the fingers of one hand into the top of my desk and propped the other hand on my hip. "I want to work remotely, traveling to the office only when I need to meet with clients or make site visits."

He blustered, a red flush creeping up his face. "Absolutely not."

"Why not? Are you afraid my productivity would suffer and you couldn't go to Bali while Wilson and I manage the office?"

"Archer, watch your damn tone."

I bypassed him to march out of the office. A stunned Wilson watched us with wide eyes, standing back like he'd been about to enter, but had changed his mind and didn't dare get close. Briony wandered out of her husband's office, her expression just as stunned.

I spun around, putting my back to Wilson and his wife. "I looked up to you. That's what I'm most ashamed of. I wanted to emulate you. I thought you were what a successful person should be. But all I was to you was a payday. You groomed me to make money so this office could be ticking while you slept with women who weren't your wife and traveled the world. I was the fallback plan when you realized Wilson wasn't as dedicated as you wanted him to be."

Mr. Truitt spoke through clenched teeth. "There were a lot of kids I could've picked."

"But I was the most gullible. I was the hick who didn't know better. I was a kid desperate for a father figure, and you swooped in. You know what? I have a fucking father. He made a lot of mistakes, but he never used people. He never gave up, and I think maybe I should take notes. Because I'm done with you. I quit."

"Where do you think you're going to go?" My former boss's voice shook. "Who do you think will hire you after I'm done telling them all what you're like?"

"I'm going home to my wife. And every time I work with manure, I'm going to think of you and your bullshit."

I spun and faced Wilson. Briony had gone to his side, her glossy red hair falling over one shoulder. The shock and concern in her gaze matched Wilson's. This time I knew that concern wasn't for me.

"You've been an okay friend," I told Wilson. My gaze jumped between him and Briony. "But y'all can fuck right off over how you treated Delaney."

A choked gasp yanked my attention beyond him. His shoulders had blocked out an additional witness.

The best apparition I could've ever seen. My wife stared

at me, her blue eyes wide and full of disbelief. She'd dressed in a loose white shirt and pink shorts with lace on the hem. The platform sandals made her legs impossibly longer.

Despite her shock, she glanced at Briony, her expression rueful. "Did he enunciate enough for ya?"

Briony made a choked sound, but I ignored her. I was done with the Truitts. I charged in Delaney's direction so fast, she took an involuntary step backward. I wrapped my arms around her and lifted, smashing my mouth onto hers.

She twined her arms around my neck, and I twirled us around.

I set her on the floor. "What are you doing here?"

"I'm making my move." Her gaze lifted over my shoulder. "But I think I'm late."

"Your timing is perfect." I draped an arm over her shoulders, tucked her into my side, and guided her to the elevator. "All I need to do is put the condo up for sale and we can go home."

Those luminous blue eyes searched mine. I didn't call the condo home. Dallas wasn't home either. My home was with Delaney.

As we loaded into the elevator, I bent to kiss her, but she put a finger on my lips. "I feel like I need to confess that I'm also jobless. And I'm homeless." When I blinked, she continued. "When I told Ma I was chasing after you, she said *good*. She wants to downsize, and eventually Kane will rent out the pastures."

"I'm sure I can get my room back at the motel. We'll figure it out." I pulled her close. "There's just one stop I want to make first. Two, because I'm gonna get you and me silicone rings we can wear twenty-four seven."

* * *

The dirt road stretched in front of us. The trunk was full of dishes and books, and the back seat was filled with shoes and clothing. The furniture we put up for sale with the condo, and we donated everything else. I gave my housekeeper and chef an excellent reference and added my own severance package.

Delaney worried about money and where to live, but I hadn't busted my ass for seven years for nothing. I had an idea for a belated wedding gift, but I wanted to wait until we returned to Coal Haven.

"It's a little flatter, but it really does look like home." Delaney peered out the window, her sunglasses perched on her nose. She had donned the only pair of jeans she'd packed. Her shirt was the same one she'd worn when she came to the office, and her hair hung loose.

My GPS prompted me to turn. Cows dotted the pastures. Short trees were scattered in the distance where there must have been a water source. I followed the road to a squat cabin with a detached garage and a fairly new shop.

There were neatly cropped bushes by the house and trees scattered around the shop and yard. Nothing like I was used to, but that was a good thing. Relief streamed through my veins as I pulled up in front of the cabin.

A tall, lanky figure walked out. He looked the same. A plaid shirt neatly tucked in to worn and faded jeans held up with a black belt. He wasn't wearing the beat-up, dirty cowboy hat I thought had been issued to him when he was born.

I parked and went around the car, but Delaney didn't wait for me to open her door and get out.

I came to a stop next to her and faced the man. "Hi, Dad."

His smile showed a few more wrinkles, but the sweltering stress from when Ansen and I were growing up was gone. "Archer, hi. And you must be Delaney. Cheryl's daughter?"

"Don't hold it against me."

He laughed, the same rusty sound I remembered. "Only if you don't hold my siblings against me." He pushed a hand through his russet hair. More gray lined his temples and was sprinkled over his head than before. "Where are my manners? Come in, come in."

He opened the door and ushered me and Delaney inside. I hadn't been worried about what I'd see, but this wasn't the house I grew up in. There wasn't one half-empty can of beer. The floor had been mopped, but not like Dad had busted ass when I'd called him and asked if I could introduce him to my wife. He kept this place clean.

Dad crowded in behind us. "Don't worry 'bout your shoes. Have a seat."

"It's nice, Dad." I led Delaney to the couch and took a seat next to her. I felt like a guest. Everything was unfamiliar. But I'd change that, starting with this visit, the first of many.

"It's a place to hang my hat." He arranged an auction ad on the end table and wiped off an invisible speck of dust.

"No, Dad. I'm really sorry for how I acted after I left for college." I hadn't meant to dive into the deep end right away, but he was moving nervously around us like he couldn't quit cleaning the place.

"There's nothin' to apologize for."

"There's everything to apologize for." I sought Delaney's hand and told Dad the story of how we met and why she left. "Being in Coal Haven, doing all the same work I did growing up, brought back a lot of memories."

Dad dipped his head, like this was hard to hear.

"Good ones, Dad. You and me and Ansen. Mama."

His eyes got glassy, and he gazed out the window. "I miss that woman. She put up with a lot."

"But you kept going, and I took that for granted."

"I made so many mistakes, Archer." His gaze grew wistful. "So many mistakes. But I'm in a good place now. And you?" He grinned and looked at Delaney. "I was happy with how you turned out before, but now I'm thrilled."

"I'm jobless and homeless." I was partially joking. My savings would get poured into my surprise for Delaney, and after we sold the condo, the housing portion would be taken care of. We weren't destitute, and ultimately that had been my goal growing up. To be able to provide for the ones I loved.

"You'll be fine." He nodded like he knew for a fact. "If I taught you anything, it was what not to do, and if I went through that special hell so you know how to do better, then I'm okay."

Dad's confidence was humbling. He was a flawed man, just like anyone. But he wasn't a user like Mr. Truitt, and he'd taught me and my brother better whether we knew it or not. "Ansen? Do you hear from him often?"

"Aw, he's as stubborn as you. But he stops in once in a while."

I bobbed my head. I had sent Ansen a message with a selfie of me and Delaney. **We have a lot to catch up on. I want you to meet your sister-in-law.**

He'd responded with **Yup. Congrats.**

Not overwhelming brotherly love, but that was Ansen. The line of communication was still open. That was enough for now.

"Y'all want to see the place?"

I had to ask. I wasn't abandoning Dad again if I was in a place to help him or, at the very least, support him. "Good owners?"

Dad's eyes crinkled at the corners. "When I don't have

to worry 'bout bein' put to the streets with kids, I don't have to tolerate as much."

"You have a good boss?"

"They're okay. They try to do right by the land, the animals, and the people on it." He rose and went to the rectangular picture window. "But I own this house and the ten acres it sits on. I stand here and think how different it would've been had I been able to raise you boys here."

I squeezed Delaney's hand. "It got us to where we were supposed to be eventually, Dad."

Twenty-One

LANEY

It wasn't the first gathering Archer and I had held at our new place, but tonight was for fun, not for moving and hauling out old equipment. I wanted nothing more than to celebrate my marriage with friends like I hadn't gotten to do three years earlier. Everyone was gathered around the area where Archer planned to have a firepit, and weather willing, one day we'd get to have an actual fire.

I dug in the cooler. "Kennedy, want anything?"

She lifted her water. "Nah, I'm good."

Liam was also at our belated wedding reception. Kennedy didn't have to worry about driving unless it was Liam's turn to get lit. The boys had been here earlier, but Liam's grandma had picked them up for a sleepover at her place.

Kennedy caught me eyeing her water. A flash of alarm ran through her expression, then guilt like she'd been busted with someone else's candy, and realization dawned on me. I mouthed, *Oh my God*. She glanced around to make sure no one noticed and pushed out of her chair.

I played it cool. Aspen was chatting with Lyric on the same camp chairs they'd packed to Medora, only with this get-together, Aspen was wearing athletic shoes. Lyric was dressed as similarly as the last time I saw her. Stetson had stopped by earlier—before Liam had arrived—to let us know he hated to miss our house warming-slash-belated wedding reception, but he had to go out of town.

He was likely skipping the awkwardness of being in the same vicinity as Liam. And the drama afterward, if his parents found out he'd socialized with his half brother.

Kennedy sidled up next to me and whispered, "I didn't want to spoil your special day, or I would've told you. I was going to tomorrow."

"It only makes the day more special," I whispered back. My best friend was pregnant. How awesome was that? "I want to hug you so bad, but then people would ask questions."

"I'm going to tell Lyric and Aspen tomorrow, and we'll do a big-brother reveal party for the boys."

"I'm soooo happy for you."

She grinned and wiggled like she wanted to do a little dance. "Thank you." She inhaled and fanned her face. "Be cool, be cool."

Holden approached. Archer had been showing him the house. "I can't believe you guys were able to get in here so fast."

"That would be my husband's doing." The ass-kissing at the draw had paid off. But I wanted to think Dan could see how much I loved this area for no other reason than it was peaceful and beautiful and I'd want to keep it that way as much as he did.

Archer came up behind Holden, looking perfect in his jeans and boots. "What did I do?"

"You called Dan the day you quit—without telling me—and discussed whether he thought he was getting a fair price for this property." I couldn't suppress my grin as I told the story. "And then you offered him more, and even more on top of that if we could get in right away."

Archer chuckled. "They were willing to pay me to help them move."

Both of us had helped them sort, pack, and load what Dan and Alice kept, and we hauled what they weren't keeping. They'd lived at this place for almost forty years, but the process hadn't been as consuming as I feared. Dan had slowly been clearing out the accumulated junk.

He had been so excited that this place would be a happy home for another couple for forty years.

I scanned my new place. The old farmhouse was in rough shape. Foam green with a leaky roof, creaky stairs, and a sagging porch, and the inside wasn't much better. Archer and I were planning the place we would build next summer. We'd have to wait for the condo sale to go through before we initiated it, but the house would do fine for another year.

As for the rest of the place—also a bit run down. Alice's chicken coop was the nicest, and she'd given me a crash course in all things hens and egg laying. Most of her customers were willing to give me a chance while I learned how to farm eggs. She was specific on the feed she used, and based on the way Holden gushed about the eggs, the feed was critical.

Then there was the ranch. Like Ma planned to do, Dan had downsized over the years. Archer and I would have a busy fall and spring of fixing fence and making improvements on the barn. Those had withstood the years slightly better than the house. Dan and Alice had put their money into the business instead of the house.

Archer slipped his phone out of his pocket, and his forehead crinkled. He glanced at our little gathering by the coolers. "Excuse me."

He moved closer to the vehicles, waving at Bruce and Willow pulling in. His uncle had been thrilled we were moving home and would be neighbors. Bruce had told Archer that his dad had called him a few days ago. The reunion thrilled Archer, and me too. The more support, the better.

Holden grabbed a beer and went to the group circling the cold firepit.

Kennedy's gaze stuck on Liam, adoration in her eyes. Was that how I looked at Archer? Stupid in love?

I was okay with that.

Kennedy let out a wistful sigh like she was anticipating having the house and Liam to herself since the twins were with his grandma. She switched her attention to me. "You're helping Kane move next week?"

"Yes, but he's not taking much. He traded in his pickup for a car, and he'll stock up on what he needs in Fargo." Unlike my husband, Kane had no issues shopping at a thrift store. "He's selling his trailer house and using that to buy furniture."

"That's so exciting. I love that Aunt Laney is sticking around."

It would've been hard to be away when Kane moved and for Kennedy and Liam's baby. All we had to worry about was maintaining what we had. Archer didn't say, but he was worried he would make mistakes that put us in the same position as his dad.

I was worried too. He'd sunk most of his money into

this property for us. But we were a little better at talking to each other than we used to be.

Kennedy noticed Archer was done with his call and gave my arm a squeeze before she went back to sit by her husband.

Archer's contemplative expression and furrowed brow weren't what I expected after a simple call. "Everything okay?"

"Yeah," he said slowly, and a slow grin spread across his handsome face. "Yeah. Remember Jaycee Henry?"

"How could I forget?" I could laugh about it now. We'd come out the other side of that client dinner stronger than ever.

"She heard I left NT Land Agency and wants to work with me since I 'had a come to Jesus.' If I walked away from Truitt and all the money, then she wants someone like that to work with."

"But she's in Texas."

"I'm still licensed in Texas." He grinned. "She never did buy that property she was looking at that was supposed to have made me partner."

"What if she doesn't buy anything now?" He could be flying to Dallas for nothing. I didn't want him to have a setback.

"It'll give me time to get qualified to be a land broker in North Dakota. If that's all right with you."

"Mm, another revenue stream and added stability. I don't know, Archer. You keep talking sexy like that and my IUD might fall right out."

He slipped his arms around my waist, and I was surrounded by his bourbon-and-citrus scent. "I can talk about investments and setting up a retirement for you." He leaned his head down to murmur in my ear. "And I'd love it if that IUD fell right out."

I pulled back and searched his face. I found nothing but sincerity. "I can make an appointment."

His grin widened, and my belly flipped. How much could my life change in a couple of months?

He was about to kiss me when Holden hollered from around the firepit. "If you two start making out, then Liam and Kennedy will start making out. And I might start canoodling with the chickens."

Archer laughed and tucked me into his side so we could join our family and friends. Two people who had fooled themselves about what they really wanted had somehow landed exactly where they were supposed to be.

While we were walking to the group, I looked up at Archer. "You know, the day you first showed up, I was thinking about life and how I was friends with Kennedy and married to a Barron, just not one I'd known as a kid, and I thought it was odd how things turned out."

The corner of his mouth kicked up. "I've been thinking the same."

"Yeah." I didn't worry anymore that he'd leave me for the next big client. He'd ditched the biggest client of his career for me. Oddly perfect how things turned out.

* * *

Holden

I entered the bar and stopped for a moment to look at the bulletin board inside the entry. There was a flyer for the football league Stetson had coerced me to help him with. It'd be for a different team—since I was in a different town.

Crocus Valley was twenty minutes away from Coal Haven. I loved seeing my cousins happy, but there were times in those situations when I had to grin and bear it. Kennedy might think no one noticed she was drinking only water, but I had. I was happy for them. I was. But only Stetson knew why it was a complex subject for me.

When she popped out some cute, red, wiggly baby, I'd be ecstatic for them. I'd say all the right things. And I'd come back to Crocus Valley and get trashed. I could usually find someone to crash with for the night. Otherwise, I always parked a couple blocks away where there was nothing but abandoned buildings and an empty lot. I had no issues sleeping it off in my truck if the good deputies of this county didn't.

I leaned my head back and took a deep breath. I hadn't come here to piss around the entrance all night. But sometimes... the feeling there was something else out there for me taunted me. There wasn't. I had tried that and lost it. I lived in the town where I was born and raised, and I was here to stay. I liked my career. I liked carrying on the business my grandparents and their parents had built. I liked being free to do whatever I pleased.

There were no screaming fights on my front porch like there had been when I was a kid. No men pretending to be my daddy. No boyfriends thinking they were going to get the land and livestock that were mine. I had a no-nonsense mom and my own place on her land.

Nothing was changing for me anytime soon, and that was the way I liked it. Once I got through football season and Stetson's incessant nagging.

I didn't do the whole kids thing, and I sure as hell didn't want to be around when everything went to shit.

Stetson was avoiding everyone tonight, thanks to Archer and Delaney's party. I'd left the party, but didn't seek him out. Maybe I'd find someone who wasn't looking for commitment I could have some fun with.

I rounded the wall blocking off the entry and was greeted by polished wood—a shiny lacquered bar top, tables that were slabs of polished wood with red-and-yellow lacquer inside, and chairs that matched the wood tones. Beams soared across the ceiling. It'd overwhelm the senses if poker and blackjack machines didn't add pops of color and break up the browns.

There were several people older than me, but all in groups. Rattler's happy hour went longer than other bars in the county, siphoning people from Crocus Valley until happy hour was over.

"Hey, Holden. What can I get you?" The server behind the bar had been the librarian in my elementary school growing up. I'd joked with her that working in a school was good training for when the crowd in this place got unruly.

"Busch Light." I wasn't looking to get lost in a bottle. As much as I liked my house, the place was quiet. It was nice to be somewhere with people, with some action, but where I didn't have to be *on*.

I slid onto a stool two down from a woman I didn't recognize. I couldn't get a look at her face, but I liked the rest of her. A generous flare at the hips, amplified by having one leg crossed over the other. Her light-brown hair was piled into a knot at the top of her head. She wore jeans and a formfitting fleece jacket. There was something about her that made it seem like she didn't fit.

When she glanced up, she scanned the bar and sighed, looking at her phone again as if she couldn't think of anything else to do but didn't want to sit and stare at the wall of stacked booze across the bar in front of her.

Her gaze shifted and landed on me. Shit. I was staring. I adopted a slightly apologetic look. "Sorry for the cliché, but you're not from around here."

An *Is this guy serious?* look crossed her face a moment

before she laughed. A loud, free sound. She didn't bother with a coy giggle; she went all out.

I liked that.

And seeing more of her confirmed my suspicion that she didn't fit. Hardly any makeup, if any. Maybe a swipe across her lashes. Underneath her light jacket, she wore a simple shirt. Her cleavage was tucked away for the night.

Damn. From what I could tell, she had nice tits. An overflowing handful.

I was a tits guy. Loved kneading and squeezing and licking and—

I shifted. This would get out of hand, and I'd done nothing more than give her a cringe line.

"You're right," she said as she caught her breath. "I'm not from around here. I knew it was obvious."

Her voice was rich. She didn't bother with breathy or light or sultry. What I saw with this woman was what I got.

I lifted my beer as a form of greeting. "Holden."

She lifted a brow. She did the same with her bottle of Bud Light. I thought she might be close to my age. A lot of the women I'd picked up lately had been younger. Twenty-five wasn't a major age gap from my thirty, but with the wrong person? Dating shouldn't make me feel ancient.

"Em," she said, and it took me a moment to realize that was her name.

I lifted a brow. "Just Em?"

She laughed again and took a drink of her beer, waiting until she swallowed before she said, "'Just Em' pretty much describes it."

My gaze stuck on what I'd seen when she lifted the bottle. A tan line on her left hand where a wedding ring usually sat.

She saw me notice it. "Divorced." She cocked her head. "Newly divorced, so now's your chance to run."

It was my turn to laugh. I hated drama. Dreaded conflict. I stayed far away and did what I could to prevent it. I'd had enough of it growing up, and I didn't need to invite more.

But I could handle a divorced woman. Newly divorced was better in a way—for me, not for her, unless she was grateful to be newly divorced. For me, it meant she wasn't looking for another Mr. Em. She wasn't into anything serious, and she was sick as hell of the drama that came with marriages breaking up. And, huge bonus, she hadn't mentioned any kids.

It meant there was a chance Em wanted to have a good time. And what a coincidence, I wanted a good time with her. I smiled and slid my beer on the bar as I moved to the stool between us. "I'm not running anywhere, Em."

———

Thanks for reading!

Is there a new surprise that will finally make Holden open his eyes and see what's been right in front of him for years? Make Me Blush

Get an extra epilogue with a peek into the life of Archer and Delaney by signing up for my newsletter. You'll get extra scenes, the latest sales and release updates, and be able to participate in my giveaways.

About the Author

Marie Johnston writes paranormal and contemporary romance and has collected several awards in both genres. Before she was a writer, she was a microbiologist. Depending on the situation, she can be oddly unconcerned about germs or weirdly phobic. She's also a licensed medical technician and has worked as a public health microbiologist and as a lab tech in hospital and clinic labs. Marie's been a volunteer EMT, a college instructor, a security guard, a phlebotomist, a hotel clerk, and a coffee pourer in a bingo hall. All fodder for a writer!! She has four kids, cats, and a half blind Corgie.

mariejohnstonwriter.com

Follow me: